STEVEN FECHTER

Encyclopocalypse Publications
www.encyclopocalypse.com

For Holly

ONE

stare at the ceiling. What do I see? Track lighting, one lightbulb burnt out. Ceiling in need of fresh paint. Skylight in need of cleaning. The sky is Parisian blue, also called Prussian blue, named for when the compound dyed the uniform coats of the powerful Prussian army in the 18ᵗʰ century. But I digress.

Breeze!

What?

Why are you staring at the ceiling?

Because I'm lying on the floor.

Breeze!

What?

Why are you lying on the floor?

I fell.

Oh. You fell.

I fall a lot.

Why do you fall a lot?

Trying to walk.

You mean you can't walk?

Of course, I can walk!

Sorry.

For three steps.

Then you can't walk, can you?

I don't respond.

I see a manual wheelchair a few feet from your body. Aluminum, nylon, lightweight. Easy to propel and push. That little baby yours?

I don't respond.

How will you get back into your wheelchair?

Like I always do.

Need assistance?

Absolutely not.

Are you sure?

Give me a minute!

Take your time.

This is the conversation I have with myself as I lie on the floor of my art studio, formerly the barn. Prior to my fall I had an upsetting phone call. In my agitation I bolted out of my wheelchair to walk across the room. Something I've never been able to do since... Obviously, I didn't make it. The first phone call came at approximately 9:00 AM this morning.

Hello? says the caller.

That voice... familiar.

Hello? Hello? repeats the caller.

I know that voice – whiny, high pitched – but where...

Hey!

Yeah? I finally respond.

This Breezy?

Who's this?

Am I speaking to Breezy Bye?

Wrong number.

Nah. This is Breeze. I'd know that voice anywhere.

Does Mr. Bye know you?

Yeah, Breeze. You fucking know me.

So, who are you?

Silence. His breathing is labored. Short, rasping breaths. Not a healthy man.

Who the hell are you? I ask again.

I'm the guy that ran you down.

What?

I RAN YOU DOWN!

He starts coughing. The kind that digs deep and tears your insides. I hear phlegm catch in his throat. It takes him a minute to clear the muck and spit it out.

What's your name? I ask.

You know it.

Yeah, and it's Mr. Asshole.

I hang up. Now I have trouble breathing, my face feels flushed.

TIRES SCREECH!

I've had crazy calls in the past, but not in years. The phone rings again. Same number. I let it ring. It stops. He'll call again. And again.

NO HEAD LIGHTS!

That's *not* when I bolted out of my chair and ended on my back. That came hours later. Later being now. Let me review, starting with the morning and two calls that followed this first call. They were disruptions, but not like the last call.

Morning started well enough, like any normal Tuesday morning. First thing I jump in the pool.

Stroke, stroke, stroke, stroke. I finish my nineteenth lap. Stroke, stroke, stroke, stroke. How many strokes in twenty laps? Four hundred and sixty. How many strokes in a painting? Hundreds. Thousands. Tens of thousands. I'm a painter. Stroke, stroke, stroke, stroke. I was once a baseball player. A pitcher. Another life ago. Instead of throwing pitches, now I paint pictures. Pictures of pitchers. The greatest pitchers: Christy Mathewson, Lefty Grove, Walter Johnson, Warren Spahn, Pete Alexander, Sandy Koufax. Stroke, stroke, stroke, stroke. I love to swim. Wish I were a dark brown seal in white-blue Antarctica.

Stroke, stroke, stroke, stroke. Every morning. In the pool by 6:00 AM. Breakfast at 7:00 AM. Paint from 8:00 AM to 4:30 PM. Read for two hours. Dinner with Salem. Watch some news.

Read in bed. Try to sleep. Most times succeed. But today's Tuesday. Heidi at 7:30 AM.

After my baseball career was over, I returned to the old farm for good. I built a pool where the corral used to be. In the corral, my mother kept two horses, a brown and white Paint, and a gray Arabian. She loved to ride. Dad never sat in a saddle. Twelve years old. I rode with Mom, she on the Paint, me on the Arabian. She liked to race. She always beat me... until the cancer.

The farm is in Middelburg. Small town in Upstate New York. You could say Middelburg is conservative. Since I don't mix with neighbors, or people in general, politics don't affect me. What I notice is the landscape: mountains, rolling hills, farms, pastures, horses, cows, some sheep, some goats. Middelburg is named after a city in the Netherlands. The Dutch were the first white settlers in the early 1700s. We still have streets with names like De Meer Lane, Gaasperdam Drive, Huygens Street. A Lutheran stone church built in 1760 is still actively in use. Local lore says General George Washington had breakfast here as he rode through with his raggedly troops. The place is soaked in history.

With swimming it's stroke, stroke, stroke, stroke. Breast stroke, backstroke, butterfly, freestyle. Each stroke consistent and precise. With painting it's stroke, stroke, stroke, stroke. Every brush stroke is different. Just as every breath is different. Some deeper. Some shallower. Some quicker. Some longer. Stop breathing for five minutes, you're dead. Why'd I say that? Why think of death now?

Swimming is far superior to walking when you can't stand up – even if you can stand. Because humans walk in an upright posture, they tower over most land creatures. Birds are an exception, but birds always are. This makes humans feel superior. Like gods. Particularly the young, attractive, well-fed, and well-off. Once I was one of them. But worse. My sense of privilege was boundless. Imagine the feeling of 50,000 fans cheering, stomping, maniacally chanting BREEZ-EEE! BREEZ-EEE! BREEZEE! Aagh! Why talk of baseball? I loathe baseball. I'd rather talk of death.

Stroke, stroke, stroke, stroke. Finishing my morning swim, I touch the pool's edge one more time. Strong arms pull my body up. Reach for handrails. Drag my body and dead legs up and into the silver wheelchair. My trusty steed. My *Wheels*, which are locked. Always lock the brakes before getting in or out of a wheelchair. I grab the towel draped over back of chair.

I propel my Wheels with human muscle – arms, wrists, hands. I am the engine. My fancy electric-powered wheelchair sits unused in the garage. I gave the thing a try... briefly. See, I love using my arms. Rolling fast, the wheelchair is part of my body. Riding in the electric, I'm a passenger. A passive, disabled passenger. Loathsome word. *Disabled*. Moving in my manual Wheels, I'm strong, independent.

With Heidi it's stroke, stroke, stroke, stroke. Her soft, oiled hands slide over my stiff cock. Blue veins fill with warm blood. Stroke, stroke, stroke, stroke. She varies pressure. Pause, press, slide, pause, press, slide. Like hands fingering strings on a violin.

I want to make you cry, she says. I want to make you laugh. I want to make you sing.

Can't sing! I gasp with pleasure.

Please sing. Or tell me to stop and I'll stop.

Stop and I'll kill you.

Ha-ha! You tempt me.

Banal sex talk but it's all in the context. Then, oh my goodness, her mouth. A large, soft, lovely mouth. Lips and tongue wrap around, pull me in. I think she'll pull my whole body into her mouth down her throat and swallow me like Noah's whale. I groan without shame. Then she mounts me. Sometimes, with Heidi's help, I mount her. Using my strong arms and hips, I give us both pleasure. Wheelchair bound does not mean sexless bound.

An hour passes, Heidi leaves. Returning Thursday. Back next Tuesday. Then back again on Thursday. A block away, like a spy, Heidi sits low in her car waiting until Salem catches the school bus. First thing, she brews us coffee. We chat about nothing.

How was your weekend? Her daughters. My daughter. Her work. My work. We make love. Then she drives off to work. Conversations blessedly short. This morning she said something surprising. On her way out she paused, turned to me, and said: I wish my husband was in a wheelchair.

Why in Christ would you ever wish that?

Might make him a nicer human being.

Based on my experience, I wouldn't count on it. Sherry would agree if she was still here.

Heidi gives me a wink and leaves.

Sherry died three years ago. Covid. She caught the virus in Spain during a film shoot. They never finished the film. A spy thriller called *The Girl from Madrid*. Sherry played a CIA agent or was it a double agent? Doesn't matter. Lead role. With violence and romance. She was excited. Then Covid came. In the beginning of the first wave no one knew how bad it would be, right? No one knew what it was. No one screamed PANDEMIC! No one even knew what the word *Covid* meant. My beautiful, nearly perfect wife had one minor imperfection. A fatal imperfection, turns out: She suffered from asthma. The asthma was well controlled. It never interfered with her personal or professional life until the virus caught her in its grip. It killed her in five days.

Two months later a black container inside a cardboard box, inside another cardboard box, arrived by USPS Priority Mail Express International. The black container is the size and shape of a hat box. No hat. Just the ashes of my wife. The box sits on a shelf in my studio. How can a full vibrant life of forty-four years be reduced to a pile of light-grey ash that weighs less than five pounds? I should do something about her ashes. Bury? Scatter? Preserved in an urn? Yes, a lovely brass urn with pink enamel background and exquisite silver hummingbirds in mid-flight. Salem wants to scatter them in the garden that Sherry loved. But ashes are all I have left of her. Sometimes I hold the box, remove the cover, and slip my hand inside. The ashes are gray-brown, odorless, surprisingly dry, and heavy, feeling more sandy than ashy. It must be from the bones. Receiving her ashes turned a switch off inside me. I shut down for a year. Sherry was not only my life but my destiny. She was... CAN'T talk about that now.

Easier to talk about Heidi. Heidi... my Great Dane. Pale, curvaceous, six feet tall, 180 pounds. She wants to lose twenty. I tell her if she loses twenty, I will find them and bring them back. Makes her laugh every time. Lustrous blonde hair tied in a long, single braid that she coils on top of her head like a golden crown, adding two inches to her height. She's a nurse. Head ER nurse. She lifts and moves broken, bleeding bodies all day or all night, depending on her shift. Some bodies can weigh well over 200 pounds. Moving your body, she says (meaning mine), is a breeze, playing on my name. She likes to lift me out of my wheelchair, carry me to bed, undress me, undress herself, touch, kiss, lick my body, then fuck me. I should feel ashamed of my helplessness. Carried like a baby. How utterly pathetic for this 53-year-old ex-jock. Yet, despite the shame, I love it. I enjoy touching Heidi's smooth skin. She perspires easily, which seems odd for a woman from Denmark. The dewy drops on her upper lip feel warm to my touch. After she removes all her clothes, she walks around the house, light bouncing off her pale-pink Rube-nesque thighs. She always looks inside the fridge. Take this morning. She grabs a container of chocolate-chip ice cream from the freezer, finishes it off before joining me in bed. After sex and snuggling, she helps me dress, carries me back to my chair, and leaves for the hospital to take care of other broken bodies.

Years ago when Sherry is still alive and Heidi and her husband are over, I decide to show Heidi my studio. I take out a few finished canvases from a rack, talk about the subjects, who they are, what they mean to me. Heidi stares at the paintings for a long time without saying a word.

I love your paintings! she finally exclaims. Show me more!

After that I sometimes invite her to see my newest work. Or she asks what I'm working on. She can talk intelligently about color, tone, light, and shape. This deepens our friendship. Sherry never appears jealous. I never ask if she is.

Heidi and her husband, Larry Weems, live ten blocks away. They have three girls. Their oldest, Brittany, is Salem's age and her best friend. The Weems moved into the neighborhood ten years ago. Because Salem and Brittany become friends, their parents become *our* friends. Larry is an ex-Marine, who served two tours in Afghanistan, earning a Bronze Star and a Purple Heart. He never talks about his time there. Now he's a lieutenant in the town's police department. You won't find a straighter arrow than Larry. Conservative in views, Christian in faith, devoted to family, trusting in law, love of country. Has a flagpole in their front yard that waves Old Glory. Each morning Larry raises the flag. Each evening he lowers it and correctly folds it. His patriotism reminds me of the good ol' Southern boys I played with and against. But I don't want to think about that.

When Sherry is still alive, the Weems occasionally invite us over for dinner. After Sherry's death I stop socializing. I see practically no one except my daughter. Then six months ago, on a Tuesday morning, things abruptly change. It's raining sheets and the wind howls like a wounded wolf. Our housekeeper has stayed home due to the storm. Salem has just left for the school bus. While clearing the kitchen table I hear the front door blow open, BLAM! I roll into the living room and see Heidi standing in the doorway. She slams shut the door. No umbrella, she's completely soaked. Hair plastered over her face like she just swam in the ocean. She pants for breath. I look out the window and don't see her car. Did she run the ten blocks from her house in the storm?

I miss you, she says between pants.

Miss you, too, I echo back.

You don't understand... I miss your company. I miss talking with you. No... no... no... that isn't it. I miss your paintings... no... I miss your face, yes, your hair, yes, your voice... yes... I think about you, dream about you... yes... yes! I... touch myself... and imagine... I miss *you*. YOU! Understand?

It's not so much her mad-tinged words but the desperate way she says them, the imploring way she stares at me. I feel something I haven't felt for a long time. Have I stepped into an Ingmar Bergman film. Maybe Heidi will walk on the ceiling like in *The Hour of the Wolf*. I don't know what to say.

Do you understand? she asks again.

I just nod.

Blood rises in my body. An electric current tingles my loins. My face feels feverish. She takes off her dripping wet coat and drops it on the floor. She approaches me and lifts my body from the chair as easily as if I were made of straw. She carries me to my bed, unbuckles my pants, and gently pulls them off. Next off, boxer shorts. For a moment she takes in my hard-on, as I do. Lord knows it's been a long time since I've had one. She removes her clothing, moistens my cock with her lips and tongue, then mounts me. She's already wet. All these transactions are done without any words between us. None necessary. I hate words. They get in the way of feeling and doing, and now I just want to feel. And I do.

That's how it begins. A relationship fueled on desire, pleasure, and loneliness. This morning, Heidi sits on my lap, facing me. I'm inside her. Vaginal muscles pulsate as she slowly ascends and descends. Lovemaking with Heidi is unlike anything I've experienced as a walking human. She performs one position that belongs in a circus. Lying on her back, she holds me up as she guides my cock inside her. Then she lifts and lowers me while I'm inside. I feel like I'm floating inside a live volcano.

Three months into our affair, Heidi says, I'm going to tell you something I've never told anyone – not even my husband.

Okay, I say, feeling both dread and fascination.

When I was eighteen, I became a sex worker.

A sex worker?

Yes.

You mean...

Yes.

So, you...

Fucked men for money.

Many men?

A lot of men... and a few women.

Here?

No! Copenhagen.

I am silent.

Shocked? she asks.

Surprised.

It paid for my college.

How long...

Two years. The Kroners were good and easy.

I bet you were...

Fantastic! My clients were quite satisfied. Except for a few. Can't please everyone.

Did you ever have a paraplegic as a client?

No. But I've had a blind client, one deaf mute, one with MS. One client had a wooden leg. He took it off during sex. They were among my favorites because they were sweet, giving, and as grateful as puppies.

Then I'm in good company.

The only difference, darling, is that I didn't love them.

What made you take up nursing? I ask to veer her from the L-word.

Larry, she says. Then she tells me about Larry.

He was in Denmark on a bicycling tour of Scandinavian countries. We met at a bar. He's alone. I'm alone. He buys me a drink. We talk. He buys me another drink. We end up in bed. Classic, right? He stays in Copenhagen the rest of his trip, the hell with the bike tour. I can't tell him what kind of work I do, so I tell him I live with my parents while going to college, which was true. When he asks me to marry him, I realize that I'll need another career. So, I go to nursing school in America. It doesn't pay as well. The work is harder. But it is legal. And I'm good at it.

A nurse, a former sex worker, and Danish. How do you beat a combination like that? Unless you add master chef. Turns out Heidi is an excellent cook and baker. For most men, Heidi would be a wet-dream fantasy. Her one drawback is that she's brainwashed from watching right-wing cable news. I blame Larry. When they used to come over, Sherry always reminded them that politics is off-limits. I tell Heidi the same. But occasionally she will talk about something she heard – like how gangs of Mexican immigrant men are raping white teen-aged girls at the border to impregnate them so they can later sell their babies. I explain that it's all wacky crap and to please drop it during our time together. She's doing better.

This morning, lying in bed after making love, she sits up and gives me a tender look.

I love you, Breezy. I mean I *really* love you. Do you know that?

We rarely use the L-word. Why complicate something perfect with its no-frills simplicity. At the time I don't yet know how complicated this day will become.

Did you know that I've loved you for years?

I think we should slow down, I say.

But she doesn't slow down but picks up the pace. She exclaims, Years! Even when Sherry was alive. That was hard. Like torture. Surely you knew. I was so afraid Larry would get suspicious.

I didn't know, is all I can say.

Bullshit! You knew.

Heidi, I didn't.

Don't lie!

I'm not!

I'm sorry Sherry's dead. I wish she were still alive, but why try to protect her?

I'm not lying! But I don't sound convincing.

Then not only can't you walk, you can't see. I was crazy about you.

I knew Heidi liked me. A lot. When the four of us got together, her gaze could burn holes in my eyes if I didn't look away. She found moments to touch my arm, shoulder, neck. Her contact looked casual but felt carnal.

At 8:30 AM is when Heidi leaves me for work. But this morning she and I are having one of our more substantial conversations. I'm anxious to get to my painting. My most important show opens in six weeks. I need to finish my newest canvases. But Heidi lingers longer than usual. She lies next to me, stroking my face.

What would you do if I left Larry?

Leave Larry?

Yes.

You're not going to leave Larry.

What if I did?

But you won't.

If I did, what would you do? Be honest.

I don't know, I say, which is true.

That isn't helpful.

Why even ask?

We could be together all the time.

Larry's a great guy. Devoted father to your daughters.

Darling, I'm the perfect partner for you.

Because we have good sex?

Because we have *great* sex. Because I love your paintings. Because I'm a nurse.

I don't need a nurse.

Living with a nurse would be a fantastic asset.

I'm not sick. I'm not an invalid. I just can't walk!

I don't know what I fear more. That her husband finds out and shoots me or that my daughter finds out and hates me for betraying her mother. I'll have to end it with Heidi soon. It's the right thing to do. I don't want to wreck her marriage. But God, I love her visits.

Finally, she prepares to leave. She kisses me, holds my face in her hands, then hits a homer of an exit line.

Even in a wheelchair, you're ten times the man Larry is.

Later, I wonder how many times the man I'd be out of a wheelchair.

After Heidi leaves, I get dressed and wheel out the front door to pick up my delivered *New York Times*. It's a long driveway, and I take my time. When Salem started elementary school, a fifteen-minute walk from our house, Sherry would walk with her to the school. She did this until Salem started fourth grade. From the driveway I would wave them goodbye and watch other fathers and mothers walk their kids to school. There were more mothers than fathers. Sometimes I could hear snatches of their conversations.

What are you doing in school today?

Our teacher, Ms. Getting, is reading a story.

What story?

'Bout a horse named Thunder.

Thunder is a good name.

Yeah, Mommy. Cause when he runs it sounds like thunder.

That's wonderful, dear.

Mommy, can I have a horse?

Sherry would sometimes ask me if I wanted go with Salem to school in my electric wheelchair. The very idea revolted me. I always told Sherry that I had to paint. After a while she stopped asking. I know now that it wasn't about my painting. It was about my pride. Thinking about this distracts me from looking out for the Old Man.

Hey, Joey! Joey! How's life?

As if I conjured up the Old Man, there he stands: Warren Stillwater, 88 years strong, my *New York Times* clutched in his blue-veiny hand. In his other hand he holds the leashes to his two long-haired Chihuahuas. Peanut and Vinny. I can never remember which is which. But as I recall, Vinny is older than Peanut by a few years. They're both rather old. I try to avoid Warren, but sometimes I'm careless like now. Warren was a friend of my parents for many years. One of the original home-owners on this block. When his wife died a few years ago, his youngest daughter, Libby, moved in to watch over him. He passes by my house whenever he walks his dogs, two or three times a day. While relatively harmless, he can be a pest. I lock the brakes and hold out my hand. Almost reluctantly he hands me my paper.

Saw you coming down the drive, Joey. Don't know how you have time to read all this small print.

Thanks, Warren, I say as I take the paper. He still calls me Joey, a name I detest and only my parents used.

Did I tell you that I beat my prostate cancer? Warren asks. He likes to begin with a tedious report on his health.

No.

The doctors gave me a shot in the ass once a week for two months. Now I have a clean bill of health. I don't know what the hell they shot in my ass, but it worked.

Glad to hear.

Not so good news for my daughter-in-law. We buried her last week. Only sixty-two. Doctors think it was an aneurysm. I never bad mouth the dead, but she was a hell-bitch on wheels to my son for thirty years. But honor the dead, I always say. Nice funeral. Priest made her sound like a saint.

Sorry for your loss.

Still painting? he asks, as he always does.

Yes, sir.

Nice to have a hobby, he always rejoins.

I enjoy it.

That's what counts I always say. Whatever you do, whether work or play, you should enjoy it.

Yes, Old Man, you always do say it. But I just nod.

What is it again you paint?

Always the same damn questions. And always the same damn answer.

Baseball players.

What?

BASEBALL PLAYERS!

Oh, baseball players. What for?

I like it.

You like it. Baseball players.

Yes, sir.

Can you really sell a painting like that?

Sometimes.

Amazing. I guess people will buy anything.

I let it go.

You used to play baseball.

Yes, sir. Now I paint baseball players' portraits.

I was known as one of the best painters in Middelburg, he says proudly.

I nod as I plan my escape from the old fart. Warren was a house painter for forty-five years and, yes, one of the best as the older residents will confirm.

I painted your folks' house and their barn.

I know.

You were just half a squirt then. I painted quite a few houses on this block alone. What set my painting apart from the others is that I never skimped on–

Coats and quality, I quickly interrupt his favorite monologue. You were the best, Warren. I'll let you go on with your walk, I say as I unlock my brakes.

Boy oh boy, I sure miss Sherry, Warren laments.

Shit. Why did he have to bring her up? I lock my brakes.

I miss her too, I say, watching Peanut (or Vinny) spin around for a spot to shit.

She always had time to chat with me on my walks with the dogs. She'd get your *New York Times*, still in her bathrobe, see me coming up the road, and wait. Yeah, she would *wait*, just so we could have a little chitchat. A chinwag. Not like you. I see you grab the paper; you'll wave at me, but you don't wait. No. You don't wait a sec. You wheel up the driveway like you seen an army of Russian soldiers marching up the block. I think you try to avoid me!

I would never do that, Warren.

Sometimes I think you do.

Glad we could have a chat.

Before he can say another word, I unlock my brakes and wheel back up the driveway. I can hear Warren yell, Peanut! Vinny! What the hell are you waiting for?

Warren and his wife Myrtle were best friends of my parents. They'd come over, play cards, and drink. My mom would always have food available so the men didn't get too drunk. They sent me to bed, but I could hear the menfolk's voices ranting away. Warren and Myrtle had one son, Rich. Though he was only a couple of years older than me, we never socialized. In high school I was a jock and hung out with the other jocks. Rich was a bully, cokehead, and dealer. He hung out with other like students. After high school he joined a white militia gang in Pennsylvania and ended up OD'ing on a variety of drugs. Warren never talks about Rich. Sometimes I think he hates me for still being alive, while his son is dead.

Stroke, stroke, stroke, stroke. It's 9:30 AM. I'm in my studio applying brushstrokes of titanium white on Matty's uniform. The studio is fifty yards off from the house. This was once a barn. Sherry called it the barn. Salem calls it the barn. Most people still call it the barn. Studio or barn, it is where I work. Tall windows on two sides. A skylight. Against one windowless wall are shelves and racks that store finished and unfinished paintings, art supplies – tubes of paint, palettes, palette knifes, wood for stretchers, rolls of canvas, containers, pots, drawing boards – a small refrigerator, a hotplate, a radio. Against the other windowless wall hang my latest paintings. On my easel I installed a battery-powered lift that can raise and lower the canvas. Who needs to stand?

For a few years I hired art students from the local college as studio assistants: to stretch canvases, order art supplies, keep the studio orderly and clean. After a while I couldn't stand having another person around while I worked. Plus, they never stretch canvases the way I like. Never tight enough or even enough. Some of the kids, who had a little talent, hoped that I would mentor them. I do not mentor. When I don't mentor they get bored. Finally, I decide to do it myself. The work takes longer. I have to get special tools. In the end, I like doing it myself. The studio isn't as clean and orderly, but that's okay. I love feeling new canvas. Reminds me of rubbing the shine off cowhide on a new baseball.

I make sketches on paper first from photographs of my subjects. Then I put paint on canvas working from the sketches. The most important stroke is the first. I feel it contains the DNA of the complete painting.

I drew and sketched all my life. On our farm I sketched the farm animals. In my adolescence, I switched to people. My middle-school art teacher, Mrs. Agnes Overbeke, tells me, Joseph, you have talent. Real talent. I hope you do something with it.

By then all I want to do is play baseball. Yet, I continue to sketch and draw. When playing in the bush leagues, on days when I'm not pitching, I sketch players on the field. My teammates call me Picasso. During the season I visit art museums and galleries in the cities and towns we play. In Chicago I spend hours at the great Art Institute of Chicago to see the Masters: Rembrandt, Caravaggio, Raphael, Vermeer. Or I go to Chicago's Museum of Contemporary Art for the modern stuff.

When my playing days abruptly come to an end, when I'm able to climb out of the pitch-black death hole of depression, addiction, and self-pity, I'm ready to paint, seriously paint. I begin with acrylics, but come to hate acrylics. When the paintings dry they look flat and lifeless. Then I try oils and fall in love with the paint's living richness. I want to give my subjects the depth, mystery, power, and nobleness of kings, popes, knights, saints, and gods. If oils were good enough for da Vinci, van Gogh, and Munch, they're good enough for me.

I paint baseball players. Only baseball players. Almost all are pitchers. The greatest pitchers that ever played the game. Pitchers I love and admire. There is something unique about the motion of a pitcher winding up and throwing a baseball to a batter. That physical action can be graceful, jerky, furious, ferocious, explosive, violent, balletic. Before each pitch, the pitcher must decide what he's going to throw, where he's going to throw it, how hard, how soft. AND he and the catcher must first agree – in less than twenty seconds.

Something else I should mention: When I paint my pitcher portraits, I don't paint the bleachers, nor the fans, nor the diamond, nor the pitching mound, nor other players on the field. There are no clouds, no sky, no lights, backstop, umpire, or batter. There is only the pitcher, alone in the universe, alone in his own time and space. I paint the pitcher from the waist up, much like Renaissance portraits. The subject is in a candid pose caught during the act of pitching, like a stopped frame in a film. The pitcher could be rubbing a new baseball before the pitch. Or he's staring down at the catcher's signs. Or he's wiping sweat off his face with his sleeve. I want to capture an authentic true-to-life image, organic and in the moment.

For me the eyes set the tone. It's where everything emanates. Eyes reveal all you need to know. How badly does he want to win? How confident is he that he will win? Watch a pitcher's eyes just before he begins his windup, and you'll learn a lot.

Something else I need to say: Pitching is not baseball. Sounds like a paradox, but hear me out. Pitching is a separate *thing*. Pitchers are uniquely different from the position players. They may even be different from other human beings. The position players play a *game*. They have *fun*. Pitchers do not *play*. It is not a game. They do not have fun. For them it is a fight, a duel to a metaphoric death. Each inning is a battle. Each game is a war. Failure is not an option. The other players are merely defenders to protect the pitcher. Should they fail, it is a betrayal. The bobbled grounder that should have been a double play; the lazy fly ball an outfielder loses in the sun; the miscues, the mental lapses, the half-hearted effort. The pitcher forgives but never forgets.

You may ask, When the pitcher wins, is there no joy? No. None. Any pleasure the pitcher feels is entirely of a masochistic nature. Pitching is a blood sport. Each time the pitcher throws a pitch he damages his body. The physical stress on sinews, cartilage, nerves, and muscles is unnatural and an absurd form of self-abuse. That is why the average working life of a big-league pitcher is less than four years. After the pitcher retires or is forced out, their pitching arm will never be normal again. It is madness to be a pitcher. No sane man would willingly do it. But if he can throw a 95-mph fastball, a curveball with a twelve-inch break, an 80-mph changeup that looks exactly like a fastball until it crosses the plate, then he is destined to be a master pitcher. This is why I paint pitchers, great pitchers. I love painting pitchers. Yet, I no longer have any interest in the game of baseball. That may also sound like a paradox, but it's the truth.

The first pitcher I painted was Christy Mathewson. My favorite old-time player. The supreme god among gods in my baseball universe. More than Babe Ruth, more than Walter Johnson, more than Lou Gehrig, more than Lefty Grove, Mathewson forever changed the game of baseball and the public's image of the professional ballplayer. He won 373 games. Only Walter Johnson and Cy Young won more. His career seventy-nine shutouts and career 2.13 ERA are among the all-time best. It's not just the records. Mathewson brought class, stature, intelligence, poise, glamour, beauty, heart, and decency to the game when the popular perception was that ballplayers were racist, drunken, ignorant louts. The fans called him Matty. He was the sport's first superstar. He was among the first inductees into the Hall of Fame. As a teenager I read everything about him. At the age of thirty-eight he enlisted during WWI. He died at the age of forty-five from inhaling poison gas in France. Matty saved my life.

Today I'm finishing a new portrait of Matty. It's my third portrait of him. He's the only player I've painted more than once. This one is from the end of his career. He's had his first losing record. His fastball is no longer fast. His curve has lost its hook. His fadeaway no longer fades. But he still has his uncanny control. He can put the ball anywhere he wants. As one sportswriter famously said, Matty could pitch the ball in your cereal bowl and never bruise the berries.

At 10:15 AM the phone rings. On the wall hangs a screen that shows incoming calls. The call is from my dealer, Jackie, of Jacqueline George Gallery. She's been a fixture in the New York art scene for decades. She can be a pain in the ass. But Jackie believed in me first when I thought no dealer or gallery would ever believe a wheelchair-bound, ex-jock could be a serious artist.

Joseph! How's it going?

She calls me Joseph, never Breeze. I love her for that.

Going fine, Jackie.

Fine?

Yeah.

You never say *fine* unless things are a disaster. Are things a disaster?

Everything's fine.

Stop saying that.

Okay.

Have you finished the double portrait? she asks for the hundredth time.

Almost, I lie for the hundredth time.

I want that double portrait. And I want a second double portrait.

I can't do two.

Yes, you can. You need two for the show.

You know I work slowly.

Then you'll have to work faster.

I don't respond.

Don't blow this, Joseph.

I won't.

I got you a solo show in the Tommy Tom Gallery, the hottest gallery in Chelsea. You'll get twenty times more exposure than your shows in my little East Village gallery. I've got commitments from *The New York Times*, *ARTnews*, *Artforum*, and *Art in America* that they'll send someone to the show. I'll also get a Whitney curator to come if I have to drag her by the hair. It's a game changer, Joseph. This could change your life.

But no pressure, right Jackie?

Ha-ha! No pressure. Absolutely! But you're used to high-stakes pressure, aren't you, Joseph?

This is the first time Jackie makes any reference to my previous baseball life. She's feeling the pressure. Betting the farm on this show. My show.

I never got used to pressure. I learned how to deal with it.

Ohh, sweetie, I love when you talk tough.

Actually, I'm kinda scared shitless. But I don't tell her that. I learned a long time ago how to put on a game face.

I like where you're taking your work, she says. You're expanding. You're taking more risks. Your palette is more complex. Don't get me wrong. I always loved your early oils, the charcoal and pastel drawings. I LOVE all that.

But...

You need to show the art world that you're a *painter*. That you know how to handle color, texture, mood, light, and space. How many new paintings have you finished?

Eight.

I want ten.

There's no time, Jackie.

The gallery requested ten – at a minimum. You'll give me ten.

Impossible.

Anything is possible if you want it bad enough. And I badly want to see you become a success.

I'm doing okay.

Okay? Okay is no good. I want FUCKING FANTASTIC. I don't say that to all my artists. In forty years very few have heard me say that. But I say that to you, Joseph, because you CAN be fantastic.

If my work is good, I'm good.

Don't act stoic, Joseph.

I'm not acting. And I'm not stoic.

Can I come visit you?

No!

I'll only stay overnight. Please!

Last time Jackie visited my studio, she stayed for a week. A nightmare. She wanted to see everything. Plus, she smokes and drinks like a film noir femme fatale.

NO! Not until I'm done. I'm not done.

Then when?

Soon, I say.

Your opening is soon, she counters.

Then sooner.

You're going to give me a heart attack.

Just don't die before my opening.

You're a beast.

You know I love you, Jackie.

Thirty years ago we'd be lovers. Maybe twenty years ago. Now, I'm too old.

Don't let that stop you.

Ha-ha! Now you can go back to work.

As a young woman Jackie wrote art criticism and lived in the East Village with a minimalist artist of minimal fame. He dumped her for a younger minimalist artist. As a result, Jackie hates minimalism. Because she knew so many starving artists in the East Village, she started a gallery there to show their work. In Jackie's telling, she slept with most of the male artists who had shows in her gallery and a few of the female ones.

Oh, one more thing, she says.

Shit, here it comes, I think.

You'll come to the opening, Joseph.

Jackie, please, we've been over this.

NOT negotiable. You will be there.

I hate art openings. Ever notice how there's never any chairs at art openings? Everyone must stand for hours! Which means I'm the only person in the gallery who's sitting. I'm a hippo in a corral of giraffes. And all the giraffes stare at the hippo. I try to position myself in the corner of the gallery, the wall at my back so no one can stand behind me. The giraffes still trot over to me and peer down. Some awkwardly crouch, spilling wine on my lap from their plastic glasses, insisting how much they LOVE the work. At my second opening, there is one particularly tall, drunk, bearded giraffe who sinks to his *knees*. The gesture is meant to be cruel, not kind. He has already shouted insulting remarks about the paintings: SECOND-RATE RIP-OFFS FROM VAN GOGH AND SOUTINE! I WOULDN'T PAY TEN DOLLARS FOR ANY OF THEM!

And so on. There are fifty frustrated, angry artists for every one artist that gets a show. And getting a show does not translate into sales. My kneeling critic may still regret his errant move. When I slam my wheelchair into his exposed knees, he screams like a stuck pig.

WHAT THE FUCK, MAN! ARE YOU NUTS! I'LL SUE YOUR ASS!

While his friends hustle him out the door, I delight in having slayed the tallest giraffe. But the incident puts a damper on the rest of the evening. I haven't gone to another opening since.

I'll send a limo – no, a van – no, a big fucking limo van! Jackie serenades. The limo van drives you to the opening. You make an appearance. Schmooze with the filthy rich collectors, the illiterate reviewers; pose for a few photos and selfies. Then the big fucking limo van drives you safely home. Is that so difficult?

Yes, and for all the things you just said. I hate New York, I hate crowds, I hate getting my photo taken, and I hate talking about my work! You'll think of a good excuse for me.

No, I won't. I'll say that Mr. Joseph Bye decided that the biggest opening of his career wasn't important enough for him to appear. That he doesn't give a shit about all the hard work his poor faithful dealer went to get him this show.

You're being unfair.

I will send the limo van. You will get in the limo van. Goodbye, Joseph. She hangs up. No pressure. No pressure at all.

It was Sherry who brought Jackie into my life. Sherry was on good terms with the Middelburg librarian, Lucille McCrory, then in her late sixties. She'd been running the library for thirty years. It's a sweet old library. All brick. Built a hundred years ago with some Art Deco touches. I often went there as a kid, checking out art books and baseball biographies. The librarian at the time, Mr. van Bronckhorst, couldn't figure me out.

More baseball biographies, Joey?

Yes, sir.

Guess you must like baseball.

Yes, sir.

And more art books. I presume for your mother? he'd always ask.

Yes, sir, I would always answer because I didn't want to hear his smartass comments.

One day Sherry brings two of my small paintings to the library – without asking me. Lucille likes them. Together they arrange a display of my artwork that will hang on the walls for one month – again without asking me. Since it is all settled, I reluctantly agree. I'd been painting for five years without showing my canvasses to anyone, discounting Sherry. It was time to show them to the public, even if it was in Middelburg. I select my best paintings, twelve in all. With the help of Sherry and Lucille, I direct where they should hang. I also type up a list of the paintings' titles and the price for each of them. My one attempt at marketing is to hang signs on some telephone poles announcing ART SHOW IN LIBRARY. I'm embarrassed to call it an art show, but Sherry insists.

The first three weeks I don't sell a single painting. Then Jackie arrives in her little red European sports-car. She's there to visit an old art curator friend who had retired from the Whitney Museum and moved upstate. Jackie sees my sign about the show. Curious or intrigued, she parks her car and walks to the library. She stares at my paintings without saying a word – I am told later by Lucille. After thirty minutes, she leaves. An hour later she comes back and buys two paintings: portraits of Whitey Ford and of Warren Spahn. They were two of my best. The woman had a good eye and knew her baseball. Then without calling first she drives to my house. Jackie must have asked a local where I live.

Are you Joseph Bye? she asks me at the front door. With the top down I can see my canvases sticking out of the passenger seat of her two-seater.

You found him.

I just bought two of your paintings.

Thanks.

You priced them too low.

I think the prices are fair.

Not for you.

You're my first buyer in three weeks.

Meaning?

Meaning no one else thought the prices were too low.

Because the people here are hicks. I don't mean that in a negative way.

How else could she mean it? But I don't respond.

I want to see your other work, she demands.

Why?

I'm interested.

I don't know your name.

Jacqueline George, but call me Jackie. George isn't my real last name, but it works better than Gorkowski in the art world.

I'm silent again as I mull over what she means by *art world*.

So, are you going to show me your work? I don't have all day. I'm due back in New York by tonight. By the way, I know who you are.

Who am I?

Hah-hah! Hey, that's good! Who am I? Very Zen. I know who you *were*. I was at Shea Stadium when you pitched a one-hitter against them. Fifteen strikeouts! You were fucking brilliant. It would have been a no-hitter except for one broken-bat blooper in the seventh inning. So, you're an artist. I saw the paintings. I read your name. Didn't put it together – at first.

She continues talking nonstop for five straight minutes about my work, about the town, about her curator friend who lives in the town. I hardly listen because of what she'd said: *You're an artist*. No one ever called me that before.

When she pauses, I say, Let's go in my studio. I pull out canvases from the last three years. Strangely, all she says is: Show me more.

Sherry brings us ice tea and a cheese plate with bread and crackers. Jackie purchases two more paintings. I charge her the same price as the two she already purchased. I ask her to pay me in cash. She does. Then she gives me her card and drives away. I say to myself, Well, that's the last of her. Three months later, she calls. Wants to give me a show in her gallery. Since then, Jackie shows my work every two years.

After Jackie hangs up I try to go back to work and almost succeed – until the next phone call. It's a number I don't recognize. I don't pick up. I hear him leave a message.

Hello. My name is Tommy Shannon, I'm a journalist. This year marks the twenty-fifth anniversary of the Immaculate

Game. I'm writing a story about it in a well-known publication, and I'd love to interview you. Please call me back.

Later.

Hi. Tommy Shannon again. I'm a HUGE admirer of your AMAZING career and all that you accomplished on the field. I'd love to get your reflections on The Game. Please call me.

Later.

Hey, it's Tommy! I don't give up. Heh-heh. Please pick up if you're there, and I won't call you again. Looking forward to speaking with you.

Later.

Tommy here. You knew my father, Gavin Shannon, sportswriter for the Chicago Tribune. He covered your career from the very beginning to when... it ended.

I remember Gavin. One of the few sportswriters on the Chicago beat that I respected. He loved baseball, loved every facet of the game, and knew its history. Sadly, he also loved the bottle. More than a few times I saw him stumble into the clubhouse after a game. Sportswriters. I never liked them. I didn't like Gavin. But he was always fair in his reporting. I respected him.

To answer a call, I don't need to pick up the phone. I had speakers and a console installed in every room. There is also a console in the right arm of my wheelchair.

I press ACCEPT.

I don't give interviews, I say to Tommy Shannon.

Thank you for taking my call.

Start talking.

It's the twenty-fifth anniversary of The Game.

The Game? What game?

C'mon, Breeze.

My name is Joseph Bye.

May I drive up and do an interview? I'm based in New York City.

Based? Are you in the military?

Ha-ha! No. I live in New York, and I travel a lot.

I. Don't. Give. Interviews. Got it?

Understood but–

I don't talk about baseball. I never again want to talk about baseball. I'm a painter. You can come to my opening at the Tommy Tom Gallery in Chelsea.

Thank you, I'd like that. But I'd also love to talk about The Immaculate Game. Nothing else, just that. I promise.

Immaculate Game? Never heard of it.

Twenty-seven outs. Twenty-seven strikeouts. Not a single ball hit fair. Greatest pitched game in the history of Major League Baseball. Arguably the greatest single-game feat in all of sports. You've never given an interview about that game. Why not?

Nothing more to add. It was nationally televised. Anyone can watch it on YouTube. Please don't call me again.

People still call it the Miracle Game.

Miracle? Batters strike out all the time.

Twenty-seven times in a row?

It was overdue. Only a matter of time. I just happened to be pitching. I was surprised that Nolan Ryan hadn't already done it.

I've interviewed almost every player and coach who was at The Game. The piece is written. Except I don't have you. Your insights and reflections would bring color and human interest to the piece. Your words would mean so much to so many fans.

How old are you?

I'm twenty-nine.

Twenty-nine. You were what? Four years old? Why so interested?

My father was there. He reported it. He loved the Cubbies. He talked about *The Game* all the time. He made it into a great tale. He coined the phrase The Immaculate Game.

I've got work to do.

My father said that The Game made him believe in God again.

I'm about to hang up on this annoying kid, but when he brings The Almighty into the story, I gotta hear this.

Why would he say that? I ask.

Dad was a lapsed Catholic. But he said only God could produce such a miracle. He said even a pitcher as great as The Big Breeze could not do it alone. Then he said – something he never wrote or told anyone else – that he saw a luminous glow on the pitching mound when you were pitching during the game. He said each inning the glow got a little brighter. By the ninth he thought he saw sparks shooting from the rubber. Dad believed it was a sign of God's presence.

I feel the hairs on the back of my neck stand up. I try to shake off the tingly sensation. But it sticks.

Listen, Tommy. The closest thing to divine power that day was my catcher. He called a fantastic game.

I wish I could have interviewed Torres. He was quoted as stating that catching The Game was the greatest experience in his life.

My fabulous catcher and best friend, Tiny Torres. He died of AIDS a couple of years after retiring from baseball. He was coaching a junior college baseball team in New Jersey. I sent flowers to his funeral. We had kept in touch over the years. I knew he was gay, and I was waiting for him to tell me. I think he was getting ready before my accident.

Finish writing your article, I tell the kid. You don't need me. Plus, I hardly remember it. You want to make it the most important game in sports history? Want to make it a cosmic, celestial event that rivals Moses parting the waters? That's your business.

Actually it was God who parted the waters, he says, trying to correct me. Bush league.

The Bible says Moses stretched out his hand. The sea parted. My money's on Moses.

Whatever.

I detect irritation in Tommy-boy's voice. Good. I decide to irritate him further.

Ever hear of Jackie Robinson? Jesse Owens? Muhammad Ali? Billie Jean King? What they accomplished dwarfs a single no-hit baseball game.

Did you know that all the players on the Chicago Cubs will be wearing your number this season to celebrate that Game? On every Cub player's sleeve will be the number 30.

These are my last words, then I'm hanging up. You begged the managing editor of some rag publication for this assignment. You promised to deliver an exclusive interview with The Big Breeze. You did your homework. That should be enough for any good journalist. But no. You had to add a touching story about your father's faith being renewed. A miracle! God's finger descends on a ball field, and your father is the only one who witnesses it. Nice hook. Maybe it's even true. You think, *This will melt Breezy's cold, hard heart. He will relent and give me the gut-spilling interview I want.* Sorry, Tommy. Heart still hard, freezer cold. Write your piece. Make your daddy happy.

There is a long silence on the phone. But I can hear Tommy breathing.

Mr. Bye, I've written articles for *The Atlantic*, *Harper's*, *The New Yorker*, and a dozen other periodicals. I don't have to *beg* anyone. In fact, it was the editor of *Rolling Stone* that asked me to write the story. My father died five years ago. And I believe his story is true. Every fucking word.

I'm sorry about your father, I say just before he hangs up.

I really am sorry, journalist Tommy Shannon, son of sportswriter Gavin Shannon. What could I possibly add? The usual clichés, the boilerplate. Did I feel invincible? Did I feel like a god? When did I realize that this game was special, different, awesome? Sorry, not interested.

What if I did talk about The Game? What would I tell him?

The ball felt different.

How different? Tommy asks.

It felt... alive.

You mean lively? he presses, madly taking notes.

No. Alive, I insist. Sounds crazy, but the ball really did feel alive. It scared me and thrilled me. I could do anything I wanted with the ball. Anything.

I stop. First time I've tried to explain what happened. It's difficult. Like trying to describe a vivid dream twenty years later.

Please, go on, he urges.

I think curve ball, inside corner. Start at the batter's eyes and drop across the knees for a called strike. The ball obeys. I think slider, outside corner. Start waist high then swoop down and outside to his ankles. The ball obeys. Batter swings and misses. But it was more than even that... The ball talked to me.

Talked to you? You heard it? Tommy asks.

It demands me to throw a four-seam fastball when I'm thinking change-up. I listen to the ball. Who's obeying who? In a game I may go through fifty to sixty baseballs. In this game, each ball feels just as alive as the last. But is it the ball in my hand I'm listening to? Or is it the ball in my head? All I know is that the ball feels alive, warm, and soft. I can mold it into whatever shape I want.

I told you that my father believed God was present, Tommy interjects.

If there was a god in that game, I don't think it was Jesus Christ, or Yahweh, or even Muhammad. For all I know it could have been the Prince of Darkness that possessed me.

Satan?

Why not the Devil? If so, perhaps God later punished me for having performed a god-like miracle. I think of the Greek ruling god Zeus, who was enraged at Prometheus for stealing fire for mortals. For his theft, Zeus chained Prometheus to a rock and sent an eagle to eat his liver for eternity.

What I don't tell Tommy is that, by the seventh inning, I feel the terror of pitching an Immaculate Game. A few times, when I have two strikes on a batter, I'm tempted to let him hit the ball fair. Break this damn spell! I hear a voice pleading to give in. Yet, I resist. FUCK YOU! I strike him out, because I can, and the hell with God or the Devil.

TWO

After Tommy's call it's back to work. The Mathewson portrait is going well – until the phone rings again. It's the Mr. Asshole who said he ran me down. It's the asshole who keeps calling. I know the asshole. I know him very well. I don't want to talk to him again. Can't bear to talk to him again. I'll regret talking to him again. Yet, I hit ACCEPT. I note the time: 3:35 PM. Salem will be at baseball practice for another hour. For the hell of it, I press RECORD.

Hello, Quincy.

Long time, huh Breeze?

Quincy Sacks. In Chicago everyone calls him Slammer – except me. Quincy spent four years in prison, thus his affectionate nickname. Attempted rape, assault, unlicensed firearm, resisting arrest. As a young man, Slammer played a few years in the minor leagues. Pitcher. When Quincy is released from prison, he tries getting back into the game. But whatever talent he once possessed has atrophied in prison. Plus, no team owner is eager to sign an ex-con to play for his team. I don't know what else Quincy tries after that, but misfortune follows him like dogshit stuck under his shoe. I heard that Lake Lemon found Quincy begging in the street near his apartment building. Lake buys him dinner, hears his story, and gives him a job. Another version I heard is that Quincy is a distant relative of Lake's – son of a cousin's niece kind of thing. Lake hires Quincy as his gofer and chauffeur. He drives Lake all over Chicago in his Mercedes-Benz. It was rumored that he sometimes gets women and drugs for Lake when asked. Quincy wants to be my gofer too, but I decline. There is something unsavory about him. He is thin to the point of boniness and has an ugly scar across his right cheek and nose. A memento from prison I guess. His slouch and shuffling walk remind me of a scavenger such as a hyena or jackal. I am protective of my precious image – as if it has any real value. Being a shallow young man, I blow Quincy off. Probably rather cruelly. I haven't seen or heard from him in twenty-five years. Ever since... the accident.

Why are you calling me?

I told you, Breeze.

Say it again. All of it. Top of the first inning to bottom of the ninth. Along with the names of all the players in the game. Take your time, Quince.

Just two players: me and Lake.

Go on.

Lake paid me.

To do what?

Like I said, to run you down.

You mean to kill me.

Silence.

Wasn't it to kill me, Quince?

Yeah.

Yeah, what?

Silence.

Yeah, WHAT!

Okay, to kill you!

I hear a long coughing jag. I imagine mucus and spots of blood on a filthy rag he holds over his mouth. The coughing subsides.

How much? I ask.

How much what?

How much did Lake pay you?

Geez... I dunno... It was a long time ago.

Better remember in three seconds or I hang up. One... two...

Okay! Ten K.

If he's waiting to hear my reaction, I give him none. Ten thousand lousy bucks. I want to scream, STUPID SONOFABITCH! YOU COULDA GOT FIFTY! Poor Slammer.

I didn't want to, Breeze! he whines.

Sure.

I loved you! You know that.

I feel sick. I want to puke. What makes men sell their souls so cheaply and thoughtlessly? Is a life that worthless? Are two lives that worthless? Mine and Slammer's? This morning I read the obituary of a woman named Esther Bejarano. She played the accordion in the Auschwitz Women's Orchestra. When a trainload of Jews arrived, the all-women orchestra greeted them with uplifting music. Esther said, We all knew that they were going to be gassed, but all we could do was stand there and play with tears in our eyes. The obit said that Esther died peacefully at the age of ninety-six at the Jewish Hospital in Hamburg, Germany. I wonder how peaceful Esther's death was.

Say something, Breeze!

Still in Chicago?

Where else am I gonna go?

Why'd you wait twenty-five years to tell me?

I'm dying.

Of what?

Liver cancer. Stage four. That's three strikes with no more at bats.

How long?

Two months. Tops.

Chicago... I'd treated Slammer like dirt. He idolized me, and

I could never take five minutes to talk to him. Now that he's dying, I can't even muster a grain of sympathy.

If you're seeking forgiveness, go to a priest.

I'm Jewish.

You're Jewish?

Yeah.

I never knew, I think, because I never talked to him. You observe? I ask.

Not since I was thirteen.

Bar mitzvah?

Yeah.

I see his whole family there, aunts, uncles, cousins, friends. Maybe a few musicians. Maybe some dancing. I wonder if his parents were Conservative Jews or Reform, but I don't ask.

I ain't asking for forgiveness! he wails. Don't deserve it. I just wanted you to know before I...

Now I know. That it, Quincy?

What are you gonna do?

Do?

With what I just told you.

Why do you care?

There is a long pause. I look at my unfinished canvas, thinking of what it needs. More red. Why red? I don't know. Needs something.

Still there? I ask.

I told Lake.

Told him what?

That I was gonna confess to you.

Why would you do something that foolish?

I wanted him to know. He threatened me. Said if I ever told you or anybody what we did, he'd kill me. Since I'm dying, I don't give a fuck. Let him kill me. Ha-ha! Doin' me a favor.

You called him?

Yeah.

Give me his number.

Why?

Just do it.

Quincy gives me the number.

You gonna call him? he asks.

Lake still in Chicago?

Nah. Moved to L.A. ten years ago.

Where in L.A.?

I don't know.

I want his address.

I don't know! Santa Monica, I think. Where the rich and famous live.

Goodbye, Quincy.

You were the best, Breeze. The best! Even Lake said so. He told me. He said, Slammer? Breeze is the greatest fucking pitcher I ever saw. Even after...

I'm not sorry you're dying, but I hope you die quick.

Trying my best. 'Cause I hate my life. I've lived a goddamn shitty life. I can't wait to die.

I'm saying goodbye. Don't call me back.

Breeze, I'm sorry. I'm so goddamn–

I hang up before he says another word.

I do feel bad for the bastard. As much as I want to hate him, I only feel pity. He drove the car that destroyed my career and almost ended my life. But he didn't end my life. I remade it doing something I enjoy. Why the hell did Quincy call me? Spilling his pathetic deathbed confession. I see him alone in a dumpy apartment in a rundown neighborhood in the Southside. Bare walls except for a calendar and some old autographed photos of Chicago Cubs players that Lake gave him. He lies in a soiled bed, nightstand filled with medications and a bottle of gin. Talking how he loved me when he tried to kill me. Why didn't he kill me? How's the saying go? A fuckup is a fuckup who will always fuck up.

But it was Lake that did it. Lake Lemon. I imagine the conversation Lake had with Quincy.

You're going to take down Breeze, says Lake.

You're kidding, right? asks Quincy, more a plea than a question.

Do I look like I'm kidding? Do I sound like I'm kidding?

N-no, Lake, stammers Quincy, who gets nervous whenever Lake gets angry.

I'm very serious. Very fucking serious.

But I like Breeze.

But I like Breeze! Lake savagely mimics.

Aw, geez, don't be like that.

Slammer, Breeze treats you like fucking goose shit.

He don't mean to.

Have you ever had a conversation with him? No, because he doesn't see you. It's obvious you disgust him. That he can barely stand the sight of you. This is the man you LIKE?

B-but I thought you liked him.

I hate him with every fiber of my being.

Why?

Breeze wronged me. He betrayed me. He deceived me in the most despicable way you can imagine. He took my woman. He seduced her. Stole my Sherry away. I was fucking this beautiful Black woman. You've never fucked a beautiful woman, Slammer, so you wouldn't understand. And now this BOY is FUCKING her! And after he fucks her, he laughs at me. Maybe both of them are laughing. LAUGHING at Lake Lemon! Do you understand?

Maybe they're not laughing.

WHAT!

N-nothing.

For that betrayal a heavy price will be paid. Breeze must pay the price. Breeze must go.

Go where?

This is when Lake takes out one of his long, expensive cigars. He enjoys lighting them over a lighter's flame, slowly rotating the cigar then moving the flame toward the center. When satisfied that he has lit a glowing red cherry on the tip, he takes his first puff as he does now.

I want you to run him down.

What?

Are you deaf?

Quincy shakes his head.

Run the bastard down.

W-what are you saying, Lake?

If you permanently cripple him I'll pay you $10,000. If you kill him I'll pay you $20,000.

K-kill Breeze? No, no! Don't ask me. Please, Lake!

But I just did.

I couldn't! There's no way...

You want to go back to the slammer, Slammer?

NO!

I can make that happen in a second, Lake says, snapping his fingers. I know what you did to that girl. Naughty boy. How old was she? Fifteen?

I didn't do nothin' to her!

Then why did I have to pay her mother off to not go to the police?

Quincy starts to weep. Lake grabs Quincy's neck with both hands and lifts him in the air like he's a raggedy doll.

You're going to do exactly what I tell you. I'll take care of the car. All you need to do is drive. You just drive. Understand, Slammer?

Quincy weeps.

DO YOU UNDERSTAND!

Y-y-yes.

Tell me what you'll do.

Whatever you say, Lake.

No, tell me what you will do!

I d-drive.

Incomplete, Slammer! Why will you drive?

To run Breeze down!

Say it again.

Run Breeze down... Run Breeze down... Run Breeze...

Lake and Quincy ran me down. What are you going to do? I ask myself. Nothing is always an option. Continue living my life; raise my daughter as best I can; paint my portraits; Tuesday/Thursday sex with Heidi. But I know doing nothing is not an option. I feel like I just awoke from a dream, and I'm either fully awake or entering a nightmare.

Since the accident, I have one recurring dream. I'm running down Chicago's Lakefront Trail along Lake Michigan. I liked to run there at dawn between my pitching starts, watching the sun come up. Then I wake up and look at my useless legs.

If Lake knows that I know, what will *he* do? Will he come after me? Will he send another assassin to finish the job he started twenty-five years ago? Or is he so confident of his power that he won't worry a twit what Breeze does? I may have once been a famous athlete, but now I'm a little-known painter bound to a wheelchair. What does he have to worry about? If I know Lake, he will worry. And that is what worries me. I wheel around the studio, considering my options.

What will you do, Breeze?

What would I like to do?

No, what WILL you do?

Blow up the world. Time travel back twenty-five years. Walk again. Never be born. Never lay eyes on Sherry. Gorgeous goddess Sherry. Burn down the Hall of Fame. Choke Lake Lemon until his eyeballs pop out, his tongue turns black, and blood shoots out of his ears and ass. With my powerful hands and wrists, I could do that.

What will you REALLY do?

MOTHER FUCKING MOTHER FUCK! Using the wheelchair as leverage, I furiously push myself up to stand. The wheelchair rolls away and flips over – because I stupidly forgot to lock the brakes. I teeter, take a step, and fall on my back. Again, JESUS FUCK!

What will you do, Breeze? asks a velvety voice by the doorway. Same velvety voice as her mother's. Shit, what's she doing here?

What will you do? Salem repeats.

I take five deep breaths to calm down. Take three more normal breaths to slow my racing heart. Take three more breaths to steady my strained voice. Ready.

Why aren't you at practice? I ask.

Cancelled. Coach was sick.

You know the rules.

Knock before entering the barn.

Studio.

It's a barn, Breeze. Built as a barn. Looks like a barn. Still smells like a barn.

See any hay? Cows? Horses? No. You see canvases, paints, brushes. Studio.

Whatever.

And yet, you still–

I did knock! You didn't answer. I was afraid you fell. You do that sometimes. Like now.

She's right. I do fall occasionally, well more than occasionally, when I try walking. Did she really knock?

How long have you been there?

A few minutes.

Only a few?

Maybe more.

Salem moves into view, baseball cap on her head, aviator sunglasses perched on the bill. The sunglasses were Sherry's favorite pair, and now Salem wears them all the time. She has on her usual practice outfit: faded turquoise over-sized tee-shirt over black denim shorts. On her right hand is a Rawlings baseball glove. She likes wearing it on her way to practice, pounding the pocket with her fist just as I did when I was her age. Her glove, bought with babysitting money, is well-worn. She pitches on the high school baseball team. Last year, she tried out for girls' softball. Boring! she complained. So, she marches over to Bernie Siskoff's office. He's the coach of the school's baseball team, all boys of course. She asks him for a tryout. Coach Siskoff tells her to go back to girls' softball. Next day Salem is back in his office and demands a chance. She reminds him that she's protected from sex discrimination under Title IX. Coach relents, thinking, *Okay, pest! This won't take long.* In her tryout she hits a ball over the fence and strikes out three of his best hitters. This year, my 14-year-old daughter is the team's number one pitcher. I've never watched her pitch. I've never attended any of the games. I haven't watched baseball since...

Salem would ask me before every game: You coming today?

Sorry, I need to finish a painting.

It's a big game. I'm pitching.

Wish I could. Pitch well, honey.

Painting. My art. Deadlines. Always excuses. Eventually she stops asking. But I know it's a sore spot for her.

Back to the present: I'm still lying on the floor.

Want me to help you up? she asks.

No thanks.

Be faster if I help.

I can do it.

Jesus, Breeze, let me help you.

I got it!

She knows I hate being helped. I turn over and, to my dismay, see that the wheelchair has rolled to the end of the studio, turned over, and is tangled in discarded canvas. It would take me twenty minutes to crawl over there, untangle the chair, and lift it upright on its wheels. I relent.

You want to help? Turn the chair over.

I'm hearing mixed messages.

Please, Salem.

She turns over the wheelchair, rolls it over to me, locks the brakes, and despite my protest, helps me back in the chair.

Thank you, I say, waiting for her to leave.

Salem doesn't leave. She remains standing by the easel, pounding her glove. Has she grown another inch in the last few months? She must be as tall as most of the boys in school. It's not that I never pay attention to her body, but maybe I should notice it more. She's now scrutinizing me in a way I haven't seen before. What's going on in that mind of hers?

I heard the phone call, she says, still pounding her glove.

What phone call?

The one before you started cursing and fell.

How much did you hear?

Enough.

Stop pounding your glove!

She stops.

Who's Quincy? she asks.

Just a poor, pathetic character I barely knew a long time ago. It's all nonsense.

Uh-huh.

I hope you didn't believe anything he said.

Every word.

Salem—

I know about Quincy Sacks, aka Slammer.

You know?

I also know about Lake Lemon.

How?

Mom told me.

Ah, Sherry, beautiful betrayer. Even after death you create turmoil.

When? I ask.

Just before she went to Spain. I'd turned eleven. Mom said, You're grown up enough. Time to tell the backstory about Mommy and Daddy. So, she told me. You and her and Lake Lemon. She talked all night and into morning. Best bedtime story Mom ever told me, and she read to me a lot – something you *never* did.

She should not have told you.

Why?

It's personal. Complicated. Adult stuff. You're not an adult.

Were you ever going to tell me?

Yes... eventually.

Bullshit.

Hey! You're not grown up enough to curse at your father.

Then don't lie to me!

I'm not lying.

So, what *are* you going to do?

I look at her. She has the same expression on her face that her mother had whenever she got exasperated with me. Eyes wide open, nostrils flared, jaw set, lips pressed tightly together, and a shake of her head. Jesus Christ. I loved her mother so much it hurt. Now I love this girl, who's becoming a young woman too fast. Independent, strong willed. Makes me wonder why she ever listens to me at all. She doesn't need me. I can't give her anything. My love seems as disabled as my legs.

Salem got her name from Sherry's favorite play. During our first months together, Sherry is cast in an all-Black, Chicago production of Arthur Miller's *The Crucible*, set in Salem during the witch trials. Sherry plays Abigail, the teenager in love with the married hero John Proctor, who lusts for the girl. Sherry makes me and the audience believe that Abigail will do anything to have him. I remember one line: Abigail says to Proctor, *A wild thing may say wild things*. Sherry is radiant on stage. I'm amazed how this woman transformed herself into a willful teenager in love with a man twice her age. Even though she ignites the events that take the life of Proctor and twenty-four other Salem residents, I feel empathy for her. She still believes Proctor loves her even when he rejects her.

You haven't answered my question, Salem reminds me.

I don't know, kid.

You gotta do something.

Push me outside.

Push you?

Yes.

You don't like being pushed.

I like *you* pushing me... sometimes.

No, you don't.

You used to love pushing me.

Yeah, like when I was seven!

Are you going to push me? I ask sweetly.

Where?

Garden.

Then you'll tell me?

Push me to the garden; I'll tell you anything you want.

Salem liked pushing me until she was ten. Then she was done. Over. No more Daddy's-little-girl crap. When she did push me, I believe it made her feel... what? Like a caregiver, though she didn't know what the word meant. Maybe it just made her feel connected to me. The wheelchair is part of Daddy. When she puts her two hands on the wheelchair, it's like she's holding Daddy. Like she's carrying him. Or like she's attached to him.

THREE

My name is Fernando José Luis Torres. But everyone calls me Tiny. Naturally, 'cause I'm nothing but. Six-four and 235 pounds. Big for a catcher. Some say too big. Yeah, I'm slow as a three-toed sloth running the bases. But behind the plate? I move like a cat. Three years in a row, I ranked best defensive catcher in the league. You wanna run on me? Oh, baby, do it, please! I love when they try to steal. I don't even get out of my crouch. ZING! My cannon arm shoots a laser to second. If they lean a little too far off first, ZING! I cut them down before they can blink. Nobody runs on me anymore. Boo-hoo. Makes Tiny very sad. Makes my pitchers very happy.

I'm the luckiest man in the world. Know why? I catch the greatest pitcher who ever played the game. The Big Breeze. And right now, I could be catching his greatest game. After three innings he's struck out all nine batters. Can't be more perfect than that. Nobody even close to getting a hit. Two foul balls. Two! Needed only nine pitches in the third inning. It's like trying to hit a feather in a hurricane. Scary. Breeze and I been battery mates for seven years. He refuses to pitch to another catcher – unless I'm hurt or on the DL. But I tell you, I'd have to be on my deathbed not to catch this guy. Pure joy!

I'm just a poor Dominican kid from the Bronx. Single mom raising four boys while working full time as a cashier in a bodega. I'm the oldest and protected my brothers with my fists and rocks. I could throw a rock farther, harder, and straighter than any kid in our 'hood. Gangs see me coming and they scatter like a flock of pigeons. Best part of growing up in the Bronx is that I could ride my bike to Yankee Stadium. I'd sit in the cheap bleacher seats, dreaming of catching for the Bronx Bombers. But an even better dream came true: catching Breeze every fourth game.

We're playing at Wrigley Field, and the hometown fans could be watching history. The score's 0-0 against our hated rivals, the St. Louis Cardinals. Best hitting team in the league. But tonight they're swinging like Little Leaguers. When Breeze is at his best he's almost unhittable. Tonight he IS unhittable. His fastball isn't just electric. It's nuclear! I've never seen him pitch so hard. Still that same smooth delivery with that high, silky leg kick. Five feet before his fastball reaches home plate, I swear it elevates three inches and explodes. His hard stuff must be hitting a hundred. Sliders are darting and slashing. Curves are dropping off a cliff. His changeup is a thing of beauty. Looks exactly like his fastball except 20 mph slower. Batters either swing before it reaches the plate or they freeze as the umpire calls STEEE-RIKE! Batter walks away shaking his head. Man, I love that!

Maybe I'll tell Breeze tonight. After the game. A week before the All-Star Game, which Breeze is starting. I've never seen him happier. This could be his best season, which is saying a lot. The team's in first place. He's in love with a gorgeous actress, Sherry what's-her-name. I've been wanting to tell him for a long time. I gotta tell someone. Tonight. For sure. We can meet at our favorite bar on North Clark Street.

FOUR

Salem pushes me past the swimming pool, down the stony path, into the garden. She has her sunglasses on, though the sky is mostly cloudy. In one of the flower beds I see our gardener, Pham, on his hands and knees spreading mulch. Pham waves at us. We wave back. He's been our gardener for twenty years. He came to the country from Vietnam with his parents after Saigon fell in '75. Sherry loved helping Pham plant new trees or spreading seedlings while he told her stories about growing up in a small Vietnamese village.

Salem pushes me past the bed of roses, past the bed of wildflowers – Black-eyed Susans, marigolds, morning glories, zinnias, corn poppies, yarrow – and past the water lily pond. Forty years ago, when I was Salem's age, this area was mostly pasture. My family owned a hundred acres of rich farmland. My father inherited the farm from his father, who inherited it from his father. A working farm in which a family, along with a few hired hands, could make a living. A *decent living* as my father would say. Decency. Respect. My father, James Patrick Bye, with my mother, Frances Rose Bye, at his side, was the last of his line. The last Bye farmer. The farm was failing even when I was a boy. It was hard just to make a living, let alone a decent living. Eventually, they could no longer afford the hired hands. Except me. My folks were forced to sell off lots to keep afloat. By the time I left home, there were twenty acres left. We had four dairy cows. My job was to milk them twice a day: 5:00 AM and 5:00 PM. From age nine until I left home. I didn't mind squeezing their teats, hearing the WHOOSH-WHOOSH sound of milk streaming in the metal pail. Made me feel close to the cows. More important, it strengthened my hands for pitching a baseball.

Eighteen years old, I'm in my first year of professional base-ball, pitching for the Chicago Cubs' minor league team in Peoria. It's a Friday in early July. The manager has scheduled me to pitch that night when my father calls.

Joey, you need to come home, he says.

What happened?

Your mother... She passed this morning.

Oh, Jesus, Dad... I thought her cancer was in remission.

It was. Then it wasn't. Doctors here don't know shit.

I'll be home as soon as I can.

After helping Dad bury her, I stay five days. During that time my father continues to work the farm but hardly says a word to me. It's almost a relief to leave and rejoin my team. A month later, I pitch a three-hitter against a team in Beloit, Wisconsin then I get the awful news: My father killed himself with his favorite 12-gauge shotgun.

Still mourning over the death of my mother, I fly home to bury Dad. This time, I plan to spend two weeks on the farm. It stretches to three weeks. I call the manager and tell him that I won't be returning to the team. He understands. See you next year, he says. I take care of unfinished business, sell off the animals, pay what bills I can. During sleepless nights there, I keep asking myself the same question: Had I stayed on the farm, would my father's grief still have overwhelmed him? I'm also angry at Dad. He left me without a word, written or verbal. Perhaps, it didn't occur to him that I still needed him.

After my father's suicide, I almost quit baseball. Seems it only brings death to my life. But I owe $30,000 to the bank on a loan to keep the farm running. I could sell the farm to pay off the loan. But I don't. I'm too attached to the damn place where three generations of Byes toiled over the land. I go to the bank manager to ask for an extension. I promise him that, by next year, I will be pitching in the Major Leagues. Turns out the bank manager is a life-long Yankees fan. He tells me the story of catching a Mickey Mantle foul ball when he's eight years old. Bank manager gives me more time. I almost make good on my promise. It took me two years, but the bank manager gave me another extension. It still saddens me that my parents never saw me pitch in the big leagues.

We should spread Mom's ashes here, says Salem.

I'm silent.

Breeze?

We've discussed this.

You know how much she loved the garden.

I'm not ready.

Three years?

It's all I have. I need more time.

Salem parks us under an eastern redbud and sits on the stone bench. She looks at me and rubs her chin. The chin rub is her tell that she's going to get serious. Sherry and I would come out here in the morning and drink our second cup of coffee before starting the day. She would push me as she hums a Broadway tune while I hold our mugs. With a free hand she strokes my hair. How I miss her fingers in my hair. Salem crosses her legs and grabs the edge of the bench, just like her mom. I can see Sherry now. I can hear Sherry.

What are you going to do about Lake Lemon? Sherry asks.

Kill him, of course.

Be serious, Breeze.

I am. I'm going to kill the bastard!

You're really going to kill Lake?

What choice do I have? There's no other option.
How do you plan to do that?
Haven't figured that out yet.

Should you be telling this to your only daughter? the woman sitting on the stone bench asks.

I stare at Sherry. No! At Salem! My daughter. Salem. I smile ironically, realizing the conversation hadn't been in my head.

Kidding! Bad joke, I say, trying to assure her. But I think of the time I wanted to kill Lake before the accident. It was after Sherry cooled things between us when I pressed her to leave Lake. We're in bed, about to make love. I couldn't stand it any longer.

You need to leave him, I say.

My relationship with Lake is none of your business, she says.

Then I guess I got no business sleeping with you.

That's up to you.

Sherry, you don't need Lake.

Really? So, now you know what I need.

He's using you. To him you're just a shiny new trophy.

Ever think that maybe I'm using Lake?

What?

He's connected me to several prominent agents, producers, and directors. Furthermore, I ain't nobody's trophy! So, don't even think of calling me that!

I get out of her bed, whip on my pants, grab the rest of my clothes, and leave.

After that we don't see each other for a month. The season has begun. By the end of April, I'm 5-0, my best start. On May 2, the day before I'm pitching, I'm asleep when I hear the apartment door open. There's only one other person who has the key. I'm about to switch on the lamp when—

No lights! Sherry cries out.

Why not?

Can I stay the night?

What happened?

Nothing! Can I stay the night?

I switch on the lamp. She turns her head – not before I see the bruise above her eye.

Did he do that?

She shakes her head.

Did Lake fucking do that!

Sherry sits on the edge of the bed, her body folds within itself. She says, Things got a little... rough. So, I left.

Will you be going back?

She shakes her head.

Come to bed.

She slips off her shoes, leaves her clothes on, and crawls under the covers.

Want me to hold you?

Just let me lie beside you.

I turn off the lamp. I hear her fall instantly asleep.

She never left me again.

Soon after, I let it be known to my teammates that I would no longer speak to the sportswriter Lake Lemon. I said it was personal and would appreciate it if they refused to speak to Lake as well. And none of them did.

Back in the garden, Salem and I are still sitting under the redbud tree.

I can help, says Salem.

I said I wasn't serious.

Yeah, you were. I'm glad.

I won't kill him.

What he did to you, Breeze? That piece of shit deserves to die.

Don't curse. And if I kill him, I go to prison. Where will you be?

Oh, yeah.

Yeah.

What are you gonna do?

Talk to Lake. If he did what Slammer said, I want to hear it from him.

Then what?

I stay silent.

I'm coming with you, she insists.

Out of the question.

You can't go alone.

Because I can't walk?

Because I want to help you! Because you need me!

Her vehemence startles me. She looks like she's about to cry. She never cries, even as a toddler. Salem holds back the tears. Good girl.

What will I do with her while I'm gone? Can't let her stay by herself. This is happening too fast.

You'll stay with Heidi and Larry, I propose.

What? No way!

You can spend more time with Brittany. It'll be fun.

Bad idea.

Heidi and Larry are crazy about you. They'll be thrilled. I'll call them tonight.

Believe me, it's much better if I go with you. Trust me.

I look at her. She breaks into a knowing grin, which I don't like.

I know about you and Heidi.

I don't say anything.

Don't even try denying it, she says.

Let's go back inside.

What are you going to do about Heidi?

I ignore her question, thinking how this day has turned into a total disaster.

It's obvious, Breeze. She loves you. And you must love her... at least a little.

Can we please drop this?

You and Heidi have been going at it for months. It's time you guys made future plans.

I stare at her. *Going at it? Future plans?* My 14-year-old daughter is offering advice on my illicit affair. Perhaps I should be proud of her. I mean, do I want a stupid daughter? I'll deny it, of course. Last refuge of poor parenting: Lie, lie, lie to your kids. And keep lying. But I can't lie. Not to Salem. Just like I could never lie to her mother.

How long have you known? I ask.

Six months.

Six months?

Yep.

Don't say yep.

Why not?

Makes you sound ignorant and white.

I'm half-white.

In the eyes of our very exceptional, very racist society, you're Black.

You're trying to change the subject, she says, and she's right.

Tell me what you *think* you know.

This is what I *know* I know. Every Tuesday and Thursday morning, Heidi parks her Volvo down the block on the corner of Brewster Lane. She waits until I get on the school bus and it pulls away. Then she gets out of the car, walks to our house, lets herself in, and for the next hour, you and Heidi do whatever you guys do.

What do you think we do?

I think she comes here to fuck you.

First, that's not true. Second, don't use foul language in this house.

We're not *in* the house, we're outside the house. And you never curse?

I'm an adult, and I don't curse around you.

I've heard you plenty.

Heidi comes here to talk. Over coffee. That's it, I say. Guess I *can* lie to Salem.

Talk?

Yes.

You talk.

Yes.

You *hate* talking. You *never* talk. Most days we exchange like three sentences: good morning, pass the bread, good night.

It's true. I'd gladly go a week without uttering a single word. Yet, here I am jabbering with my daughter like she's Alice and I'm the manic March Hare at the Wonderland tea party.

Mostly, Heidi talks and I listen, I say.

Why come here when she has Larry to talk to? she tartly asks.

Heidi's unhappy.

With Larry?

Lots of things.

I still think she comes here to fuck.

Do not use that word again.

She comes here to have sex with you. God, she must be desperate.

Thank you.

Why does she hide in her car?

She doesn't hide.

Looks like hiding to me.

If you saw her, how is that hiding?

Scrunched down in her seat so you can't see her face, though you can't miss her piled-up blonde hair. Why does she wait for me to leave?

So, we can have privacy.

To talk?

Talk... and drink coffee, I say, aware how lame that sounds.

Just because I'm fourteen, you must think I'm not only dumb but blind. Looking out the bus window, I can see Heidi's white SUV Volvo. The first time, I wondered why her car is parked two blocks from our house – for like three seconds. Later, I wondered why it's only parked there on Tuesdays and Thursdays. One Thursday I get off the bus at the next stop. I wait behind the shrubs in Mr. Snodgrass' front yard. I watch Heidi walk inside our house. An hour later she walks out all smiley balloon face and gets in her car. I know what she's smiling about, and it's not talk and coffee. So, what are you going to do about Heidi?

One of my strengths as a pitcher was that nothing ever flustered me. I was fully focused on each pitch, no matter the count or score. As a rookie, my manager said I had the mental toughness of a veteran. But now? I get upset by the stupidest, most petty things. At this moment I feel cornered by my teenaged daughter. What business is it of hers what I do while she's at school? Her smug face triggers a shameful response.

Did your mother ever tell you that I didn't want children?

Yes, she responds without a flinch.

Shit. I'm thrown off by her answer.

She told you that?

We trusted each other. We shared secrets. She was my friend. My *best* friend.

How'd you feel when she told you.

What am I supposed to feel? I'm here. Right? Can't put the toothpaste back in the tube.

No, no, no. I mean how'd that make you feel about me?

She shrugs French-like in reply. I wait for a verbal answer. She takes her time.

Didn't take it personally, she finally drawls, now Texan-like.

You don't hate me?

No.

Maybe you should. I wouldn't blame you if you did.

I don't hate you, Breeze.

Why not?

You didn't want children. Or you didn't want a kid. Either way, that's a concept.

A concept?

You didn't know me at the time. What you didn't want didn't exist because I didn't exist. Once I did exist, everything changed. Didn't it? Once you saw tiny newborn me, once you held that bundle of joy in your arms, I'd like to think you changed your mind.

She twirls a strand of hair between her thumb and index finger. Adorable. Another teasing trait of her mother's.

Do you always talk like this? I ask.

Talk like what? She smiles. Fucking heartbreaker.

Nothing.

This is how I talk, Breeze. You just haven't been listening.

This is by far the longest conversation I've had with Salem since Sherry died. We had each dug into our own interior burrows like woodchucks preparing for winter hibernation. For her it was school and baseball. For me it was painting, painting, and painting.

Push me further, I say.

How further?

Apple trees.

She stands up and pushes me along the stony path. We haven't done this together in a long time. Has it been over three years? When her mother was still alive? Ahead are four gnarly apple trees in a raggedy row. They are bent like elderly old crones, gossiping about other trees, the animals, the birds, maybe even the humans who hardly visit them anymore.

Stop! I command when we arrive under their contorted boughs. Greeting us are two weathered Adirondack chairs. Salem settles in one. The sun sits low, and the air is cool. When she sits, her shorts ride up her thighs. Strong, shapely legs. She gets them from me. All her beauty is from her mother, but her powerful legs are my gift.

How come you never ask about my sex life? she suddenly asks.

Christ, what brings this on? Did she catch me looking at her legs? Choose your words carefully, Breeze.

You have a sex life?

Doesn't everyone? she retorts, brimming with the unfathomable wisdom of all her fourteen years.

Interesting premise.

You didn't answer my question.

None of my business.

You're not interested?

Didn't say I wasn't interested. Just that, well... what you do with your body – short of harming it or harming others – is up to you.

You're weird, Breeze.

Here's weird: When did you stop calling me Dad or Daddy and start calling me Breeze?

I don't know.

When your mother died.

Hmm.

Why is that?

I don't know.

She shrugs her shoulders again in that French way, as if we're on the Left Bank sitting in the Café de Flore. She takes her sunglasses off and perches them on the cap's bill.

You do know, I say.

Everyone calls their male parent Father, Dad, Daddy, Pop. I like your brand.

My *brand*?

Breeze, Breezy, Big Breeze. None of my friends' fathers have cool names like that. They're all like Harry, George, Bert, John, Bill, Chris, Stu, Derek, Jerry, Paul, Mike, Roger...

Salem continues with her dull-daddy name list, but I stop listening. I'm looking at Sherry's old aviators, thinking of how much she loved wearing sunglasses – outdoors and indoors. She had a dozen different pair of designer sunglasses – Italian, Japanese, French, German, Israeli. Then something changes after she gives birth. Sherry never wears sunglasses whenever she's with Salem. Pushing her in a carriage or later in a stroller, even on the brightest summer day, she is sans sunglasses. One day I ask her why. I want my daughter to always see her mother's eyes, she says. That all. Doesn't tell me why that's important. Doesn't have to.

I'll take over, I say to Salem, putting my hands on the wheels.

I want to keep pushing.

You pushed enough.

But Salem pushes me down the stony path as the sun sinks further. Ahead are the last old-growth trees on the property: oaks, maples, pines, cedars. Our little forest. You can still find deer and foxes there. She stops next to an old eastern hemlock. Must be at least a hundred years old. No benches or chairs here. Salem sits on the ground, cushioned by pine needles, her back rests against the rough bark of the trunk. She rubs her chin again. Where'd she get that gesture? Me? Sherry?

Last week I let a boy touch my breast, she says as casually as telling me she loaned a boy her algebra book.

How do I respond to that declarative statement? I don't. She pulls a dandelion up from the ground and twirls it with her thumb and forefinger. I study her face. It suddenly occurs to me that I've never drawn it... my daughter's face. How is that possible? I sketch her face now in my mind. Strong chin. That could be unfortunate. Most guys are afraid of women with strong chins. At least that will weed out all the weak men. She has her mother's smokey skin tone – like a bluesy ballad sung by Abbey Lincoln. As mentioned, she's already tall. She may grow another two inches. Hazel eyes, wide mouth, small ears. She wears her hair in a braided ponytail. God, she's beautiful... like her mother. And for that, in this moment, I hate her a little. Why couldn't she be short, dumpy, pasty pale, and unathletic? Why couldn't she be happily average in intelligence and have lots of average intelligent friends? But she's not and she doesn't. I'm glad, yet I still hate her a little.

What's curious is that I don't even like him, she muses. He's sort of cute, but totally boring.

Why are you telling me this?

I don't know, she says. That damn French shrug again.

I'm your father, is my brilliant response.

Yeah, I know that.

Good.

Are you angry?

Why would I be angry?

'Cause I let a boy–

I heard you before.

We're both silent. I wish Sherry was alive. What would she say?

How did it feel? I ask. Probably not what Sherry would say.

Strange.

Did you feel...

Pleasure? Then she laughs.

Should I not ask you?

God, I dunno. Some days I think, yeah, other days, nah.

The trees cast long shadows. Fifty yards away a tawny doe grazes on the grass.

Last month I kissed a girl, she says, again as casually as remarking on a funny cloud shape.

I process this new, jolting information as I watch a fawn join the doe. The doe pays it no mind, so the fawn wanders off. Kids.

How'd that feel? I say, matching her casual tone.

Interesting... interesting.

I nod, helpless... helpless.

Am I weird? she asks.

You're young and confused like any normal 14-year-old girl, I say, sticking to a standard parent script that means absolutely nothing.

How long does that last?

You'll be fourteen for only a few more months. As to being confused, that depends.

Hmm.

There's no rush.

No rush with what?

Sex.

You mean fucking?

I decide to let that one slide.

How long did it take you? Salem asks.

For sex?

Yes.

Too long.

How come?

I was shy, introverted, and had bad acne in high school.

I don't want it to be too long.

How many boundaries am I breaking with my daughter? Should we start talking Oedipal stuff? No, that's Electra stuff. Should I ask her if she wants to sleep with me? Should I talk about a dream I recently had of kissing her thighs and waking in a panicky sweat?

Oh! And I've started masturbating, she proudly adds.

I was also late on that, I say. The threat of eternal Lutheran hell held me back.

I like talking sex with you, Breeze. We can have a lot more conversations when we go after Lake.

Don't you have girlfriends you can talk sex with?

Girlfriends? she asks with disdain, making a face like I asked if she had crabs.

No girlfriends?

Breeze, I'm a TOMBOY!

You must have a few—

The boys don't like me because I play baseball better than them. The girls don't like me because I'm bored by the girly gibberish they talk about. So, I HAVE NO FRIENDS! Only friend I ever had was Mom. I'm like you, Breeze. You don't have any friends either.

She's right.

What about Brittany? I ask.

We used to be close. Now she just talks about boys and clothes.

I love you, Salem. But you're still not coming with me.

Show me you really love me by letting me come.

You don't believe I love you?

Not all the time... Not most of the time.

How long have you felt this?

Um... Like all my life.

All this time I assumed she knew I loved her. But how could she if I didn't show it? Fourteen years? Let's say twelve years. Do I get a pass for her first two years? Maybe not. I assess with myself.

Did you hold her in your arms?

Only when I had to.

Did you ever change her diapers? Did you ever bathe her? Did you ever feed her? Did you ever play a game with her?

No, no, no, no.

Did you sing her songs? Read her stories at bedtime? Play boardgames with her? Help her with her homework?

No, no, no, no.

Ever tell her about your life? Ever talk to her about your parents and grandparents? Ever ask about her dreams, her fears, her goals?

No, no, no, no.

What the hell did you ever do to show that you loved her?

I provided her things she needed: food, shelter, clothes, school books.

Stuff. You gave her stuff. Because you loved her or because it was the least you had to do.

Can it be both?

Parenting is harder than pitching. Much harder. It was just too much for you. As a father you couldn't make bench warmer on a bush-league team. Face it, Breeze, you're a failure.

I'm going inside now on my own power, I tell Salem.

I grab the wheels and propel myself forward. She walks along. We're both silent for a minute.

We could bond on the trip, she says. It would be good for both of us.

It's not a vacation.

I know.

It could be dangerous.

Which is why I should go with you.

What about your team?

Breeze, your life is more important than a game. I love baseball. But I love you more.

Goddamn her! my brain screams.

Let me think about it, I say.

When we return to the house, it's past seven o'clock. Salem goes upstairs to do homework. I go back to the studio to get an hour of painting in. With all the disruptions today, I feel horribly unproductive. I work on Matty's mouth, brushing strokes of purple to show the intersection of fatigue and grit. Better. I set the canvas aside and pull out my double portrait.

The two figures are a pitcher and a catcher. The title is *Mound Rendezvous*. It's my largest painting ever, 5 x 8 feet. It shows the two figures from the waist up. The catcher has walked to the pitching mound to confer with his pitcher. Why does a catcher do that? Several possible reasons. To calm down a shaky pitcher, to review how to pitch to a dangerous batter in a crucial situation, to be prepared for a steal or bunt, or simply to stall while a reliever warms up.

The faces are almost there; the torsos and arms need more work. In general I'm dissatisfied with it. What are they saying to each other? What inning is it? How many men are on base? What's the score? And what's the relationship between these two men? So, I do what I always do when I have a problem. I look at the painting until I find an answer. The catcher has taken off his mask. They gaze deeply at each other like lovers. Because I couldn't find a photo of a pitcher and catcher on the mound that I liked, I painted in me and Tiny as the figures.

What if the catcher puts his hand on the pitcher's shoulder? I squirt a glob of titanium white on the palate. I brush four or five strokes to roughly outline the arm. Interesting. I lean back and look some more.

Tiny Torres joins the club the year after I break in. We

immediately click. The following season we room together on the road. By my fourth year, the club offers me a single hotel room when we travel – a perk given to only the biggest stars. I tell them I'm fine having a roomie and that I don't want the other players to know about the offer.

Tiny knows that I dislike visits to the mound unless he feels it's important. When he does visit it's always at the right moment. In my first World Series game the first batter hits a single, and I walk the next two batters. Bases loaded with no outs. We're playing the Red Sox at Fenway. It's a lion's den. Home fans are in a frenzy, screaming, jeering, chanting obscenities. They smell blood. Tiny ambles over to me. Takes off his mask and says, Some crazy-ass crowd, huh? We both crack up. That's all he says and ambles back. I strike out the side and go on to pitch a 3-hit shutout.

I'm thinking that I should work on the figures' faces. But I don't. I do something else. Something so weird it shocks me. I grab a tube of ivory black, my favorite color, and squeeze a large glob on my palette knife. Then I apply a thick, curved line three inches above the pitcher's back. I have no idea why I'm doing this. None. I stare at the black line. I stare for a long time. First, up close. Then from six feet away. That line has no business being there. I'll paint it out when it dries, I think. But no! Instead, I add more ivory black, thickening and enlarging the line. I still don't know why I'm doing this. I'm not an abstract painter! The line belongs in a painting by Franz Kline, Willem de Kooning, or Jackson Pollock. Not in a painting by Joseph Bye! I want to immediately paint over it. It scares me. The black line seems to move, wiggle, pulse. I'm afraid to touch it. What's it doing over the pitcher?

After staring at the painting for twenty minutes, I take up my palette knife, prepared to scrap off the line, when there's a knock at the door. It's not Salem's familiar three quick knocks. Instead, it's a series of five or six pounding blows. I turn the easel around. When I open the door, I see Larry Weems standing before me in his uniform. Strangely, I've never seen him wearing his uniform in all the years I've known him. Equally strange he's never visited me in my studio. It's true I've never invited him. Also true he's never shown any interest in my work. Yet, there he stands at my studio door. He looks good in uniform. A strapping six-footer, Larry is extremely fit and well-toned for a white man in his forties. Short, blond hair with hardly any gray. Their daughters are also blonde. They're an attractive blond family. However, something looks wrong. The top two buttons of his shirt are unbuttoned; he's capless; he looks distraught; and he appears at a loss for words.

Hello, Larry, I say.

He nods, says nothing.

What's up? I ask as a helpful prompt.

I... stopped by your house... Salem said you were in the barn.

Doing some touching up.

If I'm disturbing you...

Want to come in?

He nods, doesn't move. I open the door wider. He enters cautiously as if there are landmines along the way.

Larry and I have rarely had a conversation without at least one of our wives present. All we have in common is our daughters. Could this be about his daughter? My daughter? Perhaps, a local crime. Unlikely he wants advice on art. Has he come to arrest me? I lead him to the only chair in the studio, a wooden, paint-splattered, straight-back for the rare visitor. Larry doesn't sit back but leans forward, his hands dangle then clasp each other as if kneading dough. He's making me nervous. I wait for him to speak. Nothing.

Like something to drink? I ask. Coffee, tea, water?

He shakes his head.

Something stronger?

He scratches his cheek, considers.

Maybe... Yes.

There's only a bottle of Jameson... for guests.

Neat, please.

I pour him a generous shot. He downs it in one swig. I refill his glass. This one he sips before getting down to business.

I think Heidi is cheating on me.

I try to look surprised. Widen eyes. Open mouth slightly. Take a quick intake of breath. Good. I've been preparing for this moment. Rehearsing in my sleep.

What makes you think...

A feeling.

A feeling?

She's been different... for months.

In what way... different?

This will sound weird.

Go on, I say, trying to sound reassuring.

She's happier, he says.

Happier? I ask.

Yeah.

Isn't that a good thing? I ask, acting as Heidi's advocate.

I know. Sounds counter-intuitive. But it's like she's getting away with something. I've interrogated criminals and law breakers for twenty years. I'm familiar with their mind-set, that state of euphoria. Some mornings I swear, Joe, she can't wait to see me leave for work. Larry runs his fingers through his hair that settles perfectly back in place.

Are you comparing Heidi to a common criminal? I ask rhetorically.

The last three days, I followed her.

I try not to stare at Larry's holstered Glock.

Followed her? I ask, thinking *here it comes*.

He nods, takes another sip of whiskey, settles back in the chair. He's calmed down, almost enjoying his narration before a captured audience. He continues.

I'd leave the house early, drive around the street, park a block away. Then wait and watch. The two previous days she drove straight to the hospital. From there I continued to the station. But this morning was different.

Fuck! Fuck! Fuck! My worst nightmare has come true! Larry continues.

She parallel parked on Brewster Lane and remained in the car.

He stops talking and sips some whiskey. I'm thinking of plausible explanations, but none sound believable or innocent.

What happened? I ask, wanting to get this over with.

I received an emergency call on a shooting at the mall and had to leave.

No sigh of relief from me. I'm still in a shit of danger.

Perhaps she was visiting a friend, I say, still playing Heidi's advocate.

I don't think so. She stayed in the car for over ten minutes.

Larry looks at his empty glass. I offer the bottle. He nods. I pour. There's only one question to ask.

Suspect anyone?

He glares at me for a moment – then laughs.

Don't worry, Joe. You're not on my short list.

He laughs again. I laugh along. To my surprise, my laughter sounds genuine and hearty, tickled no doubt by the absurd situation.

Should I feel insulted? I ask, daring the joke further.

Hey, man, I trust you! It has nothing to do with... you know.

Yeah, man, I know, I say to myself, enjoying the irony for a moment.

Thanks, is all I say. But I think, when Larry finds out – and he *will* find out – he'll remember every word of this conversation with blackened bitterness. This knowledge saddens me because I never meant to hurt Larry. While I don't agree with his politics, I respect him as a husband, father, and public servant.

What will you do? I ask.

Follow her again until she leads me to the bastard.

What will you do if you find the bastard?

Not if, *when*. Probably rip his fucking head off for starters.

I hope you're wrong... about Heidi.

I don't think so, but thanks, Joe. I just needed to talk to someone, and you were the only one I felt I could confide in.

Anytime, Larry.

He looks around my studio for the first time.

So, this is where you make your art.

Yep.

Very cool.

Larry downs his glass, shakes my hand, and leaves.

As soon as Larry is out the door I make three quick decisions. First, I will call Heidi and tell her not to visit me for a while, a very long while. Second, I will not leave Salem with Heidi and Larry. Third, I will take Salem with me. After that I have no fucking idea.

Then, for the first time in a very long while, I think of that day twenty-five years ago, the day that changed my life... forever.

FIVE

t's my last assignment before the All-Star Game. I'm 15-2, leading the league in wins, strikeouts, innings pitched, shutouts, and ERA. Hell, maybe I'll even win thirty games this season. Koufax, Gibson, and Seaver never did that. The team is in first place by three games. Tonight, before hometown fans, I pitched a 4-hit, 3-0 shutout, with 11 strikeouts against the Atlanta Braves. My scoreless streak has reached 41 innings, 4 shutouts in a row, including my perfect 27-K game. I'm in a dream zone unlike any I've ever experienced. In three days, I'll be the starting pitcher in the All-Star Game. And I'm in love with my shining soulmate. Tonight I permit myself to feel happy.

After the last out, as usual, Tiny trotted over to the pitching mound to congratulate me. Then he said he had something important he wanted to tell me and could we meet at our usual bar. I said, Sure. Give me an hour. He nodded with a smile and headed for the clubhouse. I wonder what's on his mind.

As usual, after I pitch a complete game, I'm the last player to leave the clubhouse. I soak my pitching arm in ice water, drink a beer, shower, get dressed. When I finally leave, only the most diehard fans have stuck around for an autograph. I sign their baseballs, programs, tee-shirts, caps, bras, and head for my car.

The parking lot is deserted except for a few security and maintenance vehicles. Sherry will be waiting for me at my apartment. She always watches the home games on TV when I pitch – unless she's out of town working. I'll call her and let her know I'm meeting Tiny.

I'm five feet from my car when I hear the SCREECH of tires then the GUNNING of an engine. I quickly turn around. A black SUV speeds toward me with NO HEADLIGHTS! Mind freezes but body reacts. I jump as high as when I dunked basketballs in high school. If I don't jump, I'm dead. The SUV smashes my legs against the car. I look for the SUV's front license plate but see none. When the SUV backs up, I drop on the asphalt. Tires SCREECH again. Engine GUNS again. Mind still in shock. But body – still reacting – rolls under my car just before the SUV slams into steel metal.

Silence for the briefest moment.

I hear men shouting. I hear the SUV peel away. I see feet filling the narrow view from where I lie. I want to shout, I'M HERE! UNDER THE CAR! But my mouth is full of blood. Then I hear sirens. Then I see two peering faces where the feet were. Then I black out.

Later, much later. Hours? Days? Weeks? I hear a voice.

Mr. Bye? Mr. Bye?

I open my eyes. Two men: one mid-forties, the other early thirties. Older guy is in a suit too dark and heavy for summer. Younger guy wears a light-toned, summer suit with yellow and gray stripes. Older guy speaks.

Mr. Bye? Do you have any enemies?

Whaaar? I slur.

EN-EM-IES. Do you have any?

Three thoughts, like flickering lightbulbs, fade up in my mind. First, I'm in a hospital bed. Second, the lower half of my body is wrapped up like a mummy. Third, I'm being questioned by two police detectives. Neither look too sharp. Later, I will learn that I've been unconscious for three days.

Take your time, younger detective says, as if I'm rushing to answer.

Where is Sherry? Why has the medical staff left me alone with these bozos? How many starts will I miss?

Mr. Bye? Mr. Bye? one of them asks. Younger cop? Not sure. Yeah?

We're detectives Gumbert and Dickson, says older cop. But I'm not sure which is Gumbert and which is Dickson.

Do you have any enemies? repeats older dick.

Enemies?

Someone who hates you. Who would want to do you harm? interjects younger dick.

I'm glad he clarified what an enemy is, I think. I had no idea.

Yeah, I say.

The younger dick gets out a small notebook and a pen, ready to scribble notes. I notice that the notebook's cover is a pretty plum color, which nicely goes with his suit. Did his wife buy him the notebook as a gift? I'm tempted to say, Good choice! But I don't.

Can you give us their names? asks older dick.

It will take a while.

Why's that?

I have three hundred enemies.

Three hundred?

All the players who bat against me.

Anyone among them who would like to see you dead? asks younger dick.

About a hundred.

They ask more questions. Most I can't answer. Soon, the detectives leave. Attempted homicide one of them said. I'm a victim of a crime. In a matter of seconds, my legs, my magnificent legs, made of flesh, blood, sinew, muscle, nerves, and bone, were mashed into hamburger and grist. I still believe I will fully recover. Any pitcher will tell you that his legs are as valuable as his pitching arm.

Weeks later, still in the hospital, is when I hear the question.

Ready to talk about prosthetics?

That question is cheerfully put forth by Dr. Stewart Stumblebutt, head surgeon on my surgical team. He has a different name, but Stumblebutt suits him better. He waits for my answer. I'm too distressed to respond. He continues.

With your consent, Mr. Bye, we will customize and fit you with the latest technology and design in prosthetics. Beautiful workmanship. Made right here in the good ol' U.S.A. Not at some slave-labor factory in China.

I am silent. He continues.

You'll be able to lead a healthy, active life again. Most important, Mr. Bye, you'll be able to walk. Yes, walk! Do everything with your legs you were able to do before the accident.

I am silent. He continues.

Mow the lawn, go shopping, play golf. You play golf? Fantastic game! I'm a ten handicapper. You'll tread the back nine in less two hours. Besides your head, arms, and torso, these prosthetics can support another forty pounds you might carry. They're better than real legs: bendable, flexible, and durable. Cool stuff. Guaranteed to last a lifetime. Your lifetime, Mr. Bye. With these new legs, you will rock!

I finally gather the strength to ask the question that burns in my mouth.

Doc? Will I still...

Still what?

... be able to...

Yes?

You know... Will I still be able to...

Right! Glad you asked. I am happy to say that there is nothing wrong with your sexual functions. Go and make babies! Or go and *not* make babies! That part of your body should be fully functional.

No! I mean... Will I still be able to pitch?

Pitch?

Pitch! In a Major League game. Guess the rest of the season is out. Right? But I want to be ready by opening day of next year. Can you promise me that?

Dr. Stumblebutt glances at members of his surgical team. There is some coughing.

Mr. Bye, I'm sorry, he says. Playing baseball is out of the question.

It's not OUT of the question, Doc. It's IN the question because I'm ASKING the question!

I'm afraid you'll never be a Major League pitcher again. But I promise that with hard work in rehab – physical therapy, occupational therapy – you will lead a full, active life. A high-quality life.

I'm going to pitch again.

Sorry?

Fuck your damn plastic legs. I'm keeping mine.

They are not PLASTIC legs. They are state-of-the-art prosthetic limbs made of acrylic resin, carbon fiber, thermoplastics, silicone, aluminum, and titanium. You can't keep your legs.

Why can't I?

Because almost every bone, cartilage, and nerve from your ankles to your thighs are pulverized. Because you will never walk on those legs.

I'm keeping my legs.

Mr. Bye–

If you try to take them I will sue this hospital for every penny it's worth.

We would never–

You and your team will do everything in your power to fix them. EVERYTHING! If not, I'll go to another hospital and find another team – a team that's on my side.

Rest assured, Mr. Bye, we are all on your side.

But they aren't. They're against me. Thinking I'm crazy to keep limbs they consider useless. Paranoia sets in. I'm terrified they'll drug me and saw off my legs while I'm unconscious. Nurses tell me that in the middle of the night I scream, DON'T

TOUCH MY LEGS! DON'T TOUCH MY LEGS! PUT YOUR FUCKING SAWS AWAY!

Other times I'm in pure denial.

Doc, I'm going to pitch next season, I tell Stumblebutt.

Mr. Bye—

I'll be ready by opening day. You'll see.

Opening day?

I've pitched opening day seven years in a row.

I'm sorry but—

Okay. Maybe not opening day but...

Doc is silent but I blather on.

If I work hard I'll be back right after next season's All-Star Game.

Get some rest, he says and exits my room.

ALL STAR BREAK! I'LL BE READY! I SWEAR! my voice echoes down the corridor.

A nurse stops at the doorway, smiles idiotically, and walks by.

Later, Sherry tells me that the surgical team worked on her.

SURGICAL TEAM MEMBER #1: He'll still drive the car, do chores around the house, play tennis with you, stroll with you on sandy beaches.

SURGICAL TEAM MEMBER #2: He could get back into baseball as a coach.

SURGICAL TEAM MEMBER #3: These advanced prosthetic legs are revolutionary! He'll be almost as mobile as before.

DR. STUMBLEBUTT: Talk to him, Sherry. If you agree with us that this is the best course for Breeze and for *you*, then help him see it. We can start fitting him for his new legs by next week.

Sherry listens to their pitch, thanks them for sharing their views, and promises to talk to me. This is what she tells me: Breeze, honey, this is your decision. Whatever you decide I will love and support you all the way.

Even if I can't walk?

Listen to me, Mr. Joseph Bye. When I say all the way, I mean *all* the way.

Five months in the hospital. Seventeen surgeries spread over two years. A year of agonizing physical therapy. To relieve the tedium, boredom, and pain during my many hospitalized weeks, I draw and sketch every day: nurses, doctors, patients, and visitors are my subjects. My most willing models, though, are the nurse's aides and orderlies. They will sit for twenty minutes while I sketch them. I try to capture the empathy and exhaustion in their eyes.

I allow only Sherry to visit me. Refuse to see anyone else – no family, no friends, no teammates. No one. I'm too angry, bitter, and fragile to hear words of sympathy, their clumsy attempts at encouragement.

Big Breeze! Looking fucking good!

Shit, man, you look ready to pitch nine innings tomorrow! Ha-ha!

Everybody on the team misses you like hell and sends their love.

Hey, we brought your glove and the whole team wrote on it... To wish you... We thought... Breeze? Breeze? What's the matter? Did I say something wrong?

No, I couldn't bear it. The worst part? Seeing them walk into my hospital room with two strong, healthy legs. That would be insufferable.

I still can't take a step. With arduous effort I can stand. With a walker I can take two steps before my legs give out. From thighs to ankles, I'm covered with enough surgical scars to pass for a map of the L.A. Interstate system.

Still, I *can* feel my legs. When I touch the skin, when I squeeze the flesh of my thin thighs, I feel it... I *feel* it! I may be broken, but I am still whole. That is a small victory of sorts.

SIX

reeze. Sometimes Breezy or The Big Breeze. But mostly just Breeze. How did I get my name? My brand, as Salem calls it. I'm twenty years old playing in the Class AA league for a mediocre team in Rhode Island. After I strike out seven batters in a row, the seventh batter returns to the dugout and claims he felt a big breeze each time my fastball whizzed past him. WHOOSH! WHOOSH! is how he describes the sound. A local sportswriter hears about that and quotes him in the paper. The name sticks.

Sure, I can blow 98-99-100 mph fastballs by them. But that's not pitching. Great pitchers are artists. They sculpt the plate. They paint the corners. They aim from the knees to the chest. Better yet, they aim below the knees and above the chest, missing just outside the plate and just inside the plate. Pitchers want umpires to call those close pitches for strikes. And they want batters to chase the ball. What's the worst pitch in the world? Any ball that's hittable. Why? Because it's true. There's an old saying that probably started with Ruth: Good hitters hit hittable balls out of ballparks.

However, the start of my first year as a professional is not pretty. To show that I belong, I try to throw the ball through the backstop. Clearly, that kind of massive effort adversely affects your control. Basically, I was wilder than a flock of drunken geese. I walked as many as I struck out. Not a good ratio. During my fourth or fifth game, after walking five batters in two innings, the catcher walks up to the mound for a chat. He's a grizzled veteran named Buck Caruthers, and I think he's about to chew out my ass. But he doesn't. Buck spits out a glob of tobacco juice then pats me on the arm.

Kid, your stuff is awesome, he says. Movement on the fastball is fucking off the charts. Problem is, you're overthrowing.

I just nod, not knowing where he's going.

I want you to try something.

Okay.

As a boy, you ever play catch in the backyard with your granddad?

Both my grandfathers died before I was born.

Buck scratches his stubble.

But I played catch with my Great Uncle Hans, I say.

Hans... German?

Dutch.

Imagine you're playing catch with Uncle Hans. Tossing the ball back and forth.

Okay.

Just fastballs but nice and easy. No breaking stuff. Got it?

Yeah, Buck.

That was the turning point. I walked only one more batter and struck out seven. Buck didn't call for a breaking ball until the next game. The rest of the season, I never walked more than three and averaged nine strikeouts a game. I believe that was the true birth of The Big Breeze.

Being wheelchair bound was not supposed to be my life. This is how I viewed my life: pitch in the big leagues for twenty years; break every major pitching record – strikeouts, no hitters, wins, shutouts, ERA, Cy Youngs, MVPs; win two or three more World Series. The team calls me Iron Man. Sometimes Superman. I pitch complete games. Other pitchers feel lucky getting past the sixth inning before the manager yanks him for a fresh arm.

When the Cubs call me up, big league teams had already shifted from a 4-man to a 5-man pitching rotation. Since I'm a rookie I say nothing. I just pitch. I win 17 games, lead the league in strikeouts, win Rookie of the Year award. Manager is happy. Management is happy. Come spring training I tell our manager, Scrappy Leach, I want to pitch every four days. Scrappy is old school. He wears a black eyepatch. As a young pitcher in the minors, a line drive crushed his right eye. End of a promising pitching career, beginning of a successful managing career. He and I went on to win three World Series together. But when I tell him of my plan to pitch every four days, he cackles as if I'm joking. I narrow my eyes. Scrappy sends me to the general manager, Chick Beaumont. Back in the day, Chick was a smooth-fielding, light-hitting second baseman for the Yankees. Still wears his diamond encrusted World Series ring. He's vainly proud that he maintains his playing weight at the age of fifty-five. I tell him what I told the manager. He chortles. I narrow my eyes. He settles back in his leather chair to hear my pitch. I explain that I want to compare myself to my heroes: the old baseball gods such as Walter Johnson, Christy Mathewson, Lefty Grove; and the later gods of Bob Feller, Warren Spahn, Sandy Koufax, Nolan Ryan, Bob Gibson, Tom Seaver. But the only way I can do that is to pitch as often as they did. Chick hears me out until I finish.

Sorry, kid, he says. This is a different time, a different game. We're sticking with a 5-man rotation. It's for your own good.

Chick has a serene smile on his face as if this small matter is closed. He expects this kid to thank him for listening and then quietly leave. This kid ain't going anywhere.

A 4-man rotation is better for me. And if it's better for me, it's better for the team.

Don't say? he says, dripping with sarcasm.

Pitch me every fourth game, you'll get eight more quality

starts over the season. If the team can give me a couple of runs, that's eight more wins.

You're pretty fucking cocky, Breeze, Chick says, then he leans forward, folding his hands together on his shiny desk. With his forefinger he rubs his diamond-studded World Series ring.

Maybe I am pretty cocky. But I'm also pretty fucking good.

You had a fine rookie year. No question. We want you to have a great second year.

Then pitch me every fourth day.

Ain't gonna happen, goddamn it! That's final!

Then I won't pitch. And that's final!

As I walk out of his office I hear him yell, WE'LL FUCKING SEE ABOUT THAT!

I hold out and mail their contract back unsigned.

I don't show up when spring training opens. Chick tells the press I'm not a team player. Breeze only cares about himself, he says. Natch, press laps it up. I stay home. Chick threatens to trade me. I stay home. Halfway through spring training, Chick says he'll send me back to the minors. I stay home. I sit out all of spring training. But every day I go to Lincoln Park to jog, stretch, play catch with a few high school jocks I recruited. The season opens.

By mid-April, the team loses eight out of ten games and are mired in last place. Chick caves. He sends me to their Triple-A team to pitch a few games. First game, I throw seven shutout innings with 12 strikeouts. Chick calls me up to the big team. Scrappy pitches me every fourth game. I win 25 games. We make the playoffs for the first time in twelve years. I win my first Cy Young. I'm the only pitcher in the Majors that has the 4-day arrangement. I never win less than twenty-two games. I never have less than 250 strikeouts. I averaged twenty complete games and seven shutouts a season. They call me The Big Breeze.

When my baseball career is over, I think, I'll work in the front office, be a baseball executive. That's my plan. Funny how plans can change.

After the hospital sends me home, I finally face reality, though the reality sticks in my gut: Big Breeze will never again pitch in the Big Leagues. I dig myself into a grave-deep depression, a pitch-black cave with no chance of any light seeping in. At night I lie in bed repeating, like a dripping faucet, crip, crip, crip, crip, crip... the new nickname for myself. I take painkillers to relieve the constant pain in my legs. I drink a bottle of booze a day – bourbon, scotch, vodka. Doesn't matter. It's only to escape the pain of living with myself. I get hooked on the painkillers. I drink more so that I'll take less painkillers. Instead, I take more painkillers, then I drink even more. When I can't keep food down, I crawl to the toilet. The streaks of yellow in my vomit remind me of the yellows in Van Gogh's *Sunflowers*. Whenever Sherry leaves on an acting gig, I explode with rage. I viciously curse her. I throw bottles against the wall. She runs out in tears.

DO YOU WANT ME TO HATE YOU! she screams.

YES! I scream back.

Self-loathing wraps me in an ever-tightening cocoon. One night when Sherry is out of town, I swallow a handful of painkillers and wash them down with vodka. Down a deep well I drop, falling past flashes of my life on the farm until I land in a foul viscous void. When I regain consciousness I'm in ICU hooked up to a respirator. I'm a 30-year-old crippled drug addict wasting away. For all practical purposes I'm already dead. I've been half-dead for a year. Since I don't have the guts to blow my brains out, I take my time.

I took too long. Sherry enters the room but doesn't sit down. Everything is blurred as smeared goose grease on a dirty window pane. I can't speak. She talks to me, but I can't understand her words. I hear her cry. Poor Sherry. Wish she'd go away. Finally, she leaves. Now, I can go in peace... Won't take long.

It's the bottom of the ninth, two outs, the Reapers are ahead 2-1. I'm at bat. There's a runner on first. The count is 0-2. Down to the last strike. I can hardly see the pitcher, let alone the ball. I smile to myself. Now you know how it feels, I tell myself. How they felt when *you* were pitching in the ninth inning, the game on the line. The last batter. One run down. One good swing can win it. I close my eyes. I won't swing. Why bother?

Then I see a figure enter the room. He's not blurry at all. He wears a baseball uniform: baggy wool flannels, high socks, short-billed baseball cap. The uniform ballplayers wore a hundred years ago.

Hello, Breeze, he says. It's a mellow, friendly voice in the tenor range.

Who are you? my mind asks.

Come on, don't you know me?

I try to shake my head but the effort is too much.

You know me, he says.

He takes off his cap. Dark blond hair falls over his forehead. That dimpled chin. Over his left hand is a ridiculously small, beat-up baseball glove a little leaguer would laugh at. In the glove he holds a tan, scuffed baseball. He takes off the glove and holds it in his right hand like you'd hold a sandwich. He shoots me a big grin.

Christy? Christy Mathewson? I ask.

That's right, Breeze.

May I call you Matty?

Sure, kid.

Matty, is it true you never swore or spit or smoked?

True.

Is it true you went to church and never pitched on Sunday?

True again.

He moves closer to my bed and looks gravely at me for a long moment.

What the heck are you doing here? he asks.

Trying to die, I answer.

Why would you do that?

I don't want to live.

That's a sin.

I don't believe in sin.

Aren't you following in your father's footsteps?

I don't want to talk about my father!

Matty nods. Then he sits in a nearby chair, lays glove and ball on the foot of the bed, and looks at me without judgement or pity.

Kid, life is like a baseball game.

Okay, I reply.

You're pitching in the third inning. Your team is losing 4-0. Losing is not the same as lost. Winning is not the same as won. Your job is to keep your team in the game so they can score some runs. You're going to shut out the opposition for the rest of the game. Yeah, 4-0 may seem like a lot, but it's only the third inning. You're in the third inning right now. You've got six more innings to play.

But I'm dying.

Dying isn't the same as death. Living isn't the same as life.

I can't walk. I may never walk again.

You can still think. You can still talk, hear, see, touch. You can still move. You can still love. There's someone special that loves you. You're lucky. There are men who would trade both legs *and* an arm to be loved by a woman like Sherry.

You should be a preacher.

Mother wanted me to be a minister. She never saw the value of grown men playing baseball. Now if you want to talk about preaching, you should have heard Billy Sunday. Not a bad baseball player I heard, but when he preached it was like God batting cleanup.

If I live, what will life be like?

For you to find out.

Do you know?

Matty is silent. He runs his hand through his mop of hair. God, he's beautiful. I want to touch him, but I still can't move.

Matty, please tell me. What *will* my life be like?

Maybe not what you expect... but a life worth living. Gotta go, kid. He stands up.

Will I ever see you again?

That I don't know. But I'll keep an eye on you. Fourth inning coming up. Heavy hitters. But you've got the stuff.

Matty disappears as Sherry enters the room. I can see her! If I see her does that mean my eyes are open? Am I conscious? Sherry sits down and sets her bag on her lap. She takes out a paperback to read. She likes historical romances. She glances up to look at me. Her eyes get big, her mouth opens wide, she starts to cry. A nurse enters. The nurse looks at me, and she starts to cry. Then a doctor enters. He stares at me and smiles. He starts talking, but I don't listen to him. All I care about is that I can see Sherry... and I met Christy Mathewson. Then I fall asleep.

SEVEN

met Sherry in early March at our spring training camp in Mesa, Arizona. She's attached to the celebrated sportswriter Lake Lemon. Lake wants to do a piece on me for *Sports Illustrated*. She's twenty-two. Lake is fifty. I'm twenty-eight, entering my ninth season, coming off my best year: I led the Majors in wins, shutouts, strikeouts, and ERA. I won my fourth Cy Young, my second MVP. We took the World Series in seven games against the Toronto Blue Jays; I won the seventh game, my third win in the series. *Time Magazine* put my face on the cover.

At that time, Lake Lemon is the most famous sportswriter in America. He has a weekly sports talk show on ESPN. He pals around with political and show biz celebs. As my agent, Morrie Pelter, reminds me, Lake Lemon is a BIG FUCKING DEAL!

I hate talking to sportswriters. They're called *sportswriters* back then. Now they call themselves *journalists*. They still ask the same dumb, rude questions. Morrie tells me I should cooperate with the media. It's good for your career, he says. He's already pissed at me for turning down several generous endorsements. I tell him I won't endorse corporate *products*. Occasionally, I do a spot for a worthy nonprofit.

Nike's offering half a million! shouts Morrie.

And ten percent is fifty K! I shout back.

You think I care about my commission?

I just look at him.

Okay, I fucking care. But I care more about you.

When I look at him again, Morrie pivots back to Lake.

Lake Lemon is HUGE. No one says NO to Lake.

I just did.

Please, Breeze. Talk to him.

No.

Ten minutes.

I say ten, he'll take twenty. I say twenty, he'll take forty. It's always the same. Never enough for those sharks.

How did Lake Lemon become the most famous sportswriter in America? A few things you need to know. Lake is a stylish and talented writer. Hands down. He knows how to tell and shape a story, how to turn banal athletes into flesh and blood complicated characters you care about. A learned man, an autodidact, Lake likes to throw in quotes from Shakespeare, Milton, Homer, and Muddy Waters. People liked the idea of reading high-brow sports pieces about their favorite teams and players. But what got his fame started was a book he wrote when he was twenty-seven years old.

At the time, he's a third-string sportswriter for the *Chicago Tribune*. The book is a biography of Shoeless Joe Jackson. As every baseball devotee knows, Shoeless Joe is famous for two things: being one of the greatest hitters who ever lived and getting barred for life from baseball. Playing for the Chicago White Sox, he was accused of throwing the 1919 World Series against the Cincinnati Reds, along with seven other teammates. In writing his bio, Lake interviews every surviving player who played with or against Jackson, along with any of Jackson's surviving family members. He scours old newspaper articles during Jackson's career. He remakes Jackson. He turns a simple, illiterate man into an American story of immense tragic dimensions that indicts Major League Baseball and the entire nation.

It is a big, fat book, over 500 pages, titled *Our Shoeless Hero*, and includes a vivid portrayal of the city of his birth, Chicago, as the rough and tumble, cocky town it was at the turn of the 20th century. The book becomes a bestseller. Some call it the *Moby-Dick* of baseball biographies. Later, it was made into a successful film, staring a big-name actor. Strangely, Lake hasn't written another book since.

The other thing you need to know, that cemented Lake's fame, is his Spring Training Survey. Every year, he compiles a survey that *Sports Illustrated* publishes in their April issue. Lake rates all the upcoming rookies, based on his observations and experienced eye during spring training. After a few years, he gains a reputation for his uncanny ability at picking future stars. His Survey becomes a must-read for every baseball player, manager, coach, and executive in the Majors, along with serious baseball fans. Lake is rarely wrong with his predictions. But he was dead wrong with his prediction of me.

During spring training of my rookie year, I'm being touted by some in the press as a future star. Lake decides to check out this so-called phenom. I pitch two innings against the Angels. First inning, I strike out the side. Second inning, I walk two batters; next batter reaches first base on an error. Bases loaded. The next batter hits a grand slam. Manager takes me out, and I'm furious about my outing. After the game, while changing clothes at my locker, a guy in a beige linen suit sidles up to me. He's a large, corpulent, middle-aged man, well over six feet.

Good outing. Lousy luck.

Luck can go fuck itself, I say, annoyed that this stranger is bothering me while I'm half-dressed and still upset.

Lake Lemon, *Chicago Tribune*, he says and holds out his hand.

I act like I don't see it as I pull on my jeans.

I'd like to ask you a few questions.

Sorry. Bad time. Another day.

This is my *only* day. Now or never, Breeze.

Guess it's never.

Do you know who I am?

Yeah, you just told me.

Son, you just made a big mistake.

With that, Lake shakes his head at this poor rookie's stupidity and leaves. Of course I know very well who Lake Lemon is, but I'm not going to give him the satisfaction. I could have told him that a blister on the middle finger of my pitching hand had popped in the second inning. But why should I? He'd just think I was making an excuse.

In Lake's Survey that spring, he writes a quote that I'll always remember: *Turns out that The Big Breeze is a Wimpy Whiff. Not ready for the big leagues.* Makes me laugh now, but it pissed me off back then. I mean he could have been crueler with alliteration by writing, *Putrid Puff.* He wrote me off on the one poor outing he'd attended and our brusque conversation. After I won the Rookie of the Year Award, Lake got some ribbing from other sportswriters. In the following years, as I racked up wins and awards, Lake's detractors would delight in teasing him for getting The Big Breeze so wrong with his *Wimpy Whiff* prediction. After I won my third Cy Young Award, Lake stopped writing his Spring Training Survey.

Lake keeps calling Morrie about interviewing me. Morrie keeps telling him that Breeze is looking for a good time. One day I'm eating chiles rellenos at the Charro Café, oldest Mexican restaurant in Mesa. It's after a training game with the Giants. I'm alone, wearing sunglasses and a goofy cotton bucket hat to avoid autograph seekers.

I FINALLY FOUND YOU, BREEZE! booms across the entire restaurant.

Lake Lemon's deep, thunderous voice fills any room. At his arm is a dazzling, slim Black woman in white shorts, white tee-shirt cut at the midriff, and large designer sunglasses. When she smiles at me, I take off my sunglasses to get a better look. I want to touch her face, smell her skin and hair. I want to tell her that she's the most magnificent woman I've ever seen; then I wonder if *most magnificent* even makes sense. Tagging along Lake and Sherry is a skinny guy in a seersucker suit, mid-thirties, though he could be older. Lake doesn't bother to introduce him to me.

Go sit at the bar, Slammer, and order something for yourself, Lake tells him.

Slammer starts for the bar, stops, then gets too close to me. My name is really Quincy Sacks, he says. You've had an amazing career.

He sticks out his hand. I shake it.

Nice to meet you, Quincy. But my career is far from over.

Yeah, of course! I just meant... that meeting you is a real honor.

Alright, Slammer, enough awestruck admiration, Lake cuts in. You're embarrassing him. Now go to the bar.

See you around, Breeze, Quincy says. I can tell he wants to shake my hand again, but I turn away from him. He walks, hang dogged, to the bar.

Mind if we join you? asks Lake.

I nod. They pull up chairs.

I've been having a helluva time getting past your gatekeeper, says Lake. All I want is an hour of your time for a piece I'm doing for *Sports Illustrated*. I want to capture the Breeze the public doesn't know.

No one's interested, I say.

I'm interested, says the beauty. She takes off her sunglasses so she can flash me those beautiful honey-brown eyes.

You a big baseball fan? I ask, trying not to smirk.

I'm a big fan of yours, she quips.

Really?

Really.

You mean as in recently?

Been a Cubs fan all my life. My granddaddy, on my mother's side, LOVED the Cubs. Wrigley Field was like his second home. The two names that came out of his mouth the most were Jesus and Ernie Banks, in that order. If Mr. Banks had led the Cubs to a World Series, I bet Jesus' name would have slid down to second place. Too bad Granddaddy didn't live to see you lead them to the World Series.

That doesn't explain when you became a fan of mine.

Since I was fourteen. I still own your rookie baseball card.

I stare at her. Is she bullshitting me?

What's it look like? I ask, not in a mean way, but with a smile.

Well... you're not wearing a cap. Very unusual. How'd you get away with that? You have an impish grin on your face. You're holding a baseball in your left hand, even though you're a righty. Your uniform looks too big on you. And the uniform number is 56, not 30.

Wow, you really do have my rookie card.

You didn't believe me?

I heard that card sold for three hundred at an auction.

I wouldn't sell mine for three thousand.

Lake moves his bulk between us, giving me a wink and a wolfish smile at Sherry. You never told me that story, he says to her.

Never asked, she replies deadpan.

So, Breezy, how about that interview?

Will she be there?

My name is Bond, Sherry Bond, she cracks.

Please to meet you, Sherry Bond.

Lake says, Well, I usually don't–

Sherry cuts him off. I'd love to listen to your interview – if I can ask a question or two.

Sherry, you can ask me anything you want.

I can tell that Lake doesn't care for my flirtatiousness, but I don't give a shit. It wouldn't matter if she's his wife or daughter. I want to know her better, much better.

Lake orders lunch for Sherry and himself. Sherry is having a salad. For himself Lake orders two appetizers, four beef enchiladas, and a marbled *tres leches* cake with two scoops of chocolate ice cream for dessert. For a total glutton his eating manner is impeccable. Sherry tries to slow him down. She warns him that if he's not more careful with his diet, he'll wind up like her great aunt who lost both feet from diabetes before she died. Lake just laughs at her.

Next day we do the interview. It goes well. Lake tries to get me to trash talk other players, but I don't bite. Sherry asks the most surprising question.

Why aren't you married?

Good question.

Folks always say *good question* when they don't have a good answer or they don't want to answer.

I got an answer: I don't have time for marriage.

Time? What's time got to do with it?

My number one priority is baseball and pitching.

Priorities can change... if you meet the right woman.

Maybe our eyes meet a little too long for Lake because he abruptly butts in with a question about my workout routine during the off season.

At only twenty-two, Sherry's been in three feature films and guest starred in several prime-time TV shows. In Hollywood terms, she's a young star on the rise. So, what's she doing with this middle-aged, over-fed white man? Okay, I'm a young, well-fed white man. But I think I'm the coolest thing in cleats.

All I can think about is seeing more of Sherry. But she's always with Lake. Then one day I see her sitting alone in a front-row box seat to watch me pitch three innings against the San Diego Padres. I jog over to her.

Hey, I say.

Hi, she says, pushing up her sunglasses on her hair.

You alone?

See anyone with me?

Where's Lake?

In bed with a cold.

Gosh, that's a real shame.

Yeah, poor guy. We guiltlessly smile at each other.

Why aren't you nursing him?

He wanted me to.

But?

I don't nurse.

You don't nurse.

There's a lot of things I do well. Nursing is not one of them. And I don't mother. Any man looking for a nurse or mother better run the other way.

I ain't looking for either.

That's good.

So, you came here.

To watch you pitch.

I'm still rusty.

At what?

Pitching.

Oh.

And then she giggles in the most charming way. I'm about to make a wisecrack when she puts her hand to her chest and starts coughing. The coughing doesn't stop.

Are you okay?

Still coughing, she raises her hand, as if to say, Yes. Then I watch her calmly reach for a little leather holster hooked to her waistband and pull out an inhaler. She shakes it, blows a quick breath out, puts the mouthpiece in her mouth, and deeply inhales while pushing down on the canister. I had noticed the little holster before, always dangling from her waist, but never asked. Her coughing stops. She slips the inhaler in the holster and shoots me a resigned smile.

Do they come often? I ask.

She shakes her head and says, My mother had it worse. But it was cancer that killed her. Warning: I'm a little broken.

I had a teammate in the minors who had asthma. A good ol' boy from Louisiana named Rufus. He carried his inhaler in a deerskin pouch around his neck. I saw him use it a couple of times. Never affected his playing.

Rufus, huh? I bet you just made up that story to make me feel better.

His full name was Rufus Deberry. Played first base. And you're not broken a bit. I think you're perfect.

Rufus Deberry? I still think you made it up. But thanks.

I pitch three scoreless innings. My last inning I turn up the heat and strike out the side, just to impress her. After that we go out to dinner, skip dessert, rush to my hotel room, and make love all night. For me that's it. Case closed and throw away the key. I'm sure we're going to be together for the rest of our lives. But Sherry needs convincing.

On our third night together, we're lying in bed after some very physical love. As our breathing eases back to normal, I think I never felt happier in my life.

White boys, she says with a sigh.

What about white boys?

I *play* with white boys. I *like* playing with white boys. But I don't *stick* with white boys.

You'll stick with me.

You got some invisible white-boy glue?

Don't need no glue.

Then what you got?

Love.

She covers her mouth with one hand and laughs. I don't mind. Let her laugh.

Don't need more than that. Sticks better than Super Glue, I say.

Love... Trying that white boy bullshit. Sounds no different from Black boy bullshit.

I love you, Sherry! It's not white or Black. It's blood red, the color of my heart. No one in the world can love you more. I've got a lifetime supply of love. It's all yours. Every drop. I've been saving it all my life just for you.

STOP! ENOUGH! No more thoughts about Sherry.

EIGHT

t's Saturday, four days after the phone call with Slammer. Salem and I are having breakfast in the kitchen. I'm reading *The New York Times*. Salem is looking over her homework essay. Jasmine, our housekeeper, is making us breakfast. She used to make us breakfast every day. But once Heidi's visits started, I cut that down to weekends. Jasmine sets plates before us. On each plate is a steaming hot pie-like dish. Salem and I look at each other for a moment.

What is this? I ask.

What's it look like? Jasmine sarcastically asks back.

I don't know, which is why I'm asking.

You never saw a frittata before?

Frittata. Is that what this is?

No, it's baked lobster.

Why are you—

Made with eggs, milk, some vegetables, and seasoning. Many folks around the world enjoy it for breakfast or lunch. It originally comes from Italy.

Very interesting.

Not really.

Jasmine, I didn't ask you to make me a frittata.

Yeah. Wouldn't cross your mind. Always the same old ting: plain yogurt, fruit, granola. Every *single* day. I'm sick of looking at it. You tink you'd be sick of eating it.

This is good, Jasmine! interjects Salem, having taken a generous bite.

Tanks, Salem. See? A little appreciation. So, Mr. Bye, are you gonna at least taste it or should I trow it outside for the crows?

Jasmine is a short stocky ebony Black woman with no neck. Her hair is braided in intricate coils around her large head. While I believe she's in her late fifties, she looks ten years younger. Under her stern gaze I take a bite. It is tasty, though I'm cautious not to show it on my face. I give her a *not bad* nod and continue eating, hoping she'll return to the kitchen. But no. Jasmine stands beside my wheelchair, arms folded. Something's on her mind. She waits for me to put another forkful of frittata in my mouth.

You know, Mr. Bye, when Sherry was alive, she LOVED my cooking. Loved all the tings I cooked. Loved ALL the tings I baked. She loved to come in the kitchen and watch me cook, tell me good Hollywood gossip.

Can we *not* talk about Sherry?

No one asking you to talk about her 'cause you NEVER talk about her. I'M talking about her. You don't own Sherry memories. I got memories too.

Then KEEP your memories to yourself! My palm slams the table, startling Salem.

I will not! Sherry made coming here fun. FUN! Ever hear of dat word? Since she's gone, I feel worthless. You never want me to cook new tings. Always the same ol' breakfast. Always the same ol' dinners. I ask myself, Jasmine, what are you doing here?

We like the way you keep house, I say, hoping to placate her so she'll return to the kitchen. Jasmine doesn't move.

You like the way I keep *house*?

Yes.

So, I'm just a maid to you?

That's not—

Want me to wear a little white apron and cap like good NEGRO maids do in old Hollywood movies? Do those good Negro maids make you laugh, Mr. Bye? Makes me laugh.

Jasmine, we don't consider you a maid. You're our housekeeper and cook. Salem and I appreciate everything you do to keep our home in order.

Hmph! And with that she returns to the kitchen.

After giving birth to Salem, Sherry hires Jasmine Rivers. I don't participate in the interviews. She likes Jasmine right off. They soon become thick as thieves, laughing and whispering over God knows what. I just stay out of the way. But sometimes it's not possible. Like when Jasmine asks me if she can clean my studio.

Absolutely not!

Dat place is filty, Mr. Bye.

How would you know?

I know because I know you never clean up. Must be crawling with rats and cockroaches.

Stay out of my studio.

You tink I'm going to steal one of your priceless paintings?

Just stay out.

Jasmine never married. She lives with her twin sister, Rose, who is also a housekeeper. They cover for each other if one is sick or hospitalized. They both have had chemo and surgery for breast cancer. I like Rose better – she's sweet tempered, quiet. But Jasmine is the sister we're stuck with. She dotes on Salem, and Salem loves her like a favorite aunt.

After Jasmine returns to the kitchen, Salem speaks while still staring at her essay.

A man in a car asked me if I wanted a lift.

What?

A man in a car asked me—

When? I try not to sound alarmed, which I am.

Yesterday, she says, eyes glued to essay.

Why didn't you tell me?

Forgot.

Salem, look at me because this is serious.

She looks at me.

Hey, I'm telling you now.

I'm glad you're telling me. So, what did you say?

No thanks.

What did he say?

He said, I know where you live. It's a long walk.

Then what?

I gave him the finger and kept walking.

Did he follow you?

No. But he yelled, It's okay! I'm a friend of your father's! I knew that was a lie because you have no friends. He watched me a second longer then drove away.

What did he look like?

Ordinary white guy. Mustache, sunglasses, wore a baseball cap.

What team?

Giants.

Giants? Odd.

I know.

You did the right thing.

He was just a creep. No big deal. She goes back to her essay.

She is most definitely coming to L.A. with me. As I mull next steps the doorbell rings – at 7:30 AM on a Saturday. I look at Salem, who shrugs and heads to the front door. I'm thinking already this has been quite a morning. A minute later she returns leaning against the kitchen doorjamb.

What? I ask.

It's Coach Siskoff.

Why is he here?

Wants to talk to you.

Why?

That damn Parisian shrug again.

Okay, tell him to come in, I say.

He says he's fine on the porch.

Shit. Say I'll be there in a few minutes.

I'll tell him on my way out.

She's off. I take another forkful of frittata as I wonder what he could want. Coach Bernie Siskoff is a balding, paunchy, bespeckled man in his late forties. He's well-meaning, well-liked, and, from what I hear, a competent coach. We've met only once when I had to sign some papers to allow Salem to play on the boys' team.

He stands outside, wearing khaki cargo shorts and a red hooded sweatshirt with HAWKS, the team's name, emblazoned in gold lettering. Above that is their logo of an insanely fierce-looking hawk's head. I wheel outside onto the porch.

Morning, Bernie.

Good morning, Mr. Bye.

Call me Joe.

Sorry to bother you at this hour. Salem said this would be the best time to catch you.

Ah-ha, I think. That's why Salem dashed out of the house in a hurry. I'll speak to her later.

What's on your mind, Bernie?

Well... What's on my mind is how you could do me, but more importantly the entire baseball team, a huge favor. I wouldn't ask anyone else because there isn't anyone—

What's the favor?

I promise it won't take up much of your time... Joe. Thirty minutes. Maybe less. But definitely not more than—

Just tell me, Bernie.

Visit the team... Talk to them. It would mean a lot to the kids, and I believe help them win our division championship.

Did you say division championship?

Didn't Salem tell you?

I don't say, Of course she didn't tell me. Why would she? When I've never shown any interest in her baseball team.

I do say, Oh, right. Yeah, she did. Congrats.

Bernie sits down in one of the rocking chairs. He clears his throat for his pitch.

One week from tomorrow, Western High School comes to our school for the conference championship. They won the conference last year. Western has always been a powerhouse. If we beat them then we go on to the next round in Syracuse for the state championship. This is an awesome opportunity. So, will you talk to them?

I would if I could.

That mean you won't?

I've got nothing to offer.

Joe, I believe we have a chance... a realistic chance to go all the way to the state championship. This school has never, and when I say *never* I mean not even close to winning a championship in any sport, including chess. You could make the difference.

There's nothing bad about losing.

Maybe not. But there's nothing good about losing.

Losing builds character.

Winning builds confidence.

Did Salem ask you to see me?

No. I asked her if I could talk to you.

What did she say?

She said okay, but it would be a waste of my time. That you wouldn't help.

She was right. I'm sorry. I wish your team all the best.

Coach Siskoff rubs his hands on the top of his cargo shorts, making a sandpapery sound. I think, okay, end of our conversation. But the coach clears his throat.

As a teenager I played semi-pro baseball. It was for a local brewery in Kenosha, Wisconsin. Broken Bird Brewery it was called. Funny name. I played center field. I was pretty good and imagined I would be the next Ken Griffey, Jr. Of course, I knew

I'd never get close to Griffey. But The Big Breeze... He didn't have to pretend to be a great player. He *was* great.

That was a long time—

I remember. So do millions. You were the greatest pitcher of your generation. If you just talked to the kids. Tell them that they could be great too.

Coach, listening to you, I think you can do a better job of inspiring them than I ever could. I don't believe in greatness anymore.

Coach Siskoff is silent. He gave it his best shot and came up short. I don't feel badly, but I know it wasn't easy for him to come here.

What classes do you teach? I ask to ease his disappointment.

Science and mathematics. I've always loved numbers. Guess it's why I love baseball. All those numbers. Each one means something. Like the difference between a .290 batting average and a .310 average may be just 15 hits over the course of a season. But the significance is staggering. The Big Breeze put up some numbers that may never be broken.

It's not something I think about.

Right. Of course. You don't need to. But for me winning a state championship with these kids means everything. All my life I've pursued a dream. When all my dreams dried up, I hit bottom. For a year I lived out of my car. When I was thirty-seven, I decided to go back to college and get a teaching degree. Best decision I ever made. I love teaching. It's my life. I never married. Probably never will. Teaching and coaching high school kids. That's all I need. Talk to the team, Joe. They lack confidence that they can beat Western.

Are his eyes welling up? Oh, God, please don't start bawling on my front porch.

When is this game? I ask.

Two weeks from tomorrow.

Who do you have pitching?

Salem. She's been our best arm. Maybe our best all-around

player. I love watching her pitch. Her fastball is in the high 70s. A freshman! By the time she's a senior it will be in the high 80s. That's almost Major League speed. Haven't you ever seen her pitch?

Bernie should not have asked me that. I'm silent. But he continues.

It's none of my business, Joe, but I don't understand why you've never come to our games. If Salem was my daughter—

She's not your daughter. And you are correct, it is none of your business.

I'm sorry. I didn't mean to—

I'll leave you with this advice, coach. Maybe the soundest advice I can give. Tell your team to play their best, to play hard, and no matter what happens you will always be proud of them. Good luck. With that I spin around and wheel myself inside.

Later that day, I'm in my studio. It's after six, time to quit. Yet, I'm still staring at my double portrait and that damn black line.

What are you? I ask Black Line.
Silence.
What do you want?
Silence.
Why did I paint you?
Silence.

I wheel myself around the studio hoping, absurdly, that the line will go away when I next look at the canvas. Still there. I decide to paint that black scar out once and for all. But I don't. Instead, I add more ivory black to the line. I build it up. I extend the line down to the pitcher's waist and up to the top of his head. I can feel the energy as I apply palette knife and brush to the canvas. I look at it. Something's missing. What? I back up, staring at the looming black line that's now a menacing black ribbon. I turn around and grab the container of Sherry's ashes as if in a trance. I reach in and take a handful, say two tablespoons. I mix it in with the ivory black on my palette. I add this mixture to the line. I use my fingers to push the paint around the canvas. The paint feels warm. The line seems to breathe as if alive! It's exciting and frightening. I've never experienced this sensation before as a painter.

After an hour of looking and painting and looking and painting, I'm exhausted. But I want to keep going. I'm about to continue when there's a pounding on the door. My hands are black from the paint and ash. I turn the easel around and wipe my hands with a turpentine-soaked rag. More pounding. I wheel to the door and pull it open.

Good evening, Larry, I say.

Larry is in uniform again, just off duty no doubt. This time all his buttons are buttoned, and he's wearing his cap. But something's still not right. What? He has a two-day stubble. Very unlike him. I wait for a response. None comes.

Everything all right? I ask.

It's about Heidi, he says wearily.

Like to come in?

No... thanks. I'm fine here.

I nod and wait for the worst. Has Heidi confessed everything? I can't help but glance at that black Glock snug in his holster.

Heidi is acting... She seems unhappy, he says.

You said she was unusually happy.

She was. Then she stopped acting happy. Now she acts sad. Even depressed.

I'm sorry to hear that.

Sometimes... I can hear her weep in another room. Last night she called your name in her sleep.

My name? Really? Are you sure? I ask with innocent surprise.

She didn't say Joe or Joseph but Breezy... Breezy... Breezy. Just like that. Breezy... Breezy... Breezy.

I'm fucked, I think, totally fucked. I should confess and get it over with. Larry, I've been banging your wife for the last six months. Really sorry. Won't happen again.

That was your old baseball name, right?

Nickname, I say, as if that makes a difference.

Why would she call out your nickname? We've always called you Joe.

Heidi may have been dreaming.

Dreaming? Larry asks, looking puzzled.

In a dream, she could be walking in a storm that's very breezy... breezy.

Larry still looks puzzled. I continue.

It's possible. Especially if her emotional life is like a storm to her. From your telling, it seems that Heidi is going through some heavy shit. I remember Sherry experiencing wild mood swings as soon as she approached menopause.

Menopause... I hadn't thought of that.

His brow furrows as he considers my theory. All pure gaslighting, but I'm hoping it throws him off my track.

Joe, I gotta favor to ask.

Yeah?

I was wondering if you would talk to Heidi. Maybe with you she'll confide what's bothering her.

In the mornings... Does she...

No. She drives straight to the hospital. Maybe I was all wrong.

I'm relieved to hear that.

Has Heidi talked to you? he asks.

No... no. You sure you don't want to come in?

No, thanks. I just wanted to... you know.

Right.

Well... So, will you talk to her?

Larry, I'm going away for a few days.

Going away?

Yes.

You never go anywhere.

I'm going to L.A.

L.A.?

Some business I need to take care of.

When will you be back?

Hopefully, soon. I'll talk to Heidi when I get back.

Thanks.

We're silent for several awkward moments.

Going to L.A., huh?

Yeah.

You want us to keep an eye on Salem? Wouldn't be any trouble.

Thanks, but she's coming with me.

After Larry leaves I ponder my next move. He's right. I never go anywhere. Fly to L.A.? With a 14-year-old girl in tow? Then what? I'll need help. From who? *Think*, Breeze. Then I remember an old teammate who lives in L.A. Floyd Klebecky. Everyone on the team called him Kleb or the K-Man. He was our best middle reliever. A lefty. When one of our starters got knocked out early, third or fourth inning, and we needed someone to go long, Kleb got the call. He had an okay fastball, 92-93 mph. Occasionally he'd throw a slider. But his bread-and-butter pitch was a filthy sinker. He threw one of the heaviest sinkers in the league. It came down at you like a bowling ball.

Kleb was a big guy: six-six, 260 pounds, all muscle. Intimidating. He had huge hands. The ball would disappear in his grip, which made it harder for the batter to pick up the ball as it left his hand. He also loved to pitch high and tight if a batter crowded the plate. Once, he hit a Brave's player named Rico Santorelli. Rico always crowded the plate and had a reputation of being a hothead. The pitch hit him square in the ribs. No question it was intentional. Kleb hated batters who crowded the plate. He felt they took away real estate that rightly belonged to him. The moment after getting hit, Rico the idiot charged up the mound. Kleb stood his ground and calmly waited. When Rico got within three feet, Kleb punched him in the face. They had to carry Rico off the field in a stretcher. The umpire tossed

Kleb out of the game. The benches emptied. But it was already over.

Another thing about Kleb. He was extremely serious. He was so serious that when he told a joke, you were never quite sure if he was joking or serious. He studied hitters. Made notes during a game in a small notebook he always carried. He was a quiet guy, which I respected. Like me he was kind of a loner. I left him alone. He left me alone. But one day he did me a great service. You could say he turned my season around.

It's mid-June. I have lost three games in a row. Three! Plus, two no decisions. I haven't won a game in three weeks. My worst stretch since I was a rookie – in the minors! I can't figure it out. My stuff is as good as ever. My fastball hasn't lost any hop. My breaking balls are still hooking and diving. Even though the pitching coach tells me not to worry, it's driving me crazy. The day after my third loss I'm sitting on the bench, feeling miserable. I didn't make it past the fifth inning, and the team loses 4-2. Kleb sits down next to me. Because he had pitched three innings of relief after they took me out, he isn't needed in the bullpen. But he never sits next to me. Maybe he's trying to show support, pitcher to pitcher. Still, I wish he'd go away.

I've been watching you pitch, he says in his rumbling basso voice.

Huh?

Your last four or five starts. Been watching you. Real close.

Yeah, I respond, still wanting him to leave me alone.

I know your problem, he says.

My problem?

Actually, your tell.

I have a tell?

Everyone does. I spotted yours.

I've worked hard all my career to never show a tell.

Well, you're showing one now.

I've studied video of myself pitching.

Yeah.

I haven't picked anything up.

It's easy to miss.

Fuck! Are you going to tell me!

Kleb is silent. The only thing that's thin about him is his skin.

Sorry, Kleb.

When you throw a fastball your front foot kicks higher than on your breaking pitches.

Are you sure?

Kleb is silent. That thin skin.

How high? I ask.

Three inches, he says.

Three inches? That all?

Three inches is enough.

Go on.

Say I'm a smart hitter who studies pitchers and who's studied you for years. When I see the foot rise above your waist, I'm sitting on a fastball.

Hell. All those sons of bitches spreading the word.

If I was a batter on another team, I'd spread it, too. The question is, what are you going to do about it?

Work on correcting my delivery.

I got a better idea, he says.

Okay.

Before you make the correction, why don't you reverse it?

Reverse what? I ask.

When you pitch a breaking ball, kick your front foot higher than on your fastball.

Three inches?

Three inches.

I stare at him; he stares at me. Then we both crack up.

That will really fuck up the lineup – for a few of your games, he says.

'Cause they'll be sitting on my fastball and the breaking ball will freeze them.

Yep.

And that's exactly what I do. I win the next seven games in a row. When the hitters catch on, I correct my leg kick to remove any tell.

When Kleb is forced to leave baseball at the age of thirty-one (more on that later), he goes to college and majors in criminal justice. After graduating he moves to California and becomes an L.A. cop for twelve years, rising to detective. Then he quits the force and starts a private investigation business. I haven't seen Kleb since our Chicago days, but never forgot him. Eight years ago, a friend of mine in L.A. needed help on a delicate matter. I referred him to Kleb. The result was satisfactory. Kleb sent me a thank you card.

I decide to call Kleb.

Klebecky Investigations. Floyd Klebecky speaking.

Am I speaking to the K-Man?

There's a long pause. He's thinking, Who the fuck remembers me from back then?

Breeze?

How's it hanging, Kleb?

BREEZY! My God! Jesus! How the fuck are you?

Doing okay.

I heard about Sherry. I'm so sorry.

Thanks. You still married to...

Diane. Going on twenty-five years. I'm a grandfather now.

Congrats. How's business?

Can't complain. I have two full-time partners and a staff of five. We do missing persons, background investigations, infidelity investigation, digital data recovery, fraudulent insurance claims. I just hired another part-time investigator. She specializes in cybercrime.

Sounds like you stay busy.

Always. But I know you didn't call to catch up. So, let's cut to the chase.

I need help.

I already figured that out.

I need to find someone.

We can find people.

I think he lives somewhere in L.A. But that's all I have.

If he's alive and pays taxes, we'll find him. If he doesn't pay taxes, we'll still find him.

He's alive and pays taxes. It's Lake Lemon.

Lake Lemon! You had some history with him.

You could say that. Call me when you find him.

Then what?

Then I'll see you in L.A.

Next day, I haven't yet booked tickets to L.A. Salem goes to school and baseball practice. I sit in my studio and stare listlessly at the double portrait. I am paralyzed – which sounds like a bad joke from a paraplegic. I know I can't stay home, but the thought of flying across the country seems as daunting as flying to Kabul.

At dinner Salem asks me, When are we going to L.A.?

Soon.

Yeah, but how soon?

I say nothing.

Salem glares at me, waiting for a response. I pretend I didn't hear her. We eat the rest of the meal in silence. The sound of silverware scraping against plates stabs my brain. After dinner I return to my studio and sit in contemplation before the double portrait like a Zen monk facing an image of Buddha.

That night in bed I lie awake trying to formulate a plan. Useless. But the fruitless effort finally sends me into a fitful sleep.

I dream about Sherry. I'm pitching a game in the middle innings. And I'm losing. Sherry jumps from the stands and runs toward me. I pull her down on the mound. She raises her dress, a black and white polka dot summer dress, one of my favorites. I turn her over and enter her from behind. The crowd is eerily silent. The players on the field crowd around us to watch, including the umpire and batter. Then the dugouts empty and join the others. This only heightens my excitement and pleasure. I know I'm dreaming in that way we sometimes know, but don't want to awaken. I'm close to climaxing but hold back as long as I can. At that moment the fans stand and cheer. I open my eyes and see Heidi on top of me, guiding my erect cock into her slippery moistness. It takes me a moment to realize that this is not a dream within a dream. Her hips move in an easy allegro rhythm.

What are you doing here? I gasp, grabbing her breasts to heighten my pleasure.

What's it look like? she gasps back.

I mean—

I know.

Larry—

I know.

He'll—

I know!

Kill you!

He won't!

Her hips move faster into andante rhythm. She climaxes first and I immediately follow.

Twenty minutes later, Heidi picks up her clothing from the floor and gets dressed. You know I'm still young enough to have a baby, she says over her shoulder as she straps on her bra.

Don't even think—

Don't worry. I wouldn't do that to you — at least not now.

What do you mean *not now*?

Heidi just laughs as she slips on her jeans.

Where's Larry? I ask.

In bed where I left him.

How do you know he's—

I added some drops in his wine last night. Courtesy of the hospital's pharmacy.

He's very worried about you.

You should be worried about me.

I'm worried about a lot of things right now.

Why didn't you tell me you're going to L.A.?

It was a sudden decision.

I miss you, Breeze. I can't take it much longer. I'm going to tell him.

Please, Heidi. Don't do anything until I get back. Promise me.

I won't promise anything.

She's gone. But the scent of our musky sex lingers in the room. I know that it will be hard to go back to sleep. But I'm too tired to get out of bed.

What are you going to do? a voice asks.

I open my eyes from a drowsy sleep. Christy Mathewson stands at the foot of the bed. He's in uniform, but he doesn't have his glove. He looks older. And he's not wearing a Giants' uniform but the uniform of the Cincinnati Reds. After his pitching career was over, he managed the Reds for a few years, with moderate success. Despite his greatness as a pitcher, managing a team wasn't a perfect fit for Matty, who didn't have a mean bone in his body. His less honorable players took advantage of that.

I don't know, I answer.

What should you do?

I should kill Lake.

But you won't, says Matty.

No.

What can you do?

I'll confront him. Look him in the eyes.

Were you ever afraid to pitch to a batter?

Never.

Were you ever afraid to pitch to a 40-homer slugger with the bases loaded and no outs in the eighth inning?

I loved it. I wanted it. No manager dared walk to the mound.

What did you do? Matty asks with a small smile.

Strike the bastard out! I say, feeling my old competitive fire.

Throw your best stuff.

High heater above the chest. Curveball at the knees. Slider on his hands. Fastball on the outside corner. Freeze him with another curve at his eyes that drops over for strike three.

Matty laughs briefly then gives me a somber look. Something's on his mind.

What are you doing here? I ask. I'm not dying again, am I?

No. I came to come clean with you.

You don't need to do that, Matty.

I do... I owe it to you.

He sits down on the edge of the bed near the footboard then is silent for a long moment.

I had an affair with another woman.

Silence again but I dare not speak.

She lived in Philadelphia. A Jewess. Her name was Fanny. Dark curly hair. A small woman with gigantic energy. She was a journalist for a Yiddish newspaper. We came into Philly to play the Phillies for a four-game series. I pitched the first game, winning 3-2 in ten innings. As I left the stadium Fanny was waiting for me. She wanted to interview me for her paper. Seems the Hebrew people in Philadelphia were big fans. I learned that nobody loves baseball more than the Jews. We met for the interview at a Jewish deli. I still remember the pastrami sandwiches on fresh rye bread and the huge sour pickles. She invited me to her apartment to continue the interview. I knew where the interview was going. I accepted the invitation anyway. The affair lasted three years until she got tired of waiting for my visits during the baseball season. She married a Jewish socialist lawyer. My wife Jane never found out because I never told her. Never told anyone. But I thought about Fanny every day for the rest of my life. I still think about her.

Are you really Matty? I can't believe...

I'm not a saint, kid. Baseball writers made me into one.

I believed–

Those books you read when you were a boy?

Why? Why are you telling me this? Who asked you?

I thought you should know.

You tell no one. You die with that secret. Take it to your grave. And now you decide to spill it all out to me? No. I don't believe it. I'm dreaming. This isn't you.

Dreaming, awake. Does it matter? You gotta learn, kid. You can pitch a perfect game, even an Immaculate Game. But nobody can live a perfect life.

Then Matty stands, steps away, and disappears into the darkness.

NINE

As Salem and I enter La Guardia Airport my blood freezes. It's the sight of the crushing crowds rushing to pick up tickets as they pull their wheeled luggage. Salem pushes me past the gates. Several times airport personal offers to assist. Salem politely repels each offer. I'm as grateful for her protection as a small child shielded by his mother. Sensing my anxiety, Salem talks to me while she pushes.

We're almost there, Breeze. Once we settle in I'll get us drinks and snacks. If you need help in the restroom let me know.

Who is this incredibly kind, caring, young woman? I hardly recognize her.

In the airport, people gaze at the disabled man wearing dark glasses and wool watch cap, though the day is mild. I never get used to being the object of the GAZE. Once I was different because I could do something special with my body that no other human could do or do as well. Now I'm different because I can't do what ninety-nine percent of all humans can effortlessly do: walk.

Finally, we settle in the boarding area at our gate. Before I can breathe a sigh of relief, I hear, Are you the Big Breeze?

I look up at a bearded, heavyset guy in his forties. He wears sweat pants, flip-flops, and a sweatshirt with PENN STATE on the front. I shake my head.

Sure, you are. I watched you pitch when I was a kid. You were my favorite player, though the Pirates were my team. Man, that 3-hitter you pitched in the World Series against the Yankees. Sixteen strikeouts! Wow!

Hey, Dad, does another jerk think you're Breeze Bye?

Penn State turns red, glares at Salem, then backs away.

Thanks, honey, I say.

No problem.

It is a hideous ordeal getting situated in our seats. The flight attendants are as condescendingly helpful as to be expected. They're well trained to deal with all kinds of disabled and difficult passengers. Nevertheless, the gaze from other passengers follows me from the moment I enter the airport to when I'm seated. In the airless cabin we wait on the runway.

Howdy do, folks, says a mellow male voice over the intercom. I'm Captain Tibbets. Just a little heads-up. We are now fourth in line. Just be about fifteen minutes more to takeoff. Thank you for your patience and for flying with us today.

I close my eyes. I almost doze off, reflecting on my life. I was a pitcher. Then I became a painter. Then a father. Now I'm going to be... what? A killer? No! Never!

Why aren't you in the Hall of Fame? I hear Salem ask.

I open my eyes and look at Salem. She's taken out her ear buds and gives me a fiercely serious look. When she was four years old, I thought it was cute when she gave me that look. But not now. Hall of fucking Fame. Call it the Hall of Shame. Last thing I want to talk about. But I will try.

To get in the Hall, sportswriters vote you in. The threshold is seventy-five percent.

Did they ever vote for you?

No.

Why not?

They have rules.

What rules?

To be eligible for the ballot you must play at least ten Major League seasons. I played nine seasons. Actually, eight and a half.

It's a bullshit rule!

Keep your voice down.

Will they throw me off the plane?

Why are you asking about this now?

I've always wanted to ask, but you're hard to talk to. Always holed up in the barn. When you weren't, you *never* wanted to talk about baseball. Now you can't hide. We're stuck with each other.

Girl's right, damn her. I'll try to get through this as quickly as I can.

All the rules of eligibility were written by the Hall since it opened in 1939. There's nothing more to say.

Salem makes a face and says, It's still a bullshit rule.

Let's drop it.

See? Always wanting to drop stuff.

You still want to talk about the Hall of Fame?

Yes!

Why Fame? I ask her.

Huh?

The word: Fame. Why?

I don't...

Why not Hall of Excellence?

I don't think Excellence is—

Or Greatness? Or Winning? Or Achievement? Or Heroes? Aren't they heroes in the eyes of kids? Hall of Heroes sounds pretty good. But Fame? Really? Fame is fleeting, ephemeral.

No! I don't agree! Fame is perfect! Greatness, winning, heroism, courage? They're all wrapped in fame like a burrito. To be famous, really famous, is like being immortal. You were famous. I know all about your career. I've Googled you. I've read your biography.

I groan. That trashy, unauthorized bio full of misinformation, exaggeration, and plain lies. I was going to sue the author but decided it wasn't worth my time. Right now I'd rather jump out of the plane than continue talking about this. But Salem has latched her shapely nails into this topic and won't let go until satisfied.

I call it the Hall of Shame. Know why?

No, obviously.

What happened to professional baseball in 1947?

You're really asking me that? Really?

The plane finally taxis down the runway. We take off into the cloudless blue sky. Salem looks out the porthole. I wait for my ears to pop.

You wanted to talk. So, talk.

Salem gives me a dramatic sigh, then recites, In 1947, Jackie Robinson broke the color barrier in Major League Baseball when he played for the Brooklyn Dodgers.

That's right. For over sixty years, African American players were not allowed to play in the big leagues. Of course, there was nothing in writing. One of those unofficial, unwritten understandings much like Jim Crow in the South. Most of the team owners, general managers, managers, and many players were racists. Shamefully, even the players who were not racists never publicly protested this injustice. They just went along. Imagine if Babe Ruth had said, I'm not playing another game until I see some men of color in uniforms on the playing field.

There were the Negro Leagues, Salem interjects.

Yeah, there were the Negro—

I'm not defending it! But maybe the white players thought that was good enough.

I can't respond. Why am I even talking about this when it hurts my head and heart?

I won't interrupt you again, Breeze. Please keep talking.

I'll say one more thing, and then we'll stop. That okay?

Yes.

I believe that any players in the Hall of Fame whose careers ended before 1947 don't belong in the Hall. They didn't compete against the best baseball players in the country. It's like electing a player into the Hall who only played in Triple-A.

Even Babe Ruth? Sorry.

Babe Ruth, Lou Gehrig, Ty Cobb, Walter Johnson, and all the rest. They don't belong. So, I don't want to be in a Hall of Shame. Understand?

But those great Black players in the Negro Leagues are now in the Hall of Fame.

I don't care. The injustice is too great, too grave. Imagine if Joe DiMaggio or Ted Williams batted against Satchel Page and Smokey Joe Williams in their prime. Or Bob Feller had to pitch to Josh Gibson and Cool Papa Bell.

But you paint portraits of Hall of Fame pitchers who played way before Jackie Robinson broke into the Majors. Are you saying they don't belong in the Hall of Fame?

Pitchers like Christy Mathewson, Lefty Grove, and Walter Johnson would be just as great if they pitched against the best Black ballplayers. Sadly, they didn't get that opportunity. I would still put them in the pre-Robinson Hall of Fame.

You belong in the Hall, Breeze. You were the best. I don't care what you say.

She puts her ear buds back in and closes her eyes. I take out one of the books I brought, a new translation of Pablo Neruda poems. It was my old catcher, Tiny Torres, who turned me on to Neruda. Man, Neruda can paint an image better with words than any painter with oils. But after reading a few poems, I set the book aside and pull out a novel. It's a Scandinavian crime mystery, easier to concentrate.

I'm not bitter or angry. If they ever elect me to the Hall of Fame, I'll politely tell them to go fuck themselves. I don't need a plaque to tell me how good I was. But I don't tell Salem that. There's something else I don't tell her. But if I do ever tell her, this is what I will say.

Imagine a boy who loves baseball more than anything in his

life. On his twelfth birthday, his father takes him to Cooperstown, NY to see the Hall of Fame. It's a three-hour drive. But the journey seems forever to the boy, who has been thinking and dreaming about this trip for months. Then imagine this boy now inside the Hall of Fame Museum and entering the Plaque Gallery, the most sacred ground in all of baseball. To him it is the grandest cathedral in the world. Baseball's version of St. Peter's Basilica in Vatican City. Inside, are pairs and trios of middle-aged men wearing baseball caps and baseball jerseys. On their jerseys are the numbers of their favorite players. As they walk past the plaques, the men speak to each other in low tones, like the murmurings of monks in a monastery. But the boy pays them no attention. He is the only true believer there. He reads every plaque in the Gallery. *Every* plaque. It takes the boy two hours to read all the plaques. When they finish the tour, his father tells his son that he will buy him copies of three vintage baseball cards. The boy may choose only three. It's an impossible task. But he chooses. He picks Christy Mathewson first, of course, then Walter Johnson, then the great lefty, Sandy Koufax.

No, I won't tell Salem that story. Too sentimental and nostalgic. There is another Hall of Fame story I won't tell her. That one is neither sentimental nor nostalgic but something worse: coldly cynical.

I've been in the hospital for three months. By that time I've had four operations. In two weeks, I'm scheduled for my fifth round of surgery. I've accepted the fact that I'll never play baseball again. Now all I want is to walk again. I try to be optimistic. But optimism seems like a rare religion worshipped only among tribes in the highest peaks of the Andean Mountains. The phone rings next to my bed. I'm not in the mood to chat, but I pick it up on the fourth ring.

Hello?

Hey, Breezy!

Hello?

This is Emanuel Windgate, Commissioner of Major League Baseball.

Hello... Commissioner.

How ya feeling, son?

Why do older men feel they have the right to call young men they do not know, *son?*

Hanging in there, sir.

Right. Glad to hear it. I just want to let you know that the Commissioner's office and the entire Major League Baseball community are rooting for your recovery.

Thank you, I say, not believing a word.

If there's anything – ANYTHING – my office can do, you let me know pronto.

Thank you.

I mean it. PRONTO.

Thank you.

The ballplayers call Commissioner Windgate *Winnie*. He is not a beloved figure. In fact, most players have zero respect for him. His prior connections to Major League Baseball are paper thin: He is a former congressman from Maryland who had season box seats at Baltimore Oriole games; he is a close buddy of the owner of the Orioles. The record will show that Winnie's head is stuck deep in the ass of the owners. When the Players Union decides to strike for better health benefits, he sides with the owners. He doesn't care about the players nor does he have a natural, deep-rooted love for the game. What he loves is the power and prestige of his office. So why the hell is he calling me?

I also wanted to share with you some news before it goes public, he says.

News?

I wanted to be the first one to tell you.

Okay.

I just heard from the president of The Hall of Fame. He informed me that they won't make any exceptions to the 10-year eligibility rule. As he put it, rules are rules.

I am silent. The commissioner clears his throat.

As you know that rule states that a player must have played at least ten years in the Major Leagues to qualify for election into the Hall of Fame.

I am still silent, wondering why he is telling me this.

Did you hear what I just said?

Yes, sir.

Well... there has been a movement among *some* members of the press and *some* players and, frankly, many fans that the Hall of Fame should make you an exception. Personally, while I would love to see you in the Hall of Fame, I believe that it is in the best interests of baseball...

Hall of Fame... baseball... Hall of Fame... baseball... Hall of Fame... baseball... Hall of Fame... baseball... Hall of Fame... baseball...

I tune Winnie out and stare at the phone. I notice that it has the same off-white color as the hospital walls. Is that intentional? I try to name its shade of white. Egg-shell white? My mind sinks down a white-colored rabbit hole...

Ivory white, satin white, cloudy white, snow white, golden white, cool white, ice white, baseball white, Dodger home-field uniform white...

Then I hear, BREEZE!

Commissioner?

I'm very sorry that the Hall of Fame wasn't able–

Tell the Hall of Fame that I have no interest in ever being considered.

What?

No interest... EVER...

Breeze! It's not a question of your great contribution to–

Sir... I'm very tired now.

Of course. I'll call you back when–

I hang up, knowing that he will never call me back.

Then I let out a primal scream. I rip the tubes from my body. I shove the overbed table so hard it goes crashing against the wall. With all my pathetic strength, I part pull, part roll myself out of bed. My useless legs do not break my fall to the floor. Two nurses and an attendant rush in. By then I'm laughing my ass off – until one of the nurses sticks a long needle into my arm.

After that episode, I forget about any more Hall of Fame nonsense. *You wish.* Fast forward one year later, start of the baseball season. My agent, Morrie Pelter, calls me and says he just received an intriguing offer. A prominent team owner wants to sign me to a 1-year contract in order to pitch to one batter in a game. That game would officially count as my tenth season and thus qualify me for the Hall of Fame. I tell Morrie to inform the prominent team owner that I will not, under any circumstances, participate in a cheap stunt. Morrie later receives similar offers from two other team owners. He gives them the same answer.

Finally, I think, no more Hall of Fame foolishness. Fast forward four years later. I've been out of baseball for five years. In 1954, the Hall of Fame installed the 5-year waiting period. That means a player must be retired from baseball for five full seasons before being eligible for the Hall of Fame. Now that I've been *retired* from baseball for five years, there is a renewed effort to get me in the Hall. A group consisting of two Hall of Famers, a few sportswriters, and an Illinois senator are urging people to write to the Hall of Fame's president and board of directors asking them to make me an exception to their 10-year rule. The group's slogan is *THE HALL NEEDS THE BREEZE!* The group reaches out to me for my support. I instruct Morrie to tell them that I want no part of it. I will neither help nor hinder them. The campaign gathers steam. The Hall of Fame schedules an emergency meeting. That's when Lake Lemon enters the picture. From his lofty platform as America's favorite sports-writing personality, he leads a counter campaign. His group includes Hall of Famers, sportswriters, and a famous actor who played Babe Ruth in a popular movie. Their slogan is *NO ONE IS ABOVE THE RULES!* The Hall of Fame comes out of their emergency meeting and calls a press conference. Standing on the steps of the Hall of Fame, the president of the Hall speaks to hundreds of reporters and onlookers.

We understand the high interest in the case of Joseph Bye, known to his many admirers and fans as The Big Breeze. He had an exceptional career. Many believe a Hall of Fame career, cut short by a tragic accident. However, the Hall of Fame stands by its rules and long-time policy. We cannot make any exceptions to the 10-year rule.

I was not surprised by their decision. In fact, I was relieved. FINALLY, I'll be left alone from this nonsense. I never wanted a fucking plaque in the Hall of Shame. Never. I know what I accomplished. The players who played with me and against me know. The fans and sportswriters who watched me know. That's the only thing that ever counted... the only thing.

TEN

'm pinching myself and thinking: Tiny Torres, can you believe the game you're catching? Can you believe the game Breeze is pitching? Well, you better believe 'cause it's fucking happening. It's the fourth inning, two outs. I go into my crouch after Ducky Downs, the Cardinals' rookie catcher, strikes out. The crowd roars. Everyone stands up. The big scoreboard lights up.

ELEVEN STRIKEOUTS IN A ROW! A MAJOR LEAGUE RECORD!

And Breeze is still pitching a perfect game! Every pitch is working. At that moment, Jim McQuaid, the home plate umpire, whispers in my ear.

Jesus, Tiny, Breeze's fastballs are so quick I can't see the damn ball.

I whisper back, Don't worry, Jim. If it hits my glove and I don't move, it's a strike.

Thanks, Tiny.

Then we share a quick laugh over his joke before the next batter steps to the plate. McQuaid is in his thirtieth year of umping, and I hear it will be his last. He's one of the best. If his calls lean at all, they slightly favor the pitcher. That's great when

I'm catching, not so great when I'm batting. Tonight, I'm glad he's umping.

Here comes Billy Stoney, the Cards' power hitting second baseman. Struck out looking at a big curve in the first inning. He'll be first pitch swinging. Billy's anxious. He sure don't want to be strikeout number twelve. He's looking for a fastball. I signal for the hook. Breeze never nods or shakes his head like other pitchers. No need. We are *muy sincronizado*. If he don't like my call, he'll just stare at me a second longer. He goes into his motion, smooth as a malted milkshake. The ball hangs in the sky, a beautiful full moon. Then it drops like a tossed snowball across Billy's waist, who swings at nothing but air. I signal for another curve. Just to fuck him up. The fat moon orbits above his head then drops on the outside corner. Billy chases and misses by a foot. The next pitch is a low fastball on the inside corner. Billy's mind is so fucked up he turns to stone as the ball cross the plate. He looks at me with a pleading expression.

That fucking shit is fucking unfair, Tiny!

Like fucking life, Billy.

Twelve strikeouts in a row. Perfect game. Grown men don't even dream about this kind of game. Maybe boys do. Some boys. Nah. Not even boys. Too... impossible. We all dream about being heroes. Hitting the game-winning home run in the ninth inning. Pitching a 1-0 shutout. In the stands sits the prettiest girl – or handsomest boy – in town, looking only at you, throwing you a kiss. Those the kind of dreams boys dream. Not this. This is Greek mythology shit. Be like Zeus or Apollo changing into a mortal and performing some impossible warrior deeds. Like slaying giants or killing Medusa or defeating an entire army single-handed... Or striking out every damned batter in a game.

I turn and look at Breeze, who sits at the end of the dugout bench like he always does. No one goes near him. We know to leave him alone. But tonight the guys hardly talk to each other. When they do, they speak in soft voices. Nobody mentions the strikeouts and the perfect game. Never seen them like this.

Never. Me? I'm a chatterbox. I like to talk, make the players relax. Not tonight.

The opposing pitcher, Felix Berroa, is a journeyman. Bounced around the minors and Majors for years. Tonight, he's pitching the game of his life. A two-hit shutout. I struck out and bounced out. I look down at my catching hand. The palm is red and burns from all the fastballs I've caught. I wrap adhesive tape over my palm for extra padding. I want to tell Breeze to keep burning my hand.

I remember when I joined the team as a rookie. Breeze has only been with the team for two years, but he's already a star. During spring training, the veterans ignore me. I get it. Why bother? I'll probably be sent back to the bush leagues. But Breeze... Fucking Breeze.

Hey, rook, welcome to camp, he says.

Thank you, Mr. Bye.

Mr. Bye? Better call me Breeze if you want to be my friend.

Thanks! ... Breeze.

I need to warm up my arm. How about catching me?

And that was it. Made me feel like I belonged. That's why I want to tell him about... how I am. Cause I know he'll understand. I wonder if he already suspects. Breeze, I'm gay. I'm gay. Just two little words. Five letters. I'm gay. That's all I gotta say. Why's it so hard?

ELEVEN

'm sitting in a plane with my daughter flying to L.A. This is a sentence I never imagined I would ever say. It could not be more foreign to me if I said, I'm in a rocket ship with my daughter flying to Mars. I turn my head to look at Salem. She eagerly stares out the porthole. This is not her first flight. She flew with Sherry several times to Chicago to visit Sherry's parents while I stayed home and painted. We have first-class seats, for the extra room, extra privacy, and to spare me from navigating down the long narrow aisle.

As a player, I flew hundreds of thousands of miles. I would usually sit next to my catcher, Tiny, or the pitching coach, discussing pitching strategies for the next series. We'd go over the lineup: who was hot, who was cold, how they hit me in the past. I didn't want to just outpitch the opposition. I wanted to out-think them.

But I haven't been in the air in twenty-five years. As our plane continues to climb, I break into a sweat. Salem has her earbuds in, listening to whatever she listens to. What does she listen to? No idea. Have I ever asked? No. Maybe I'll ask her... Maybe not.

I try to sleep but only drift. Thoughts buzz around my brain like stinging mosquitos. This is crazy. Crazy that I'm going. Crazy that I brought my 14-year-old daughter. Crazy that I have no plan. Crazy that I don't feel crazy. What do I feel? Numbly foolish. I always had a plan before pitching a game. Start with lots of fastballs through the lineup. Second time through the lineup, mix in the breaking stuff. Third time around, go back to the hard stuff. When I broke in as a rookie, my only plan was to fire the ball past them – I learned. Once we arrive in L.A., a plan will come together... I hope. I go back to the novel.

Going to L.A.? asks a voice to my right.

I turn my attention from the novel to a male passenger on the opposite aisle seat. Late thirties, business attire: a well-cut, shark-gray suit, white shirt, no tie. On his tray is a sleek laptop. I'm struck by his hair: wavy, black, and slicked back. With his square chin and wide-set eyes, he would be considered good looking if it wasn't for his nose. By its crooked shape it looks like it has been broken, maybe more than once. His toothy smile indicates that he's trying to be friendly. Who asked him?

If this plane doesn't crash, I say.

Ha-ha! Good one. I meant is L.A. your destination.

It is.

Me too. Unfortunately, it's all business. No time to enjoy the sights. What about you?

Some business, some personal.

Interesting. Personal but not pleasure?

This stranger is trying too hard to be engaging. I don't do engaging. Meanwhile, Salem has her eyes closed and ears plugged.

My name is Henry Watt.

Joe, I say and go back to my book.

I do consulting work for rich people in trouble. Pays exceptionally well and there is no end of rich people getting in trouble, right? What's your line of work?

Nothing as interesting as yours.

I hope I wasn't prying.

No harm.

Is that your daughter?

Enjoy L.A., I say, trying again to end the conversation.

Lovely girl. You must be very proud.

I didn't say she was my daughter.

It's obvious. I see the resemblance.

As Salem would say, this is getting creepy. When I don't respond, the stranger's warm smile drops twenty degrees. He returns his gaze to his laptop. I can tell he's watching an action flick. On his screen I see a bridge blow up and a leather-clad guy on a motorcycle – Tom Cruise? – fly across the chasm. I return to my Scandinavian crime mystery, a loan from Heidi. She hooked me on Nordic noir: Stieg Larsson, Jo Nesbø, Henning Mankell, Karin Fossum, Anne Holt. This book takes place in Iceland. The hero is a 50-ish police detective named Lars Tovan. He has a serious drinking problem, and his wife is having an affair with the city's corrupt mayor. While Tovan is aware and troubled by her affair, he does nothing. The murder victim is a woman who was running against the mayor in the upcoming election. The victim was also an ex-lover of our hero. Complicated.

After reading a few pages I wonder if Henry Watt, if that's his real name, was sent by Lake. Put a fake mustache on him and he might be the creep that tried to pick up Salem. Or am I getting paranoid? I hope I am being paranoid. Henry doesn't talk to me the rest of the trip. He takes a nap, purchases a dirty martini, and continues watching the action flick.

I try to get into my novel again, but instead I think of Dawn... Dawn Gold... 24 Karat Gold. The genuine deal. Dawn. The one before Sherry. A dancer for the Joffrey Ballet Company in Chicago. Breathtaking. Long, shapely legs that seemed to start at her throat. Auburn hair she kept short. All angles: hips, shoulders, arms, high cheekbones. As light on her feet as fine blown Murano glass.

How did we meet? During my playing days, I have season

tickets to the Joffrey in Chicago. I meet her at the company's season opening party for members. We eye each other from across the ballroom. We gravitate closer. She doesn't know who I am. Couldn't care less about baseball. We end up in her bed that night. We stay glued to each other for two years. But when I meet Sherry it's only Sherry. Nothing else matters. Breaking up with Dawn is the hardest thing I ever did up to that point. I try to be gentle. It doesn't go well. In fact, quite badly – screaming, crying, pleading, cursing, smashed glasses. I love her. But what I feel for Sherry is beyond love... beyond words.

After our breakup I don't hear from Dawn until my accident. She tries to visit me at the hospital. But I don't allow anyone to see me except Sherry. After I'm home she calls me, leaves messages. I never call her back. Silence for twenty years until Sherry's death. When she calls again, this time I answer. I'm cordial, guarded, and keep the conversation short. Dawn tells me she lives in L.A. to be close to her son, who works in the television industry. She gives me her address.

She says, If you're ever in L.A. you better visit me.

Okay.

I mean it.

I will visit you.

Promise.

I promise, I say, thinking I will never come to L.A.

Had I never met Sherry, had I never left Dawn, how different would my life have been? I have avoided answering that question for a long time... as I do now.

Salem and I check into the Santa Monica Paradise Hotel. After going up to our rooms and quickly unpacking, first thing I do is head for the pool. Their pool is heated, state-of-the-art, four times the size of my pool at home. It has two diving boards, one low, one high, a 3-foot wading section for the tykes, purified water, and a separate sauna. I pressed hard for details about their pool before booking.

Wearing swimming trunks under my shorts, towel draped

over my shoulders, I wheel myself to the pool patio, excited to swim long laps in its pristine water. When I sail into the patio I'm confronted with a pool teeming with adults, old and young, and kids, playing and shrieking. Around the pool, sitting in lounge chairs, is a ring of chattering mothers. Undeterred, I roll near the pool's edge. I slip off my shorts, set towel aside, ease myself off my Wheels, and wait. On cue the adults stop swimming, the kids stop shrieking, mothers stop mid-chatter. Everyone either stares or looks away. Then comes the urgent, overlapping commentary.

Mommy, is the man in the wheelchair—

Quiet, Timmy.

Is he going—

Never mind.

—in the water?

Yes!

Eeeoow!

Time to go, Bethie!

I don't—

Out!

—want to!

Now!

WAAAH!

Peggy, is this allowed?

Carol, can you—

Don't they have a—

—believe this?

—special pool for them?

Or at least have some—

Out, out, out!

Rules!

I take my time getting into the pool. Make a show, like it's a struggle, dragging my body the last few feet. This creates quiet pandemonium. The pool and most of the patio empties. I dip myself into the refreshing water without even glancing at the disgruntled guests who remain. Then I swim my laps. No hurry. I take my time. Stroke... stroke... stroke... stroke. Breast stroke, side stroke, free style, back stroke, butterfly. Ahh... pure joy.

I remember recuperating during the final surgeries. Part of my rehab is swimming in the hospital's pool. To strengthen my arms and whatever living leg muscles I have left. There are other patients in the pool. One is a young Chicano. He has one arm, his left. His right arm had to be amputated due to severe gunshot wounds in a gang-related ambush. He swims with powerful strokes with his one arm, and his ferocious 6-beat kick thrusts him forward like a torpedo. We become friendly. To encourage each other, we race against each other. Half the time he beats me, inspiring me to work harder.

Thirty minutes later, I'm sitting under the shade of an umbrella table, reading my Scandinavian mystery. Police detective Tovan has uncovered a second related murder: the victim is another woman from his past. Meanwhile, his wife's affair with the mayor has intensified and it's beginning to torment him. Guests are back in the pool. A few mothers keep a wary eye on me. My attention is drawn to Salem, who just entered the patio. She's wearing a purple one-piece I haven't seen before. New? With her long muscular legs and broad shoulders, she looks stunning. Most of the men watch her. She comes over to me, drops towel, sunglasses, and book on a lounge chair next to me then heads to the pool without a word. Instead of jumping in the water, she climbs the ladder to the high board. Now she has the attention of every guest, even the kids. When she gets to the top, without hesitation, she springs off the edge of the board and does a perfect jackknife. A few people applaud. Salem swims back to the board, climbs up, and does a flawless swan dive. More guests applaud. Salem swims a few laps, returns to the lounge chair, wipes herself with the towel, and stretches out on the chair.

Where did you learn to dive like that? I ask.

My high school has a great pool. Everything else at school is old and falling apart. I think some wealthy alumni dude, who loves swimming, donated big bucks for a new pool.

Yeah, but *how* did you learn to dive like that?

I just watched some guys on the diving team. Then I practiced on my own. They're not hard dives, Breeze.

I never see her swim in our pool. I assumed she doesn't like swimming and/or pools. Yeah, right. I go back to my novel. Salem opens her book and starts reading. I notice that she occasionally highlights a passage with an orange highlighter.

What are you reading?

To the Lighthouse.

By Virginia Woolf?

Of course.

Why?

I'm writing an essay on it for my English class. I don't want to fall behind in my classes while I'm gone.

Virginia Woolf. That's pretty advanced stuff.

My teacher thinks I'm ready. I'm not like a genius, but I'm smart for my age.

I say nothing because I don't know what to say to this. *I've always known you were brilliant* would be a pure parental bullshit cliché. Salem is still looking at me.

You never read my report cards, do you?

Of course I read them. I'm your father.

What were my grades last semester?

Last semester?

Yeah.

Straight A's.

Wrong. I got A-pluses in history and English.

By straight A's I'm not including A-minuses and pluses.

I didn't get any A-minuses. It's okay, Breeze. I don't need your approval to do well in school.

She returns to Virginia Woolf, a literary giant, who wisely never had children. I knew bringing Salem along would be hard, painful, even scary. But I wasn't prepared for how humbling it would be. Now I'm prepared.

A few hours later I'm sitting in the hotel restaurant, waiting for Salem. She says she needs more time to dress for dinner. I'm looking over the menu when my cell buzzes. It's Jackie. I don't want to answer, but she'll just keep calling. Reluctantly, I answer.

Joseph! I got confirmations! MOMA is coming! The Whitney is coming! *ArtForum* is coming! Fucking *Art in America* is coming. Now you MUST come!

Sorry, Jackie.

What? You're sorry? No, no, no, no. I'm the one who's sorry for ever helping you.

Can't we let my paintings speak for me?

Absolutely. As soon as you're as famous as Jackson Pollock. But you know what? Even Pollock, that bipolar drunk, who was terrified of openings, went to his openings.

I have no response.

Pleeease, Joseph. Do this one little thing for me, and I'll never ask you again.

I'm in L.A., I say.

There follows such a long silence I think we're cut off.

Jackie?

How strange. It sounded like you said you're in L.A., which is impossible. No, unbelievable.

It's true.

How the fuck could you go to L.A.?

Business.

Business?

Serious personal business. Couldn't be helped.

I can't get you to ride in a limo for a two and a half-hour trip to New York, and now you tell me you flew 3,000 miles to L.A.? How do I process that? Do you know how much I talk about you at my therapist's? More than about my mother, who was a total monster bitch.

Jackie—

You should be home finishing your paintings!

Listen! If I complete my business successfully, I will... go to the opening.

What if you don't?

If I don't... then it won't matter.

What won't matter?

Goodbye, Jackie.

For the first time in years, I want to have a drink. I sip on my seltzer water. Then Salem enters. She wears a dress – a dress! – I've never seen on her before. It's short, sleeveless, green, and looks dazzling on her. She's put on a little lipstick and eyeshadow and pinned her hair up. I see men turn their heads. I can't help but smile. She smiles back at me as if to say, What do you think? I think *no more little girl*. She moves across the room with a grace I've never seen or noticed.

Time stands still. I see Sherry glide toward me in a silver, slinky, strapless evening dress with a high slit up one thigh. We're going to a fancy party thrown by a producer friend of Sherry's. I feel like the luckiest man alive.

How do I look? Sherry asks with an impish smile.

So good it should be illegal.

I like that.

You should.

You're staring at me, Breeze.

Salem stands before me, her hands on her hips.

Am I?

Yeah. But I like it.

You shouldn't like it.

Why?

Because a father shouldn't stare at his daughter.

Why?

Sit down and look at the menu.

She sits and studies the large menu with mindful attention. My thoughts wander to the black ribbon hovering over the figure of the pitcher in my *Rendezvous on the Mound* painting.

What is the meaning of that shape? I feel that it's important to the life of the painting. But what does it have to do with the life of the figure? What does it have to do with the life of the artist (if I can call myself that)? Now that Sherry's ashes are embedded in the ribbon, it's too late to scrape it out.

Can I have a small salad and a crab cake for appetizers? Salem asks.

Yes.

Can I have the grilled scallops for my entree?

Yes.

Can I have a glass of white wine?

No.

What! Why not?

Do I really need to tell you?

She shrugs petulantly.

Shrug all you want. This ain't France.

After dinner I decide to take a cruise around the hotel, maybe go down to the Santa Monica Pier and watch the waves come in.

You want me to come with you? Salem asks.

No, thanks. I need to think.

I can't tell if she looks disappointed or relieved. Maybe both. Maybe neither.

The hotel is wheelchair friendly – another thing I thoroughly checked out with the front desk clerk before making the reservation. I grilled the poor woman, named Kayla, on the phone.

You sure there are ramps? I ask.

Elevators and ramps throughout the hotel, inside and out, sir.

Are there sidewalks outside the hotel?

Yes, there are sidewalks.

How are the sidewalks?

Excuse me?

The sidewalks. How are they?

They're just sidewalks, sir.

Are the sidewalks in good condition?

I'm pretty sure they are, says Kayla, sounding not so sure.

Just pretty sure?

Kayla is silent.

Don't you walk on the sidewalks?

I drive to work... sir.

You do take an occasional walk, right? During your lunch break?

There's a coffee shop in the hotel.

Now I'm silent.

Sir? Would you like me to complete your–

Listen, Kayla, and listen carefully. For a wheelchair-bound person, knowing the condition of sidewalks is very, *very* important. Are they sufficiently wide? Are they uneven? Are they full of cracks? Are they in crumbling condition? Do you understand?

I think so, she answers tentatively. I take a deep breath and exhale slowly.

Let's try this. Who in your hotel would know about the sidewalks?

I don't know. I just work at the front desk, take reservations, and–

Kayla... Can you ask one of your maintenance people about the sidewalks?

He may be outside or in another part of–

I can wait.

I'm not supposed to leave my desk.

Then you better hurry.

I'll put you on hold, she says curtly.

Ten minutes go by before Kayla is back on the line. She sounds breathless.

Sir! I spoke to Emilio. He does outdoor maintenance. Emilio said that the sidewalks are in very good condition. *Muy bueno,* he said.

I'm outside the hotel. Temperature in the high 70s. The sky is hazy from smoke drifting from three wildfires up north. Still, the ocean breeze intoxicates my senses. I feel that I'm starting to get my bearings in this alien place. The sidewalks are wide, even, and no cracks! This makes me a happy paraplegic. The sidewalk is at the top of an embankment. Below flows the Santa Monica Freeway like a surging river. A chain-link fence runs along the top. I count fourteen lanes of steady, heavy traffic in either direction. The sidewalk, I note, is deserted. No one walks in L.A. I may be the only person in Los Angeles who wants to walk.

I wheel forward to get a closer view of the ocean. Small rippling waves barely reach the beach. Low tide or can an ocean feel tired? Am I projecting my own fatigue? Already I feel coming here was a mistake. Might as well return to the hotel and head right to bed. I'm beat. What's Lake Lemon thinking right now? Is he thinking of me?

I remember the last time I saw Lake. It's a few weeks after Sherry left him for good. Every other day he sends her flowers. Every day he leaves messages on her answering machine, imploring her to take him back. She tosses the flowers in the garbage and doesn't return his calls. Later, Lake's messages become more aggressive, hinting that he could destroy her career, that she'll never work in Hollywood. Sherry tries to laugh it off, but I know it's gnawing at her. One night, when our game is cancelled due to rain, I go looking for Lake. I head to his favorite Chicago watering hole, the historic Twin Anchors Tavern on North Sedgwick Street. He likes their steaks.

He sits at a big round table with other baseball writers I recognize and a few young women, who don't look like their wives. I go over to the table, grab somebody's beer, tip Lake's chair back until he falls on his back, then douse his face with the drink. Nobody at the table moves.

No more calls! I shout down at Lake. No more flowers! No more notes! Stop following her in your car. If I catch you bothering her again, you'll get more than beer in your face! I look at the others. They still haven't moved, uncertain whether to laugh or curse. I turn around and see everyone in the tavern staring at me. Let 'em stare. Then I leave.

I'm walking south on North Park Avenue when I sense a car moving slowly to my left.

GET IN! shouts a voice from the car. I turn my head to see Lake's Mercedes.

Piss off!

Come on, Breeze! says Lake.

Fuck you!

Five minutes. That's all. I've got an offer for you.

Against my better judgement I open the back car door. Slammer is at the wheel. Lake sits in the back. I slide in. Lake's face is dry, but his hair is still damp. Instead of looking furious, he has a grin on his face.

What you did was impressive, he says.

Wasn't meant to be, I say.

But it was! Total humiliation. Public place. Before my esteemed colleagues of the fourth estate. They knew better than to laugh, but I know they thought it was funny. They may still be laughing now. It's a good scene that I'll include in my book.

What book?

My book about The Big Breeze.

You're joking, Lake.

Couldn't be more serious.

Then you're crazy.

At times, but not about this.

Quincy, you can let me out now.

First hear my offer. I will not press charges for the assault back there. I'll stop communicating with Sherry.

Completely?

Completely.

In return?

In return you will remove the gag order you put on your team. And, most important, you'll cooperate with my *authorized* biography of your life and career. I have taken the liberty of speaking to several major publishing houses. They are salivating for such a book. Why are they salivating, you ask? First, it will be only my second book in over twenty years, which the sports world has been eagerly waiting for. Second, there has never been an authorized bio of your life and spectacular career. I expect a bidding war into the high six figures to option my book. I expect sales will be in the millions. How does a fifty-fifty split sound?

You would trade Sherry for the money you'll make on my bio.

Sherry's value is priceless. But I expect that she will come to her senses and return to me.

Lake takes out one of his long cigars. Perhaps he thinks that by leisurely lighting up it will give me time to consider and accept his offer. He may even believe that he's being generous, even kind. I let him light up and have his moment – until his first puff.

If you leave Sherry alone, completely, I'll take the gag off the team. But it will be a chilly day in hell before I help with your book. If you still try writing it, I'll tell everyone who knows me not to cooperate. Feel free to write the *unauthorized* biography of Breezy Bye. But it won't be worth the paper it's printed on.

Do you know why I haven't written another book in twenty years?

I'm silent since I know he's going to tell me.

After the spectacular success of my Shoeless Joe bio, what could I do as an encore? It wasn't writer's block. It was subject block. I couldn't think of another figure that inspired my imagination – until you came into my life. From farm boy to baseball superstar to sports deity. The chapter on your Immaculate Game alone will be worth the price of the book. I've already filled a thick binder with notes. Give me this chance, Breeze, and I promise that you will never regret it.

My answer is the same,

I believe we can work as a team. You and I have so much in common.

Like Sherry?

Forget Sherry! I'm talking about our humble backgrounds, our deep ties to Chicago, our towering ambition, our love for the science, poetry, and myth of baseball. I think of us as close. I dare say that I could be a father-figure for you.

A father figure. For me. Seriously?

If you'll allow me.

I start laughing, and I can't stop. The idea is too ridiculous. During my fit, Quincy glances nervously in the rear-view mirror. After my laughter subsides I look at Lake. Surprisingly, his face shows no signs of anger or disappointment, but remains relatively impassive. That impassiveness is Lake's *tell*.

Do you know how I became a sportswriter? he asks.

Gonna tell me a story? Not interested.

Course not. Nobody does or ever will – unless I write my memoir, which I may someday.

Let me out, Quincy!

Five more minutes, then you can go. Keep driving, Slammer.

Lake takes a puff on his cigar and stares out the window.

I became a sportswriter because of two people: my mother and Early Wynn. My father died when I was six years old. All I remember of him is his thunderous laughter and whiskey breath. I was an only child. My mother, a lifelong Cubs fan, decided she would take me to baseball games because that's what my father would've done. Being a fair-minded woman, she took me to Wrigley Field when the Cubs were in town and Comiskey Park when the White Sox were in town. On my eighth birthday my mother asked me which team I preferred. I told her the White Sox. That was probably the best choice I ever made in my life. After that she only took me to White Sox games. In 1959, the White Sox won the American League pennant. It had been a 40-year drought since the last time they appeared in the fall classic – as you know that series was the infamous 1919 Black Sox Scandal. My favorite player on the White Sox was Early Wynn. He was thirty-nine years old and led the team with twenty-two wins. Won the Cy Young Award that year. He won over twenty games five times. Ended with 300 wins. Played twenty-three years. Had over a hundred pinch hits, including a grand slam. You ever hit a grand slam, Breeze? Were you ever used as a pinch hitter?

A rhetorical question I don't answer.

I just loved his name. Early Wynn. One of the great baseball names for a pitcher. Like yours, Breezy. In early September of '59, my mother and I watch Wynn notch his twentieth win. My mother turns to me and says, Let's get Early's autograph. We had never done that before. I don't know how, but my mother knows which gate the players exit from after a game. We rush down and wait. Half an hour later the players start to exit. I see their dazzling young shortstop, Luis Aparicio. Followed by their great second baseman, Nellie Fox, walking with third baseman Bubba Phillips. I recognize pitcher Bob Shaw, one of their aces. But no Early Wynn. I am beginning to believe he will never show up. But finally I see him walking with the reserve catcher Earl Battey. But there is no mistaking it's Early with his burly body and moon face. He wears a leisure suit and no tie. I'm too shy, if you can believe it, to call his name. My mother waves her arms in the air like she's drowning, calling, MR. WYNN! OVER HERE! He looks over our way and smiles. He seems even bigger to my eyes. He ambles over. My mother says, My son is a huge fan of yours. Would you mind autographing his program? Early looks down at me and says, My pleasure, ma'am. What's your name, son? I tell him. You plan to be a ballplayer? he asks. No, sir, I say. I want to be a baseball writer for the Chicago Tribune and write stories about players like you. Early laughs. But not at me. He takes my program, pauses a moment before writing with evident care. Then he gives the program back. I thank him and tell him the Sox are going to win the World Series. Hope you're right, son, he says, and off he goes.

I don't read what he wrote until I get home. In surprisingly neat handwriting, he wrote: Wishing Lake a Hall of Fame career as a Chicago baseball writer. All the best, Early Wynn. His words and autograph are like being blessed by a saint. The Sox did win the pennant. But they lost the World Series to the L.A. Dodgers in six games. I was crushed for a good two weeks. But Early Wynn's wish became my mission: To have a Hall of Fame writing career. I feel I've done that. My bio of you would be the capper. You want a bigger cut? Name it. It's not about the money.

Lake's story surprises me. Underneath those thick layers of ego and arrogance, exists a human being. I can even admit that Lake and I have something in common. That as boys we both decided we would do something special in baseball. And that we were both inspired by a Hall of Fame pitcher. But it stops there. We are nothing alike. For him sports writing is a means to power. For me pitching is a means to enter the company of baseball legends. Not for the glory but to push myself to unimaginable feats. That was my unspoken madness. It was also the fuel that fired the engine of my career.

Nice story, Lake. The bit with your mother is a nice touch. But you're wasting your time.

You really don't know who you're fucking around with.

I don't fuck around. I deliver. Quincy, pull over! I'm getting off!

Quincy looks in the rear-view mirror. Lake nods. Quincy hits the brakes. I get out, naively thinking that this is the end of it. I take the gag off the team. Lake leaves Sherry alone. But this is not the end of it. Lake has other ideas. And I completely missed his tell.

Pleasant evening for a stroll.

A male voice behind me breaks my Chicago reverie. I'm back in L.A., pushing my way along the sidewalk. The voice continues.

Unfortunately, the smoke from the fires does mar the view.

The speaker sounds familiar.

Mind showing yourself? I ask.

I was at the game when you pitched a 2-hitter in San Francisco. My father, may he rest in peace, took me to that game for my birthday. He was a big fan of yours. We're sitting behind the backstop so close to home plate that I can hear the crack of the ball hitting the catcher's mitt. You struck out fourteen and their only hits were a bunt and a cheap roller down the third base line. I wanted to get your autograph after the game, but my father was in a hurry to beat the traffic.

You want my autograph? I ask.

No.

What do you want?

That's a hard question. You mean right now? Or in my life?

He still hasn't shown himself. I push my Wheels faster. His footsteps keep up.

You really should have stayed in New York, he says, huffing for breath. You really should. You were safe in New York. The City of Angels is not a safe place for people in wheelchairs. This is strictly a car-culture town.

I hold my hands on the rear wheels to slow down and stop. But my chair rolls faster, now pushed by the stranger.

You like sushi? There's a fabulous sushi joint on Wilshire Boulevard. Koko-Oh. Ten-minute drive, can't miss it.

Let go of my wheelchair!

Koko-Oh! Remember that name! Just don't order the raw tuna on Sundays.

He picks up the pace. The sidewalk is still deserted.

Hey, Breeze, the Dodgers are in town. I could get you box seats. I love L.A. I lived here for seven years until I got into a little trouble with the LAPD. A total misunderstanding.

Are you going to kill me? I ask, wondering if I have time to get to my cell phone in the wheelchair's side pocket. Probably not.

Kill you?

Are you?

What are you talking about? I'm your friend. We have a lot in common.

How is that?

We both came to L.A. We both wish we hadn't. Our trip was

initiated by the same source – and keep your fucking hands on the arms of the chair.

Please, I have a daughter! I feel ashamed bringing up Salem. But I don't want to die. Not yet... Not now. Not here.

Yes, you have a daughter. Many men have daughters. Many men have sons. I have a son. About your daughter's age. He's a moron, but I still love him. Some men have both a daughter and a son. Some men have several daughters and sons. Yet, they will all die eventually. Does it matter to me that you have a daughter? Unfortunately, it does matter.

You wouldn't harm her, would you?

Harm your daughter? Do you think I'm a monster? Harm a beautiful girl with a bright future? She's like a blue star. Do you know what makes blue stars special?

I don't answer, knowing that he truly is a monster and that he would harm Salem.

Blue stars are the hottest stars in the universe. That's why I say your daughter is a blue star. A burning, blue star... Pity, she was on the plane with you.

If I shout for help, who would hear me?

Almost there, Breeze! he says as if to assure me.

Up ahead the chain-link fence has been cut, exposing a wide opening. I see his plan. My heart sinks, stomach turns, sphincter tightens. Still not one pedestrian in sight. Who walks in this fucking city? The stranger pushes me through the gap and down the embankment. Over the Pacific horizon a blazing sunset explodes in flaming oranges and reds. The freeway lies fifty feet below. I could try pushing myself off the chair. Then what? Lying helplessly on the ground he would still kill me.

DID LAKE SEND YOU? I shout.

Silence. Or do I hear a chuckle?

The ground is rocky with small white stones. What are they? Quartz? I see the palm trees sway in the breeze. Another hit and run. They'll say some poor fool in a wheelchair rolled into the freeway. What will Salem think of me? No matter.

Will she be safe? After my death the value of my paintings should go up. Good for Salem. But who will take care of her? There's an aunt on my mother's side who lives in Minneapolis... NO, YOU FUCKING IDIOT! Salem won't be safe!

Last thoughts and make them quick. I have a ton of regrets, but the only one I can think of is throwing a changeup instead of a fastball to Cal Ripken in an All-Star Game. I had already thrown a changeup for a called strike two. I figure he's expecting the heater. I shake off the sign for a fastball. The catcher, Pudge Rodríguez, jogs over to me.

Breeze, why the fuck you shaking me off?

He's expecting the fastball. I want to go with the changeup again.

You got away with a pissy changeup. Today the fastball's your best pitch. Trust me.

I'm going with the change. Outside and low. He'll either freeze up or wave at air.

Throw your fucking heater tight and inside.

I'm throwing the change.

Pudge glares at me, shakes his head, then slowly walks back behind the plate, cursing in Spanish. I can't believe that he still calls for the fastball. I shake him off. Ripken hits my change a country mile going the other way for a 2-run homer that wins the game.

The freeway looms twenty feet away. Hell. They'll call it suicide or an accident. Please not suicide. My assassin sprints the final push. I wait. Ten feet... five feet... NOW! I press hard on the hand breaks. The action of the sudden stop causes the killer's head and torso to snap forward across the back of my chair. I grab his head and twist hard. He shrieks. Then, super-charged with adrenalin and using all the strength in my arms and shoulders, I throw the scumbag over my shoulder. The wheel-chair tips over. I tumble to the ground as I watch his body roll down the last few feet of the incline and into the traffic. I see two cars then a truck run over his body before I turn my head away.

TIRES SCREECH! I hear several cars crash into other cars. I did catch a glimpse of the color of his suit. Shark gray. The man on the plane. Henry Watt... Henry Watt, hired killer. Henry Watt, no longer available for business.

NOT THIS TIME! I scream. Henry Watt, whose body is now a crushed sack of blood and shit. Henry Watt, whose moronic son is now fatherless. How will his son process the news of his father's grisly death? Did he really believe that his father was a consultant? The boy may wonder why Dad killed himself or why he would try crossing a busy freeway on foot. Perhaps he'll want to investigate his father's background and learn that his dad's consulting was of the unsavory sort.

Now, how do I get up the embankment? I hear multiple sirens from emergency vehicles: ambulances, police cars, fire trucks. Traffic must be backed up for miles. I fold up the wheelchair. Clutching it in one hand, I drag it along as I crawl up the grassy incline. I'm a caterpillar inching up a tree, dragging a leaf with only half its legs working. It's slow going. I turn my head and see flashing red lights as horns blare. I need to escape before they find me. The scene must look like an accident or suicide – not a homicide. Can't get caught... Can't get caught! Must not get brought in for questioning. More sirens. Men shouting. C'mon, Breeze! Keep going! Show me what you've got! I got nothing. Arms feel dead. But if I don't make the top in two minutes, the cops' flashlights will spot me.

POLICE! STOP! STAND UP! SHOW US YOUR HANDS! BOTH HANDS! STAND UP! FUCKING NOW! TURN AROUND! STAND UP OR WE'LL FIRE! STOP! When I fail to stand up and show both hands, a rain of bullets rakes across my back and head. The first officer to shoot is a shaky rookie, who empties all fifteen rounds in his clip.

Breeze! Hurry up! Right now! I'm not waiting another second! Are you listening to me?

I raise my head and see Sherry standing at the top of the embankment in heels, a short purple skirt, and a silky silver blouse — just the way she looked for the Joseph Jefferson Awards given every year in Chicago. Sherry was nominated for an acting award, and she was nervously excited. I was having trouble getting into a tux for the first time.

Come here and let me fix your tie!

I crawl toward her. She laughs at me.

Stop laughing!

But I'm laughing too. She holds out her hand to pull me up. I reach up to grab her hand. But it's just air.

I'm at the grassy top of the embankment. I unfold my trusty Wheels, set the brakes, pull myself up, settle in. Below, I see EMTs lift a sheet-wrapped body onto a stretcher and into an ambulance. Then I break down, weeping, no, sobbing, my entire body shaking. I don't know why except for the fact that I'm alive and that I just killed another human being. Despite his intent to murder me, he didn't hate me like Lake does. Henry Watt was a professional – though a bit too chatty. With tears running down my face, I head back to the hotel.

I'm outside the hotel, but I don't enter. I must make a call. I dial the number. I wait. Someone answers.

Hello?

It sounds like his voice but I don't speak.

Hello? Is someone there?

It is his voice, but a hollow version riddled with croaks and cracks. Like a worn-down LP. The booming baritone is gone.

Hello! He asks more sharply.

Now I answer.

I'm still fucking here, Lake! Surprised? I'm surprised.

Who is this?

It's not Henry.

What?

That's right. Watt. Henry Watt.

Henry?

Henry not here. Henry gone. Henry no more. Hope you

didn't pay him in full. Of course not, you cheap bastard. Too bad he didn't finish the job.

Who the fuck is this?

Who the fuck do you think it is?

I don't fucking know!

Remember Sherry?

Sherry? Sherry who?

Sherry's gone. But she stayed with the cripple. She told me that when I was in the hospital, you tried again to get her back. She laughed at you. Now it's just you and me, Lake.

Breeze? Is this Breezy Bye?

Strike one, Lake. Swing and miss. I'm throwing high heat. YOU HEAR ME? HIGH HEAT!

Where are you?

We're going to talk soon. Face to face. You and me.

I'm hanging up.

No, I'm hanging up, Lake. When you're ready to talk, call me.

I enter the hotel and go straight to the bar. I find a table in the corner. A barmaid immediately comes to my table. There are perks to being disabled. Faster service. I order a double scotch on the rocks and a large glass of water. When she puts the glasses on the table, I stare at the scotch. My hand reaches for it. My fingers wrap around the glass. I feel the cool condensation.

Five minutes pass. My hand is still around the glass when I feel someone's hand on my shoulder. I look up and see my daughter's face. She looks worried, which I find comforting.

Are you going to drink that? she asks.

No, I say.

Good. Why'd you order it?

To look at. To feel it.

Why?

During the aging process of scotch in charred oak barrels, the whiskey turns a translucent gold. Then they color it artificially with caramel to produce an amber hue. Such a lovely color. Reminds me of fire.

Where have you been?

I did a little sightseeing around the hotel. Didn't realize I'd been out so long. Got back a few minutes ago.

What happened to your clothes?

My clothes? For the first time I notice that my clothes are streaked with grass stains, one sleeve has a rip.

And your face. It's cut up. She presses a napkin against my cheek then shows me blood on it. My cheek must have rolled over a sharp stone. My war wounds, I think, feeling almost proud. Salem hands me a napkin. I dab it on my cheek.

I fell.

Fell?

Or tumbled.

Breeze!

No biggie. I fell or tumbled out of my chair going down a hill.

What hill?

I took a detour. There was a hill.

You look like you were dragged across three football fields.

Are you hungry? Shall I order some bar food? Calamari or onion rings?

No thanks. I'm going to bed. Just let me know the next time you decide to take a tour.

Salem's gone. I need to have a talk with her. Topic: What to do in case I die in L.A. I don't want to die. Especially not in L.A. But there is that possibility. Perhaps even that probability. My odds, I guess, are 50-50. Maybe less. As a pitcher I never liked being the favorite. I perform best as the underdog. In my first World Series I pitched the seventh game with three days of rest after going ten innings in the previous game. We lost in the eleventh inning. In that seventh game, I pitched against Turk Cannon, the American League's best pitcher, who would win his second Cy Young. He had four days of rest after pitching only six innings in a lopsided 9-2 win for his team. According to all the wise baseball pundits, the odds were against me. I beat Turk 3-2. We each went the distance.

I order a coke. It arrives and the tempting scotch is taken away. I down the coke and rehearse my *If I Die in L.A.* conversation with Salem.

First thing, call Heidi. You have her number. Second thing, say nothing to the police without a lawyer. Here's the number to my attorney in New York: Leo Meyerwitz. An honest man, rare for a lawyer. Third thing, cremate me. No burial, no funeral, no memorial. No coffin. If they have a cardboard box, take it. Fourth thing, spread my ashes with your mother's ashes anywhere you want. ASAP. Don't keep me inside a handsome vase in the house for years. Get rid of my ashes. I'll give you three months. Fifth thing, forgive me for being a shitty father. Sixth thing, believe me when I say that I love you very much. Seventh thing, have a great life. Do whatever makes you happy. Love whoever you want. Eighth thing, go to college. Ninth thing, sell the house so you can afford to go to college without taking out a loan.

I know there are four or five more things, but I can't think of any. I really hope I don't die. Not in L.A. Please not in L.A. Definitely not in Santa Monica.

TWELVE

The following afternoon I'm occupying a shady spot on the pool patio, reading the *Los Angeles Times*, when a huge Polish dude enters the patio. Floyd Klebecky. Like I said, he's a very large man. Now he's larger. He put on another thirty pounds but still looks rock hard. He wears tea-green linen pants, a Hawaiian shirt with a tropical fruit pattern – pineapples, passion fruit, coconuts – round metal Ray Ban sunglasses, loafers, shaved head, grayish goatee. He's quite a sight and a sight for sore eyes.

Then I notice his left index finger. The tip of the finger, just where the fingernail would begin, is missing. His pitching hand. The one that once threw the filthiest sinker in the league. His sinker was a thing of beauty. A batter would flail weakly at air as the ball sank to their ankles or the dirt. I know how and why he lost part of his finger.

Kleb has a lot of admirable strengths. But he had one notable weakness. He loved to gamble. Never on a baseball game, but just about everything else: basketball, both college and NBA; football, both college and NFL; hockey; golf; horses; dogs. He'd bet on cockroaches if they had races. He also liked playing high-stakes poker. He was a good gambler and generally won more often than he lost. But one year he hits a wall as big as the one in China. I mean it is a massive losing streak. But Kleb doesn't stop. He gambles more. It gets so bad that his first wife leaves him. From credible sources I hear that he's in trouble with some unsavory, high-rolling gamblers. He owes them in the tens of thousands. They give Kleb a deadline. He ignores it. Late one night, after leaving a poker game, a gang of six jump him. They need all six thugs to take Kleb down. When they do, they cut off the tip of his left index finger. They warn him that if he doesn't pay up in two weeks, they'll take the rest of the finger and his thumb.

When I hear what happened, I give him a loan to pay off his debt. But without the tip of his index finger, he can't throw his famed sinker ball. He makes adjustments, tries other pitches, but it becomes clear that Kleb is through. I was surprised hearing that he was accepted into the LAPD Academy. He must have had enough finger left to fire a handgun.

When Kleb approaches me first thing he says, Please, don't stand up.

I only stand for pretty, young women, I deadpan.

We both laugh. Then he bends down and crushes me in a hug.

You look good, Kleb. Like you could pitch a couple of innings in relief.

How would you know? You never let me relieve you.

That's because I wanted to win the game.

Fuck you.

He sits in the sun lounger next to me. He even removes his loafers. I notice he wears no socks. His face relaxes, but his eyes sweep across the pool area, taking in every person, entrance, and exit. He was the same as a player. He watched every player on the field. He observed the opposing manager and pitching coach in the dugout. He took note of the body language of the opposing pitcher. He would have been a great manager. Had he not left the game the way he did, he might have gone down that road. But I never asked him, and he never volunteered that information.

It feels strange and familiar talking to an ex-teammate. Something I haven't done since the accident. I tell Kleb everything: Quincy's call, why I came to L.A., Henry. Kleb's reaction, for him, is almost extravagant. He sits up, takes off his sunglasses, and looks at me.

Okay, Lake tries to kill you by sending a hired assassin. Hired assassin finds you and tried to kill you. Instead, you kill hired assassin. And you've been in L.A. for twenty-four hours. Damn impressive, Breeze.

Thank you, Kleb.

So, what do you want?

I want to confront Lake. I want to see that bastard confess to my face.

When's the last time you've seen Lake?

Twenty-five years ago. What happened to him?

Don't you know?

I shake my head. I don't tell him that I made a point of shutting out anything to do with Lake. After Sherry left him and moved in with me, Lake became my harshest critic. If I had a subpar game or a tough loss, he'd say on his show that my fastball lost its zip, and that I was washed up. He called me a selfish, gutless player, who only thought about himself, never a team player. His digs were vicious and personal. I ignored his taunts, but sometimes it was hard.

A small beach ball bounces over to Kleb. He picks it up with one hand. Two young boys in the pool jump up and down, waving their skinny arms for the ball. Instead of a soft toss, Kleb throws one of his bullet-like sinkers. When the ball splashes in front of the boys, a torrent of water slams into their faces. One of the boys starts crying. Kleb nods with satisfaction then turns his attention back to me.

I remember his show on ESPN, he says. I enjoyed his

commentary and interviews. Then Lake changed. Kleb goes silent as if deep in thought or just typically being Kleb.

Changed how? I ask.

His comments were always blunt. But they became more shaded with sexist and racist allusions and stereotypes. Like his criticism of Black managers, Black players, and Black sports announcers were more negative than their white counterparts. People noticed. There was a backlash. Advertisers pulled out. His TV show was cancelled. Then his radio show. And *Sports Illustrated* fired him. You'd think that's the last of Lake Lemon.

Kleb again goes silent. He hates saying more than three sentences at a time. Must drive his clients crazy.

Was it? I ask.

A right-wing cable station hired him for their primetime slot. His language got coarser, more sexist and racist. His political views became more outrageous. Yet, he becomes more popular than ever. Then came the MeToo movement.

What happened? I ask after another Kleb shutdown.

What do you think?

I can guess, but you tell me.

A bunch of women went public. Accused Lake of sexual harassment. One woman said she was sixteen when Lake touched her inappropriately. That was the last straw.

Kleb searches in his breast pocket for a cigarette. A sign he's tired of talking.

You can't smoke in the pool area.

We're outside.

I don't make the rules.

Fuck.

Take me through Lake to the present.

Kleb glares at me.

Do the short version, I tell him.

About five years ago, Lake kinda disappeared from the scene. His career was shot, but he was still rich. Bought a villa on the beach. Became reclusive. Married two or three times to young actresses. After a few years they bail. In his last interview he said he was working on a big book.

What kind of big book?

Who fucking cares?

I want to know.

Let me think... Kleb searches for a cigarette again until I clear my throat. He curses, closes his eyes, opens them.

Now I remember. His autobiography.

Autobiography. Are you sure?

Pretty sure.

He ever publish it?

Far as I know Lake hasn't published a word for five years.

I couldn't help but start laughing.

What's so funny?

Nothing.

Listen, says Kleb, turning serious. When you go to see Lake, I'm coming with you.

That won't work. I'm pretty sure he'll only see me if I'm alone.

He tried to kill you twice. He'll try again.

Maybe.

It's too dangerous.

It was dangerous when Lake used a third party. But what if it's only me and him, face to face? I'm betting it's a different story.

Now you're a betting man? Kleb folds his massive arms.

Sorry. Bad choice of words, I say.

If I still gambled I wouldn't touch those odds.

We silently watch a buxom teenager in a maroon bikini play with her little brother in the pool. After a couple of minutes, Kleb puts his loafers on and stands up.

I'll be in touch, he says in that deep rumbly voice.

What's your retainer?

Zero.

What does that mean?

I'm doing this pro bono.

That's not necessary.

I know.

I can pay.

I know.

So, why not let me pay?

No.

I want to pay.

No. And don't fucking ask me again.

We look at each other for a long moment in the same way we did in the dugout. Brothers of the mound.

Thank you, I say.

Kleb is silent but still looks at me. I wait for him to say something or leave. He does neither. Just stands there looking at me. Fucking Kleb hasn't changed.

I saw Scrappy, he finally says.

Scrappy?

Yeah.

Scrappy Leach?

What other Scrappy is there?

When?

Recently. Like last week.

Where?

West L.A. He's in a veteran's nursing home.

I recall that Scrappy was a Marine during the Korean War. He never talked about it. I once heard from the pitching coach, also a vet, that he'd fought in some big battles: Chosin Reservoir, Bloody Ridge. That's where he got his nickname. He was a tough little guy, who wasn't afraid to fight anyone, any time, any place.

How is he doing?

For an old dude, okay. Like, he doesn't drool or wear diapers.

How do you know about the diapers?

He showed me.

Kleb pauses then says, He gets around in a wheelchair.

I'm glad he gets around.

Kleb nods.

What did you two talk about?

Baseball. What else? He follows the Dodgers. Still loves the Cubs. Still hates the Cards.

We're silent for another minute. We watch the girl climb out of the pool. It's like we're in an old French film: two middle-aged guys at a pool completely mesmerized by the ripe beauty of a teenaged girl in a maroon bikini climbing out of the water. Another way that Time taunts us.

He asked about you, says Kleb.

Scrap asked about me?

Couple of times. I told him you would be in L.A. He said he'd like to see you.

Why does he want to see me?

He wants to ask you a question.

Ask me what?

He wouldn't say. But it seemed important to him.

My time here is rather tight, I say.

Kleb nods.

I'll drive you there, he says.

You don't have to—

Tomorrow okay? Or do you have a date?

I'll need a van.

Got a van. We use it for surveillance.

Aren't you busy with other clients?

I got time. Tomorrow. That work for you?

It's clear that Kleb is not going to let me avoid this. Scrappy loved Kleb because he was tough. And Kleb loved Scrappy because he protected his players. Scrappy got tossed out of more games for arguing with umpires than any skipper in the game. If there was a fight on the field he was the first to jump in.

Yeah... Tomorrow's fine.

Visiting hours begin at 10:00 AM. I'll pick you up at 10:30.

Then he saunters off. I start to take out my pad and charcoal to sketch the girl in the maroon bikini, but she's gone, too.

Next day, Kleb picks me up promptly at 10:30 in a gray van. Printed on the side of the van is the logo KZ'S INTERIORS & DESIGN. I smile. KZ'S Pub was a favorite bar of Kleb's in Chicago's Southside.

The VA nursing home is a complex of several buildings with a campus. The oldest buildings have a charming Spanish missionary look. Kleb says he'll wait outside. When I enter the nursing home, I see some old folks in wheelchairs. They stare at this wheelchair-bound youngster. I go to the reception desk to find Scrappy. The receptionist is a pleasant-looking Asian-American woman.

Good morning! How may I help you?

I'm looking for Scrappy Leach.

Scrappy?

Right, I think. He'd be under his real name here. What the hell is it? The receptionist pleasantly waits while I search my memory.

Herman. Herman Leach, I say, smiling at a name so unsuitable for the Scrappy I knew.

Ah, Herman! Such a funny man. He would probably be in the recreational room now. Down that hall and to your left.

I enter a large room. There's a 50-inch flat screen on one end running what looks like CNN. The volume is very loud. In the room are various round and square metal tables with patients playing cards, checkers, chess, backgammon; board games like Scrabble and Monopoly; and there's a threesome working a jigsaw puzzle. Half the patients are in wheelchairs. The wheelchairs look new and are top brands. I know my wheelchairs.

I spot Scrappy. He's wearing a worn-looking Cubs baseball cap. Could it be the same cap he wore twenty-five years ago? Still the same black eyepatch. He sits alone and gazes out the large picture window with a view of the well-kept grounds with palm trees, garden, fountain, benches. There are a few patients in the garden with visitors. On a small table next to Scrappy is a bowl of sunflower seeds. While gazing ahead he reaches into the bowl, grabs a handful, pops a seed into his mouth, chews, spits out the shell, and eats the kernel. There's debris of chewed shells on the floor. To be cleaned up later by an attendant, I suppose. I remember during my playing days how Scrappy would go through a big bag of sunflower seeds during a game. I wheel over, swivel next to him, and gaze out the window. He pays me no mind.

I can go nine, I say.

What are you talking about? he asks then spits out a shell.

I'm good for nine.

Nobody goes nine anymore, he responds, still gazing out the window.

I do.

Bullshit.

Leave me in.

I got two fresh arms warming up. You're coming out.

Tell 'em to sit their asses down. I'm going nine.

Who's the fucking manager?

You.

That's right!

Do you recognize me? I ask.

He turns his head and stares at me.

Why wouldn't I recognize you, Breezy?

Hello, Scrappy.

What took you so long?

I got married, raised a daughter, became an artist, I say.

Scrappy stares at my wheelchair and shakes his head.

Better put that wheelchair back. They're only for patients. It's not something to goof around in.

This wheelchair is mine.

I'm serious, Breeze.

So am I.

Knock it off!

I can't walk anymore.

Can't walk?

I was in an accident. That's the truth.

What accident?

I was hit by a car.

He stares at me a long time, blinks several times, nods.

Oh, yeah... Now I remember. Sorry, Breeze.

It's all right.

Don't you hate being in a wheelchair?

I'm used to it.

Bullshit!

I don't mind.

I don't mind, he repeats in a harsh whiny voice. I remember, not fondly, how he could ladle dripping sarcasm in the clubhouse, mostly aimed at rookies, but no one was spared.

What do you do now? he asks.

Like I said, Scrappy, I'm an artist. A painter.

A painter?

I paint pictures.

Pictures of what?

Pitchers.

I heard you.

Good.

Pictures of what, goddamn it!

Baseball pitchers.

You were a baseball pitcher.

I know.

The best... the very best.

Is there anything I can get you?

Yeah, get me out of this nuthouse.

Wish I could.

The best. Nobody ain't even close. I saw Gibson, Ryan, Koufax, Drysdale, Carlton. You were the best.

Kleb said you had a question for me.

A question?

You told Kleb you wanted to ask me something.

Scrappy blinks his eyes again, pops another sunflower seed in his mouth, spits out the shell, then gazes out the window. A drop of mucus hangs from the tip of his bulbous nose. He seems unaware. I wait for the drop to fall but it just hangs on. Scrap was a good manager. We were in five World Series and won three. He eventually got elected into the Hall of Fame. While few players liked him, everyone respected his deep knowledge, tenacious spirit, and love of the game. He wanted to win at almost any cost.

Scrappy silently eats his sunflower seeds. We sit staring out the picture window for a few minutes. I wonder what the hell I'm doing here and figure it's time to tell him goodbye.

Why didn't you hit the motherfucker? he abruptly asks.

Hit who?

The motherfucker!

What mother–

You disobeyed an order.

What order?

To hit the motherfucker! You fucking deaf?

I heard you.

Yeah, you heard me. Bullshit!

He angrily pops another sunflower seed in his mouth, chews, and spits out the shell. Now I remember the motherfucker Scrappy refers to.

The incident occurred in my fifth year with the Cubs. In early July, we're playing the Cardinals in St. Louis. We're neck and neck for first place. They won the first game; we took the second. In the rubber match we're ahead 3-2, and I'm on the mound. In the top of the fourth inning our cleanup hitter, Kyle Drayman, gets drilled by a fastball on his elbow by the pitcher, Dickie Munger. Clearly payback for hitting a 3-run homer off him in the first inning. Kyle drops to the ground, rolls on his stomach, holding his elbow, no doubt in agonizing pain. The trainer and Scrappy help him to his feet and take him into the clubhouse. Later, X-rays show that his elbow is only badly bruised.

Scrappy returns to the dugout and sits next to me, which is a big no-no when I'm pitching. It's been made clear for years that nobody sits next to me or talks to me when I pitch. But there's the sonofabitch sitting so close I can smell the sunflower seeds on his breath.

Hit Gardens, he says.

I don't respond. I don't look at him. I'm thinking this pudgy little old man better leave me the fuck alone. But he doesn't leave.

Gardens comes up first this inning. Throw two balls then drill the motherfucker.

Ty Gardens is the Cards' cleanup hitter. An All-Star first baseman and all-around classy guy. Last year he won the Roberto Clemente Award for his community work to help the under-served youth of St. Louis.

I'm not hitting Gardens, I say, still not looking at him.

What?

I'm not hitting Gardens.

Yes, you will.

Nope.

You protect your teammates. That's your job. Munger purposely hit Kyle. You retaliate.

I might knock him down. But I won't hit him.

I want to see your best fastball drill him. You can choose where.

Not going to happen, Scrap.

Better do it, he warns. Then he leaves. I look down the bench where my teammates are stealing glances in my direction. No doubt they heard our words. I wonder whose side they're on. Probably the skipper's. They want me to drill Gardens. Well, fuck them too!

Next inning I'm so upset that I walk Gardens on four pitches, all outside. Scrappy immediately runs out signaling for a relief pitcher even though no one is warming up and we're still ahead 3-2. The ritual is that when the manager comes out to the mound signaling for a new arm, the pitcher hands the ball to the manager, who pats his pitcher's butt as he makes his way to the dugout. But I don't budge. And I don't hand over the ball to Scrappy when he reaches for it.

Give me the ball.

No.

You've got three seconds to hand over the fucking ball.

And you've got two seconds to get off my fucking mound.

Scrappy swings at me. I block his punch and push him off the mound, maybe harder than I intended. He falls back on his ass. I mean, I'm not going to hit this 60-something-old-man, as much as I want to. He gets right up, takes another swing that I block, and I push him off again. This time even harder. Again, he falls on his ass. Now he's livid, red-faced, screaming curses. Before he can take another swing, Tiny runs up to the mound and grabs him around the waist. Meanwhile, the umpires try to restore order. The opposing team looks flummoxed. I'm still furious but allow three players from my infield to escort me off the field. Ironically, it's Kleb who gets the call to relieve me, one of the very few times he ever did.

Why didn't you hit the motherfucker? Scrappy asks again.

You mean Gardens?

Of course I mean Gardens! Who else are we talking about?

Because you told me to.

What kind of fucking answer is that?

Nobody tells me what to do on the mound, even the manager. If I hit a batter, I'll decide when and where.

Get out of here! Get out you snotnosed bastard!

You want me to leave because of something that happened almost thirty years ago?

Whataya talking about? It was only two or three years ago.

Scrap, look at me. I'm fifty-three years old, I say.

He looks at me, but I can tell he only sees that young, brash pitcher who embarrassed him in front of his team and 30,000 fans.

Get the fuck out! GET THE FUCK OUT BEFORE I KILL YOU! He waves his arms, tears in his eyes. He starts coughing, practically gagging. I see a nurse come running in our direction.

After nine years of playing for Scrappy, helping him take the team to five World Series, winning three, this is what he most acutely remembers. All reduced to one hard, bitter nut of resentment inside a thick shell of rage and rancor.

When I roll outside I see Kleb waiting by his van having a smoke.

How'd it go? he asks.

Let's get out of here.

Riding in the van, staring out the window as we pass palm trees and ugly strip malls, I ask myself: Why didn't I hit Gardens? If I had hit him the ump would've automatically ejected me for intentional retaliation. It was in the fifth inning, meaning that I wouldn't qualify to get the win. Plus, with a runner on base and dangerous hitters coming up, we could lose the game. Most important, and the real deal breaker, was the clumsy way Scrappy handled it. He didn't ask me what I thought. He *told* me to hit Gardens. He *ordered* a veteran and the most valuable pitcher on the team. That displayed disrespect. He made a mistake. Yet, he never apologized to me. And I never apologized to him.

As we leave West L.A., I see a billboard with an ad for the Dodgers. There is a giant image of a handsome, middle-aged man's face. As if coming out of his mouth are the words: DON'T WAIT! GET TICKETS FOR THE NEXT DODGER HOME STAND TODAY! The face belongs to Teddy Peacemaker, the Dodgers' color commentator on TV.

Do you know Teddy Peacemaker? I ask Kleb.

Teddy? Sure, I know him.

How well?

I know just about every ex-ballplayer in L.A. As clients,

ballplayers and ex-ballplayers are my bread and butter. They love the fact that a P.I. played in the Bigs.

Okay. But *how* well do you know Peacemaker?

I occasionally run into him at baseball functions in L.A. and elsewhere. We both play golf and are members of the same country club. So, we see each other on the links. Of course, I pitched against him. Man, he was tough. Fucking impossible to strike out.

I'd like to talk to him, I say as casually as I can.

Okay.

Can you call him for me?

Not a problem.

Good.

What do you want me to say?

Tell him... I'm in town and to give me a call.

That's it?

Yeah.

We don't say anything for a while, but I feel Kleb glancing at me.

Didn't he hit you pretty well? he asks.

Yeah... pretty well.

Teddy Peacemaker played shortstop for the L.A. Dodgers. We faced each other during most of my career. He's a full Creek from Oklahoma. Grew up on a reservation just south of Tulsa. His father, I'd heard, was a big deal chief in the Creek Nation. Teddy was the most graceful athlete I'd ever seen in or out of baseball. And you can throw in figure skating and gymnastics. He was also the fastest player in the Major Leagues. Almost every year he led the league in triples. I loved watching Teddy play baseball. Whether it was going deep in the hole to snag a hard-hit grounder, laying down a perfect bunt, stretching a single into a double, stealing third base. And for a shortstop he had pop. He averaged twenty-five homers a season. To top it off the man was damn good looking! Jet black hair, chiseled features, prominent nose, a chin you could hang your coat on. The whole package presented a proud bearing. You couldn't help but admire the guy. He played his entire career with the Dodgers. In his first year of eligibility, he was voted into the Hall of Fame.

Here's the thing. Teddy Peacemaker owned me like no other player. Whenever I faced him, it was like I was pitching against that other Teddy – as in Ted Williams. All told, he tattooed me for a .380 average and seven home runs, more homers off me than any other player. It seemed that every dinger he hit off me cost us the game. The costliest by far, the one that still hurts and haunts me, the one that I will take to my grave, came in the seventh game of the National League Championship Series when we played the Dodgers in L.A.

If we win this game, we go to our third consecutive World Series. We had won the previous two. To win three consecutive World Series is a rare achievement, and our team wanted it badly – no one more than me. I had won the first game and fourth game. Now I have the ball for the seventh deciding game, which is exactly where I want to be. We're leading 4-3 in the ninth inning. Teddy has already tagged me with a two-run double. There are two outs and a runner on first, due to a rare error by our steady third baseman. Of course, it's Teddy Peacemaker coming to bat. The count runs to three balls and two strikes. One of the balls should have been a called third strike but the umpire missed it. I'm not going to give in and walk him. He fouls off the next three pitches. I pound the outside corner, painting the dish. But Teddy reaches over and somehow flicks each one foul. Tiny signals for a fastball, high, tight, on the inside corner, like he's reading my mind. Best case scenario: Teddy either swings and misses or lets it go for a called strike three. Mid-case scenario: he fouls it off. Worst case scenario: I walk him. There is no way in hell he can hit it fair.

I go into my stretch and throw a four-seam fastball exactly where I want it. Here's the weird and uncanny part: Unbelievably, before the ball reaches the plate, Teddy leans back, tucks in his hands, and swings, pulling a high fly ball down the left field line. I wait for the ball to hook foul. And wait. Time slows down. I think of the next pitch I'll throw him, a slider on the outside corner. I'm watching the ball... The ball hooks. But will it hook enough? Yes... Yes!... NOOO!! The ball curls just inside the foul line two rows back.

I watch Teddy round the bases. He doesn't look at me once. Not even a glance. I watch his team mob him as he touches home plate. I watch them carry him off on their shoulders. A hero. An epic feat that will add to Dodger lore. When I finally go into the dugout, I sit down, bury my face in my hands, and cry. It is the only time I ever shed tears over a loss. All these years later I'm still trying to figure out how he did it.

At the age of thirty-five, Teddy announces his retirement, which stuns the entire baseball world. While he may have lost a step, his baseball skills have not declined an iota. In his last season he leads the league in hits, triples, runs, and wins his sixth Gold Glove Award. As soon as his playing career is over, he moves into the Dodgers' broadcasting booth to do color commentary. As a broadcaster, Teddy Peacemaker is just as smooth in the booth as he was on the field. It's enough to hate the guy.

The next afternoon I'm sitting in the hotel bar. Few people are there. Everyone's either at the beach or sightseeing. Salem's in the pool. At breakfast I tell her I'm meeting Teddy Peacemaker.

I thought you hate baseball, she says.

Still do, I reply, not wanting to get into a conversation.

You hire a detective who played on your team.

Yeah.

Yesterday you visit your old manager.

Yeah.

Today you're meeting an arch-rival you played against.

And your point?

You don't see a contradiction?

Should I?

She does her French shrug just to annoy me. She succeeds.

Stay around the pool or on hotel grounds. Don't go to the beach alone.

She kisses her fingers, waves them in the air, and off she goes. And yet I love her.

Teddy Peacemaker enters the bar area right on time. His hair is now long and tied in a ponytail. It's still jet black with some streaks of gray. He's still handsome and fit, still carries himself like a prince, and the clothes – tangerine tee-shirt, off-white chinos – look casual and stylish. He takes his sunglasses off as he enters and breaks into a big smile. He offers his hand. I take it. We shake firmly like old, opposing ex-combatants after a long war that ended in a truce.

Mr. Breezy Bye himself. This is indeed an honor.

Same here, Teddy.

He sits down at the table and crosses his legs. He's in no hurry.

I sure was surprised when Kleb told me that you wanted to see me.

Why surprised?

I mean... never expected you being in L.A.

I appreciate you giving me the time on short notice.

Are you kidding? I'd drop anything to meet with The Big Breeze.

How do you like broadcasting?

It's awesome. Keeps me in the game. I love the Dodger organization. They're the greatest. They've been like family to me my whole adult life. They just know how to take care of their people...

He goes on espousing Dodger Blue's deeply held commitment to its baseball people and the L.A. community. It almost sounds like the dogma of a religious order. I don't buy it for a second. I wait until he's done, half listening. I offer a half-smile.

Come on, Teddy.

What?

Tell me... what it's really like.

Teddy looks at me and grins.

Is it too early to order a drink?

Never too early for that.

We order drinks. Teddy orders a Bloody Mary. I order the same without vodka. We chat about the Dodgers' strong start, tied for first with the Giants. The cocktails arrive with a bowl of tortilla chips. We toast and drink. I never spoke to Teddy before except at All-Star games, and it was just banal baseball talk. Meanwhile, my question hangs in the air like a child's big red helium balloon. I didn't need to ask again.

To be honest, Teddy says, when I'm in the booth broadcasting, I feel lonely as hell.

Lonely?

Yeah.

Explain that.

I'd rather be playing than watching these overpaid, over-coddled, underachieving athletes.

You had a great career, Teddy. One of the greatest. You left the game on your terms. I respect that.

I still had a lot of quality baseball left. Had I played three more years I would have broken 3,000 hits. Maybe won another World Series. Sometimes, I wonder if I left the game too soon.

Better too soon than too late.

Teddy's face suddenly looks distraught.

Hey, Breeze, I'm sorry.

About what?

Spilling this puddle of self-pity when you... Christ... You left the game way too soon. Man, I'm such a fucking jerk!

It's okay.

It's not okay!

I don't know what to say. Neither does Teddy. So, we sip on our drinks and eat chips.

You're a painter now, right? Teddy asks, eager to change the subject.

Trying to be.

If you're half the painter you were as a pitcher, then I bet you're a great artist. You sure could paint the dish.

Thanks, I say and sip on my drink.

But Teddy doesn't pick up his glass. Instead, he looks at me in a different way. It's the look he gave when he came to the plate. He would look me in the eyes. The only player that did that. Most players avoid looking at the pitcher's face. All they're focused on is the baseball and the arm that flings it at them.

You're probably wondering why I wanted to see you, I say.

That did cross my mind. I mean it's not like we were buddies and hung out together.

I want to ask you a question. It's something that's been on my mind for a long time.

Okay.

Teddy's body glides into an alert position. It's so subtle and smooth you'd miss it if you weren't watching. He's both intrigued and guarded. Maybe he's having a flashback to when we faced each other in a game. That competitive fire never completely dies.

How were you able to hit me the way you did?

That's your question? That's what you wanted to ask me?

You were the toughest out I ever faced – by a mile. Nobody even close.

Teddy laughs. But my eyes stay right at him, waiting for his answer.

What are you talking about? My rookie year I couldn't buy a hit off you. I was 0 for 12 and struck out 8 times. Damn humiliating. I remember like it was yesterday.

But after that... you were a completely different hitter against me.

I got better, he shrugs.

No, Teddy. You didn't just get better. Something happened. I want to know. I need to know.

Hey, man, that was thirty years ago.

How the fuck did you hit that home run off me in the seventh game of the League Championship?

He laughs and drops his face into his open palm. I can't help smiling. I never disliked Teddy. I just disliked what he did to me at the plate.

Sweetest moment in my entire Major League career, he says. The modest pride in his voice still ticks me off.

We went on to win the World Series in a four-game sweep, he continues. My only ring. You have three. Three! I'd like to know how you did that.

He's trying to change the subject, but the toothpaste is out of the tube.

I saw what you did.

Did?

Yeah.

I got lucky.

You leaned back in the batter's box. Immediately after I released the ball – as if you knew ahead of time where the ball would cross.

You sure about that?

Come on, Teddy. If someone was tipping you the signs, I won't say anything.

No one was tipping me off. I swear it!

Then how did you do it? Not just in that game but all those years. Nobody ever hit me like you did. You *owned* me.

Teddy picks up his Bloody Mary, but Mary's all gone. He sets the glass down, looks for the barmaid, but she's also gone. Then he looks at me.

I dreamed it, he says.

Dreamed what?

How you would pitch to me.

I stare at Teddy and wait for him to say more.

It's not like it just sort of happened. You could say that I willed myself to dream it.

Why? I sputter.

You were the best pitcher in the Majors – the fucking universe! When the Dodgers called me up, you were already a superstar. I wanted to be a great hitter. But to prove myself I had to hit the greatest pitcher. It was my test. I had to beat The Big Breeze.

How did...

After my rookie season I went to my father and told him of my quest. He told me it was a stupid, childish quest. When I convinced him that my success would benefit the entire Creek Nation, he told me to talk to my grandfather, John Quiet Hawk, who still lived on the Rez. I did and stayed with him for three days. He told me what I had to do. It's a pretty intense ceremony. I can't share it with you, but I can say that it includes reciting a Creek prayer. The warriors did this just before going into battle against enemy tribes or paleface soldiers. They would dream how their enemy would attack them so that they would be prepared to defend themselves and defeat them. This is what I did the night before facing you.

I stare at him in disbelief and wonder if he'd put on war paint and danced around a fire, beating a drum, while chanting the prayer. But I don't ask that.

Teddy... I don't know what to say.

I've never told this to anyone before.

At that moment I think of Sherry and her half-Haitian blood. She too could foresee the future when she wanted to. One day she shared her darkest forecast.

I'm going to die before you, she tells me.

No, you're not, I quickly reply but am shaken nevertheless by her cursed prediction.

I'm sharing this not to upset you but to prepare you. I'm not sad. So, don't you be.

How will you die? When?

I don't know how. Before I turn fifty.

So soon?

She says nothing.

What can I do?

Take care of Salem. Love her... love her.

Hey, Breeze, says Teddy, while Sherry's *Love her* still echoes in my mind.

I'd really appreciate...

I will never repeat a word of this, I say. You have my promise. Thanks for telling me.

Now I have a question for you. It's something that's bothered me for quite a while.

What's that?

Do you think I cheated?

Cheated?

By dreaming how you would pitch to me.

Even knowing the location and kind of pitch I'd throw, you still had to get good wood on the ball.

True, but...

The greatest relief pitcher in the history of the game, Mariano Rivera, basically had only one pitch: the cutter. Every batter knew what was coming. But they still couldn't hit him. So, no, I don't think you cheated.

Thanks, Breeze.

We look at each other, I feel, with comradely affection. We are no longer old foes. Instead, we're something approaching friends.

Teddy looks at his watch.

Shoot. I need to head to the stadium. Big series. Dodgers and Giants.

Before you go, I have something I want to give you.

Teddy's eyebrows rise. I reach into a pouch on the side of my wheelchair and pull out a 5 x 7 pencil and ink drawing. The paper is backed on cardboard and covered in cellophane. I hand it to Teddy, who pulls back the cellophane covering the image. It's a sketch I made of him during our playing days. It shows him in the air as he completes a double play. It almost looks like he's taking flight, his arm is cocked back like a wing to throw out the runner at first. The drawing is one I've always liked. Teddy stares at it and shakes his head.

Wow. Breeze, this is... awesome! I don't know what to say, except thank you!

It's titled *Flight*.

THIRTEEN

Man, this is crazy, unreal, totally nuts! Tiny, I'm asking to myself – but softly so the ump can't hear me – have you died and gone to heaven? Nah, this is better than heaven... way better.

Sixth inning, two outs. Seventeen strikeouts in a row. Seventeen fucking strikeouts! Here comes right fielder Chase Toney, the Cardinals' cleanup hitter. That dude is even more bulked up than last year when he hit fifty-one homers. Everybody knows he's on steroids, but nobody talks about it. He always struck out a lot but hit a ton of homers. He still strikes out a lot but now hits more homers and they go farther. Breeze will crowd him with inside heat. Yep. I can settle back and watch the fun. Here comes the heater tight and inside. Chase swings, but he's too tied up to do anything. Second pitch shatters Chase's bat at the handle. As he goes to get another piece of lumber, I think how steroids almost shattered my friendship with Breeze. It was my own fucking fault, too. I had hit the age of thirty. My body was starting to break down from years of getting battered behind the plate. So, a DR brother on another team tells me about steroids. Says he takes it and it's a wonder drug. Like how it heals the aches and pains of playing and makes you feel stronger. That stuff is magic! he says. Every player he knows is doing it. Even the superstars. He gives me a sample. He calls it anabolic androgenic steroids. I try it, and, yeah, the stuff works!

What is that? Breeze asks as he enters our hotel room.

We're in Pittsburgh playing the Pirates for a three-game series. I didn't think Breeze would be back so soon from his run.

Nothing, I say, trying to hide it without looking like I'm hiding it.

Nothing?

Yeah.

Then why are you trying to cover it up?

I'm not—

What is that shit?

Nothing, Breeze.

Say nothing one more time, I'll kick you out the window.

Steroids.

Tiny, are you a fucking idiot?

Don't call me an idiot.

You are an idiot if you use that shit.

Everybody uses it.

I don't.

Maybe you should.

Why would I do that? he asks.

Well... You could be better, I say, getting myself into deeper shit.

Better? So, I'm not good enough?

No, man! I'm not saying that.

I'm asking for a new roomie.

What?

I'm not rooming with a junkie.

Junkie? What the fuck! Who you calling a junkie?

You start taking that shit, you're no better than a junkie. You'll want more and want it more often until you start looking like the other freaks I see on the field. Heads like bowling balls, bodies like NFL linemen. They no longer look like baseball players. You want to take it. Go ahead. Be like Superman. I won't stop you. But I won't room with you.

Nah! Don't say that, Breeze!

When we get back to Chicago, I'm asking the front office for another roommate.

I start weeping like a baby. But Breeze walks out. He doesn't speak to me for the rest of the road trip.

When we get back to Chicago, I tell him I won't use it. Isn't worth losing his respect for me. He gives me a hug. A big hug. I'm so happy that I cry on his shoulder.

Chase is back with a new bat. I signal for a curve on the outside corner. Did Breeze just smile? It's a sumptuous sweeping pitch that starts at eye level until it sharply bends into the pocket of my mitt knee high. McQuaid punches the air as he calls steee-RIKE!

FOURTEEN

TIRES SCREECH!

NO HEADLIGHTS!

My body rolls under the car – but the car is gone!
ENGINE ROARS! ENGINE RINGS! Rings?

My ringing cell pulls me out of the dream. It's been years since I've had that nightmare. In one dream, when I jump my body keeps rising like a helium balloon. As I float above the scene, I watch the SUV ram my car again and again. I float all the way to my apartment where Sherry waits for me. In other versions, I see different drivers at the SUV's wheel – people who I have hurt and betrayed in my life, which is almost everyone I ever befriended. I pick up the cell. 4:10 AM. Heidi. I've been ignoring her calls up to now but decide I better take it.

Good morning, Heidi.

I left Larry.

Three words I've been dreading to hear for months.

Did you hear me? I left–

Where are you?

Home, of course.

If you left Larry...

Actually, Larry left after I told him I was leaving.

Where? I ask.

I don't know, she says.

Did you tell him about us?

Not yet.

Good.

I did tell him I was in love with someone else.

You didn't.

Oh, yeah, I did.

How did he take it.

Let's say not well. First, he starts crying. Then some objects got broken, including his favorite chair.

I try to envision Larry breaking the chair. Recliner? Wingback?

Are you alright? I ask.

I'm unharmed if that's what you're asking.

Yes, and I'm glad.

I do plan to tell him about us, says Heidi.

Considering what he did to the chair, you think that's a good idea?

I hate lying. I'm an open person.

You never told him about your sex work.

That's not lying. I just didn't tell him.

Just like you didn't tell him about sleeping with me.

Larry will find out soon enough. He's a very good detective.

Really? Just so you know, I'm not on his list of suspects.

How do you know?

He told me he trusts me.

Ha-ha!

That wasn't meant to be funny.

That's what makes it funny.

When I get back we'll sort this out.

When will you be home?

Soon.

How soon?

When I finish my business. It's delicate.

Hmm.

How's Brittany doing?

You're changing the subject, Breeze.

Am I?

I told her about us.

What!

She's for it a hundred percent. I think she has a tiny crush on you. So sweet. I made her promise not to tell Larry. She kept asking me when we'll all live together. Isn't that adorable?

It takes me a few moments to take all this in.

Hello? Breeze? Are you there?

I'll call you back later today. I miss you.

Last night I heard that caravans of released Mexican prisoners are headed for L.A. Most are drug lords and murderers. Please be careful.

Heidi, there are no caravans of Mexican prisoners.

But they showed video clips of–

Stop watching Fox News! It will poison your mind.

Do you love me?

Heidi...

Do you? 'Cause if you don't love me then all we were doing was fucking. And if it was just fucking, it doesn't matter if I tell Larry.

I love you! I tell her for the first time. I love you! I tell her again.

I love you, too. With all my heart.

Good night. I hang up.

Did I just say, I love you? Is it true? And will I be able to get back to sleep?

I wake up at dawn. In six hours I'll see another Dawn... Dawn Gold. The one before Sherry. To call Dawn merely a dancer is like calling a Monarch butterfly an insect. Soaring and spinning in the air like a weightless bird is what I remember about her. That was back in Chicago. Dawn now lives in Burbank. I call a limo company that provides accessible wheelchair SUVs. Then I talk to Salem. As expected, she peppers me with questions.

Burbank? What's in Burbank? she asks.

Someone I know, I reply.

Who's that?

An old friend.

Another ex-baseball player?

No.

Does your friend have a name?

Dawn Gold.

I never heard you mention *Dawn Gold* before.

I knew her before your mother.

Ohh. An old lover.

Just a *friend*.

Who was your lover.

Stop, Salem.

No. Was it like serious?

No comment.

Was she beautiful? she asks.

I pause.

Yes.

An actress like Mom?

A dancer.

Same thing.

Quite different.

Did you break her heart?

Stop.

No. Did you break her heart, Breeze?

I don't know.

You broke her heart.

I've got to go.

Why are you seeing her?

Just to say hi.

Going all the way to Burbank–

Not that far.

I think you're going to fuck her.

Don't say... Salem, I promised to visit her if I ever came to L.A.

Can I come?

No.

Why not?

Because this is personal.

Then you *are* going to fuck her.

You can say fuck fifty more times, but you're not coming with me. Will you be okay here while I'm gone?

Expecting any trouble, sheriff? Shall I round up a posse if you don't come back by sundown? She says this while tucking her thumbs in her pockets. Not cute.

Stay in the hotel or hang out by the pool. Don't go anywhere else.

Breeze, this is Santa Monica. It's not like we're in the middle of Islamabad.

Islamabad? Salem reads *The New Times* when I'm done with it. She likes to stay abreast. Smart kid.

The limo company sends me a Chrysler Pacifica minivan. Not top of the line, but it will do. The driver is a young Hispanic man, short and wiry, clean shaven, closely cropped, bristly black hair. He wears a navy-blue sports coat with the company logo, crisp white shirt, blue tie. There is a blue baseball cap on top of the dashboard, which I learn he doesn't wear. Surprisingly, he isn't wearing sunglasses. He takes my folded wheelchair and sets it in the back. Besides *Good morning, sir* and *My name is Javier* said in a heavy Spanish accent, he doesn't say a word to me. As we get on the freeway, I ask Javier where he's from. There is a long pause.

El Salvador, he finally says. Nothing more.

I decide not to ask him any more questions. And I don't.

Half an hour later, the Pacifica pulls up to a single-family ranch house. No grass in the front yard. Instead, there are plants, trees, cacti, some artsy-shaped rocks. I nod with approval. She wants to conserve water. I see white stucco walls, Spanish tile roof. Lots of windows. Thankfully, no steps to the front door. The entrance, in fact, looks inviting. When I called Dawn, she told me that she'll be home. I tell Javier that he can either wait here or come back in an hour. He says he'll go have lunch and come back. I roll up the driveway toward the front door. The door opens. A woman steps out and waits for me, a big smile on her face. Dawn. I know she's twenty-five years older, but it's as if time had stood still. In my eyes she hasn't aged. Her body's lovely angles are still there, not as sharp but rounded off.

We sit in the sun room, all screens, glass, and white walls, sipping on hibiscus-ginger ice tea. A lean black and white cat watches us from another chair. The cat is named Isadora, after the dancer Isadora Duncan. Set on a coffee table are a bowl of grapes and a plate of homemade oatmeal cookies, still warm. When we were together, Dawn never baked and barely cooked.

She settles down in a rocking chair. We haven't yet talked except for the banal pleasantries of arrival chatter. *How are you? Fine. Lovely home. Thank you. This way to the sun room.* There is original artwork on the walls, mostly watercolors. On the shelves are vases and tchotchkes that look Native American. I should start a real conversation but am tongue-tied.

You're here, she says, almost with a sigh.

Yes.

Really here.

Yes.

I can't believe it.

I can.

Here in my sun room.

In the flesh... more or less.

We both laugh at our silliness. She covers her face like a 5-year-old. Then her laughter dissolves into tears. She cries just the way she cried the last time I saw her. I say nothing as I hold the tall sweaty glass of tea in my two hands. What did you expect? I ask myself. Did you think this would be easy? A few laughs while catching up? No. I did not. Isadora jumps on Dawn's lap and curls up. This has a calming effect as Dawn rubs the back of Isadora's head.

You know... she begins, falters, wipes her eyes with a tissue. I set my glass down.

When you left me, Breeze, I thought I would die.

Now it begins. Warm-up pitches are over. The game has begun. There will be no winner in the game. Only losers. Yes, the game must be played. The pitcher must pitch. The batters must swing. No home runs. Only errors, walks, singles, attempted steals. At best a tie game due to exhaustion.

What else could I do? I answer.

Stayed with me.

That was impossible. You know that.

I didn't know it then. I don't know it now.

It wasn't your fault.

Why do men who leave women always tell them *It wasn't your fault*?

I loved you.

Love? Don't talk to me of love. You told me you'd love me *forever*. No one could have loved you more or better than me. That is what I do know for sure... Did she love you well?

Dawn, please.

Did she love you better than me?

I can't...

Can't what? It's a simple question.

She loved me, and I loved her. To the very end. I can't compare.

But you did compare, Breeze. You compared two women who loved you. You chose one over the other. That comprises the act of comparison. You found one superior, one inferior; one pleasing, one unpleasant; one precious, one dull. You chose one, rejected the other.

I shake my head. We are silent for a few minutes. Or is it only thirty seconds? I try again.

Tell me about your life. I'm interested, I say, glancing at her wedding finger – no ring.

Not married, she says with a half-amused smile.

Ever been?

Twice. First guy was sweet and gentle – until he wasn't. Then he was mean and violent. Why do guys wait until you marry them before they show their true colors? Second guy cheated on me until he stopped trying to hide it.

Sorry to hear.

I like being single. The thing that bothers me the most is all that fucking time I wasted trying to make bad marriages work.

Any children?

A son from the gentle-mean guy. Anthony. He lives in West Hollywood, determined to succeed as a filmmaker. He's made a few short films that hit the film festival circuit. The first one is about a young ballet dancer. I did the choreography for that. My son is not brilliant and never will be. But he works hard, has some talent, and he loves what he does.

You still dance?

I teach ballet and modern dance to children and teens.

Here?

I rent a studio close by.

You like teaching?

I love it. Especially watching the little girls gaining confidence. Seeing what their young bodies can do. Defying space, time, and pain. The first time they successfully do a demi-plié. Moving to the rhythm of music until they're inside the chords. I have a piano in my studio so I can play as I call out the movements.

Your life sounds... good. Are you–

Happy? No.

I was going to say content.

Oh. Maybe. I've never thought about it.

I'm out of questions. We are being careful. She folds her long limber legs underneath her. How well I remember those legs. During sex they would wrap around my torso. When she climaxed, they almost squeezed the breath out of me. I remember waking up in the morning, seeing her legs tangled in the sheets, her arms stretched out, as if she's caught in a jeté. Once she danced nude for me while I sat up in her bed. She played a recording of Schubert's *Death and the Maiden*. For the next twenty minutes she performed a dance that was part ballet, part modern, part ecstatic. Leaps, spins, splits, falling and rolling on the floor, all made up on the spot. When the music ended she collapsed, so exhausted I had to pick her up and carry her to bed. It thrilled and frightened me. I told her to never do that again.

Do you still dance?

You already asked me that.

Yeah, I did. But you didn't answer.

No.

Why not? I ask.

Dawn strokes Isadora. The cat purrs.

A few years after you left me... I was in a car accident.

Jesus, what happened?

Totally my fault. It was late at night. I fell asleep at the wheel. Luckily, I hit a street light and not a vehicle. But the injuries ended my dancing career.

I'm sorry.

A few months before my car accident is when I married. Big mistake. I knew it was a mistake, yet, I still married him. I stopped asking myself why I would do something I knew was stupid and self-destructive. Sometimes life doesn't provide any answers. You were right for me. I knew it the moment I saw you at that reception. I'm not angry anymore. I'm glad I met you. Am I talking too much?

No, Dawn. Not at all. But I do have to go.

You just got here. Can't you stay longer?

No, I...

I'll make us dinner. I'm a good cook now. Can you believe it? There's a guest room. We could really catch up.

I have to go back.

Stay. Please! she pleads.

My daughter's at the hotel.

What's one night?

I can't...

Yes, you can... if you want to. You owe me one night, Breeze.

I owe you more than one night. But I still can't stay.

Then Dawn does something that totally surprises me. She moves Isadora from her lap, stands, steps toward me, kneels, and lays her head on my lap. I rest my hand on her head. This is her way of saying goodbye, I think. Sweet. Then I hear the sound of a zipper.

No, Dawn... Don't, I whisper, her head still on my lap, her hand now inside my pants.

This is not a good idea, okay? Just let go, please.

I feel her slip my cock out of my underpants. Oh, God. I try to speak again, but the words fill my mouth like water. I push her back gently, but she holds on. I push harder. She holds on. I push her roughly. This time she falls back with a thud. Isadora hisses and scampers out the room. I wheel toward the front door as Dawn screams.

I FEEL LIKE A WHORE!

I don't turn back. Just as I reach the door, an object flies past my head and crashes against the wall. Outside, I'm relieved to see Javier and the SUV waiting for me at the curb. As I roll down the driveway, I hear Dawn shrieking incoherently inside.

FOOL, FOOL, FOOL, FOOL! an accusing voice howls in my head. This is not how I wanted us to part. What did I want? Forgiveness? Friendship? Love? Redemption? I reach the minivan, stand, climb inside while Javier folds my chair and throws it in the back.

DRIVE! I yell.

Javier jumps in the driver's seat and hits the gas. We take off.

I close my eyes. Dawn's last words burn in my brain like hot lava blistering through moist moss.

We have been on the road for about ten minutes. Javier wordlessly drives, occasionally changing lanes. If he has any thoughts about his paraplegic passenger's desperate escape from a raging woman, he's keeping them to himself. I'm still thinking of Dawn, still feeling miserable. Should I call her when I get back to the hotel? Should I call her later? Should I never contact her again? I'm in one of those black moments, when you wish you were anybody else but yourself. I stare dismally out the window. Another busy L.A. freeway that means nothing to me. I look ahead and notice Javier repeatedly glancing at the rear-view mirror with a frown.

Anything wrong, Javier? I ask.

He doesn't answer. I turn around and see a dark green, 4-door Jeep Wrangler with a tinted windshield tailgating us. I look back at Javier, who is now glaring at the rear-view and muttering in Spanish. He changes lanes. So does the green Jeep. He changes lanes again. So does the Jeep, still hugging our rear like a mutt in heat sniffing a bitch's butt. Javier speeds up to 75. So does the Jeep. He speeds up again, hitting 80. So does the Jeep. Asshole.

The next moment I feel a hard jolt. The Jeep rammed us! Our vehicle swerves into the other lane. Car horns blare until Javier straightens us out. What's the driver's problem? The Jeep rams us again, even harder. Shit, this is no accident! Another hard ram! Fuck! The Jeep is using its hardened steel front fender like a battering ram.

GET OFF THIS ROAD! I shout, though I don't know why I'm shouting. Javier nods.

Fortunately, there's an exit up ahead. Javier takes it, tires squealing. As does the Jeep. Then Javier makes a sharp right turn on another road. Ditto Jeep.

Bastardo! Javier grunts and takes an even sharper left turn on another road, just missing an oncoming pickup. The Jeep stays glued. My eyes stay glued on the Jeep.

I've seen plenty of car chases in movies. While thrilling to watch I never believed they were real. Closeups of an actor's sweaty face at the wheel but driven by a trained stuntman. This is real, baby. No actors, no stuntmen here. Despite the tinted windshield I see two men in the Jeep.

I can see Javier's dark brown eyes in the rear-view mirror. That they show no fear brings me some comfort. I imagine the brutal violence and daily hardships he may have experienced and escaped from in El Salvador: gangs, drug cartels, corrupt cops, poverty, disease. Welcome to the peaceful security of the USA.

Our two-lane country road is twisty, hilly, with narrow lanes. Road signs read SPEED LIMIT 35. Javier does 60, taking the turns at 50. The Wrangler is not far behind. I am faintly hoping that Javier can lose them when I hear a CRACK! Then another CRACK! I turn around and see two jagged holes in the rear window. Jesus Christ, the Jeep is firing real bullets at us! I duck my head down.

WHO ARE THOSE FUCKHEADS! Javier shouts. His first words of real anger since the chase began. His question in the context feels fitting and fully justified.

I DON'T KNOW! I shout back.

But I do know. I know very well who those fuckheads are. But there is no time to explain this to Javier, who I've grown to admire in the last few minutes. His exceptional driving skills and steady nerves have so far kept us alive. Perhaps dodging bullets is something he is familiar with in his home country. We still must lose the Wrangler. And if we can't lose the Wrangler, then we must stop the Wrangler. But how?

I peek over the back of the seat to spot the Jeep when my eyes lock on my wheelchair, neatly folded in the back. Where I live – low mountainous countryside – one sees many Jeeps. Most are for show for people with money to spend who want to look rugged and cool. The one flaw in Jeeps is that they can easily flip

– a shortish wheel base and too much weight at the top. I gaze at my beloved, faithful Wheels. I hate the idea, but I have no choice.

Can you open the trunk from up there? I ask Javier.

Yeah!

Then do it!

Why?

Just do it! NOW! AHORA!

Javier touches something on the dashboard. The trunk door rises open. Using my hands and arms, I pull myself up and I climb over the back of my seat as a bullet whistles by. I hear it crack through the windshield. I crawl on my stomach next to my wheelchair and push it to the edge of the open door. The road momentarily straightens. Javier speeds up, the Jeep is forty feet behind.

JAVIER, SLOW DOWN! I yell, my voice getting ragged.

SLOW DOWN?

SÍ! A LITTLE! UN POCO!

He eases up on the accelerator. I wait for the Wrangler to move closer. I pick up the chair, take aim, wait, then pitch it. The wheelchair sails, dives, and drops beneath the Jeep's left front tire. At such high speed, the effect of the folded titanium metal getting pulled under hyper-spinning rubber lifts the entire left side of the Jeep. I watch with wonder as the vehicle flips like a charging rhino slammed by a seizure. The Jeep rolls off the side of the road and continues rolling as it crashes down a shallow canyon.

STOP THE CAR! I yell, my voice sounding harsh and frayed. Javier slams the brakes. I crawl back over to my seat to see Javier grinning at me. His first smile.

That was cool, man! He raises his palm to high five me.

I ignore his palm and say, Get my wheelchair!

Javier's grin vanishes.

What?

My wheelchair!

No way!

I'll tip you fifty dollars extra.

You're crazy! LOCO!

One hundred!

Javier curses in Spanish and English. But he jumps out, runs down the road, picks up my mangled Wheels on the side of the road and dashes back. He tosses it in the back, closes the trunk, gets in, and hits the gas. In five minutes we're back on the freeway to Santa Monica. That is when I ask him.

Did you look at the Jeep?

He shakes his head. After several moments, he says, Un poco.

What did you see?

Blood. Two bodies. Not moving. Bad men.

Yeah. Bad men... very bad men, I say, thinking: Men just doing their job and the bodies are piling up.

As we head to the hotel I explain to Javier that there is a serial number on every wheelchair. When the police arrive on the scene, they would certainly trace that serial number... right to me.

No police! No! *Por favor!* pleads Javier, shaking his head.

No police, no police, I agree. I figure Javier doesn't have a green card and wants no part of our fabled criminal justice system.

At the hotel Javier gets a porter to bring me a wheelchair. When that is done, I pay Javier $100 in cash.

Muchas gracias, he says.

De nada, I reply.

We firmly shake hands. Then I look at the minivan. The back fender and tail lights are crushed. There are jagged holes in the rear and front windows.

I'm sorry about what happened, I say. I'll pay for any repairs.

Javier also looks at the minivan then looks at me.

No importante.

I raise my eyebrows.

My uncle owns the business.

We both let out a laugh. But there is one more thing I need to ask.

Javier. Are you married? Do you have children?

He smiles, takes out his cell phone, and shows me a photo. I see a pretty Hispanic woman and two young girls, a toddler on her lap and perhaps a 5-year-old at her side.

Muy bonita, I say.

Gracias. You?

One 14-year-old daughter. My wife is dead.

I'm sorry.

I shrug. We shake hands again.

Stay well... and safe, I say. He nods.

Then Javier gets in the Chrysler Pacifica and drives off. Later, I call Kleb and tell him what happened.

I know a place that sells wheelchairs, Kleb says.

Do you know a place that repairs wheelchairs?

Ten dead seconds slowly go by.

No, but I'll look into it.

Thanks. I'll pay whatever it takes.

Amazingly, Kleb does find such a shop. In two days I get my Wheels back, as good as new. Even better than new. I did not want to lose her.

After my call with Kleb, I make one more call. A female-sounding machine voice tells me to leave a message. I leave a message;

It's me, Lake. Now you've got two strikes. Another swing and miss. Miss again and you're out. You better see me before that happens.

I hang up, expecting that Lake will take another swing.

FIFTEEN

The morning after the death of Henry, I bought a copy of the *LA Times* in the hotel lobby. I hastily searched for any news of his death. Nothing. The following day I did the same. Zero. Perhaps, I think, Henry's death has been ruled an accident or suicide. Therefore, nothing of real interest to write about. Just another senseless death. I allow myself to feel a little relief. Paradoxically, I'm also disappointed. Shamelessly, I'm like the rookie I was after pitching a good game. So eager the next day to read about myself in the Chicago papers. That shallow vanity wore off by my sophomore year. But I had never *killed* a man before. This is a whole lot different from a well-pitched game – even a 2-hitter with twelve strikeouts and no walks. Henry was a bad man. Sure, he was a human being. But he tried to kill me and threatened my daughter. I'm glad he's dead.

On the third day I'm sitting at the pool, once again paging through the *LA Times*. Still no story. I should relax. But it makes me a little angry that this city doesn't give a shit that a man was struck dead by numerous vehicles on a major freeway.

I look for Salem. She's in the pool with a teenaged girl. Perhaps a year or two older than Salem, though physically smaller. Slender of frame, almost delicate. I've seen them hanging out together for the last two days. Sometimes they swim side by side. Sometimes they sit by the pool. The girl's mother, an attractive woman of about forty, lies on a lounge chair reading. She never goes in the water. No father around. Is he at a business meeting? Is there a father? Salem and the girl, still dripping wet, walk toward me.

Breeze! This is my new friend, Oriole Wong.

Oriole? Like the bird? I ask the new friend.

Yes, says Oriole. Like the bird. Oriole symbolizes simplicity, joy, and balance.

Very nice to meet you, Oriole.

She bows her head and says, I am honored to meet Salem's father. Her eyes widen, hand over her heart. Her voice almost sing-song.

Is your family on vacation? I ask.

Vacation for me and my mother. Business for my father. She wrinkles her nose when she says *business*.

Where is home for you?

Sometimes Singapore. Sometimes Beijing.

I'm glad Salem has found a friend to—

Come on, Oriole. Let's swim! Salem cuts in.

She takes Oriole by the hand and off they go. They dive off the edge and knife into the water. They stay under for almost half the length. I haven't seen Salem this happy since Sherry was alive. I had forgotten what she was like in that state. I take out my drawing pad and a pencil to do a quickie sketch of the girls. But after making a few lines of Oriole, I set my pad down. Could this be Salem's first love? First love, young love. Should I envy her or fear for her? If only Sherry was still alive. She would help Salem navigate through the rushing rapids of desire, fulfillment, and inevitable rejection.

Simplicity and joy, Oriole had said. But her eyes didn't look simple or joyful. Her eyes are her tell. They didn't narrow. Just the opposite. They widened when there was no reason to widen. I believed almost everything about her sincerity: her bow, her smile, her hand over her heart... but not her eyes. No need to widen the eyes... unless you're faking it. Should I warn Salem? But warn her of what? Stop her from what?

Betrayal, I say softly aloud.

What is betrayal? Spell it out.

Betrayal is an important and painful experience of life.

Go on.

Even if I could prevent it, should I? Would Salem even listen? It would sound like the gibberish of her old. white father.

What will you do?

Wait, let it happen, and be there when it ends.

Then what?

We go back to New York. Oriole Wong goes back to Singapore or Beijing.

And Salem?

She will suffer. She will heal. And she will love and be loved again by someone else. Who, most likely, will betray her or she him/her.

You sound like you know a lot about betrayal, right? ... Right?

Yes... yes.

My name is Caprice, she says.

Caprice? Like the car? I ask and try not to grin.

Yeah, like the car.

Now I grin. I wait for more. She tells me more.

My family has a thing for cars.

Oh?

My mother's name is Impala. My sister's name is Pontiac. My brother's name is Dodge.

I think you got the best name.

So do I.

Caprice is a tall, shapely redhead and has a laugh so big it could fill a crowded ballroom and turn every head. She's 32-years-old and a pure sex machine. I'm a 20-year-old sexual novice.

Her husband is Scottie Wiggs, a tall, rangy, side-winding left-hander, and our team's ace. A three-time twenty-game winner. Four years ago, he won the Cy Young Award. He's six-four and

230 pounds of fury and meanness on the mound. Enhancing this unnerving persona are long stringy hair, a ragged goatee, and a glowering stare. His stuff is nasty with lots of movement. Scottie is always among the league leaders in hitting batters, which he takes pride in. At the age of thirty-six, his fastball is not the weapon it used to be. But he recently added a very good cutter. And he's still wily smart and mean as ever. During spring training, Scottie never went out of his way to show me the ropes. Why should he? He was the ace, and I was an unproven rookie. After spring training I'm sent down to their Triple-A team. After I burn through the opposition for a month, the Cubs call me up. Now that I'm in the starting rotation and pitching well, Scottie talks to me. Like, Good fucking game tonight, rook. Or, Hey, rook, after the game me a few guys are going out for beers. Join us. The other guys are veteran pitchers. I join them. Scottie's not only the ace but the undisputed leader of the staff.

Caprice is my first real adult sexual relationship. She's all I think about. I don't know what she sees in me. I wouldn't call myself ugly, but I'm far from handsome. At twenty, I'm still on the skinny side. But I can pitch. Yeah, I can pitch. And Caprice loves the way I pitch.

I *adore* watching you pitch, baby, Caprice whispers into my ear as we float back down after our first climatic fuck.

Why is that? I ask.

Because it's beautiful! The most beautiful thing I've seen on a baseball diamond. Like a cobra about to strike.

The fact that I am having an affair with a teammate's wife makes it even more dangerous and exciting. We meet in motels. Always. Too risky to meet at her place or mine. Two hours of heavy sex. Sometimes three. Then we get in our cars and drive off. She makes the rules. I gratefully follow. If I'm not scheduled to pitch that night, she brings a bottle of booze and makes cocktails. I go to some games pretty wasted, praying that they won't need me for emergency relief.

As the season moves into August, Scottie begins to fade

while I get stronger. With two weeks to go, we clinch a playoff spot as a wildcard. Scottie isn't happy that the manager, Scrappy, hasn't yet tapped him to pitch the first game of the playoffs. The press speculates that I'll be chosen. From dugout gossip I hear that Scottie and Scrappy had words in his office. I warn myself to end the affair with Caprice, but that seems about as doable as trying to end sleeping or eating.

A week before the end of the season, Caprice and I decide to spend a whole day together. I call in sick on the morning of a night game that Scottie is scheduled to pitch. We check into our favorite motel. We like the king-sized mattress' firmness and view of a church cemetery. This will prove to be a mistake. We should have gone to a different motel, one we've never stayed in. We enter the room, lock the door, close the shades, drink our first cocktail, strip off our clothes, and dive into bed. By now I've learned a lot from Caprice and have come up with my own moves and variations. In the field of fucking, Caprice took me from primary school to graduate studies. In our buzzy intoxicated state, dizzying sexual pleasure, and with the shades drawn, we don't notice that it begins to rain. And that the rain continues unabated. Critically, we are also unaware that the umpires have canceled the game due to the rain.

Caprice and I lie back in bed. We sip on our fourth round of cocktails, preparing for another round of cock and tails, when we hear a tremendous CRACK! followed by the sickening sound of splintering cheap plywood that comprises the motel room's door. I don't ask who is at the door. I KNOW who's at the door. Caprice clasps both hands over her mouth to muffle her scream. This tells me she knows something I don't know, something scary.

OPEN THE DOOR, CAPRICE! OPEN THE FUCKING DOOR! Scottie shouts. But Caprice, still muffling her screams, appears incapable of opening the door.

YOU'RE DEAD! DEAD!!! YOU'RE BOTH FUCKING DEAD! roars Scottie.

The last image I see in the room is Scottie's bloody fist punching through the door. My last thought in the room is the hope that it isn't his pitching hand. Then like a cartoon character (think Wile E. Coyote), I leap out of bed, grab my shoes and clothes from the floor, and jump out the window. As a precaution we always ask for a room on the first floor. It's still a good 8-foot drop. I land awkwardly, feeling a needle of pain shoot up my ankle. But I don't think about that as I part run, part limp buck naked through the parking lot, cross the street, cars honking, and climb over a mesh fence into a church cemetery. Hidden by the moonless night I pass out between two graves, a departed couple named John (1875 – 1919) and Emily Fitzgerald (1881 – 1957). At dawn I awaken, dress, hobble to my car, and drive home.

All that day I ice my sprained ankle. Luckily, it doesn't look too bad, but I know that I'll miss at least one start. I miss two starts. Scottie isn't so lucky. It *was* his pitching hand that punched through the door. He tells the manager he got in a bar fight when a drunk insulted the team. A hairline fracture in his middle finger will sideline him for the rest of the season through the playoffs. Scottie is keenly curious of my injury. Like a prosecutor, he keeps asking me how I hurt it, as if testing the consistency of my story. Before a game he stops at my locker as I put on my uniform.

How did you hurt it? he asks.

Again?

Tell me.

I've told you ten times.

Guess I forgot.

I fell off a ladder, I say.

What kind of ladder?

Seriously?

What kind of ladder?

Stepladder.

Why were you on a ladder?

Stepladder.

Why were you on the stepladder?

Moving some clothes on the top shelf of my closet.

What kind of clothes?

Sweaters.

Sweaters... In the summer? Scottie persists, trying to trick me.

Making room for new summer clothes.

How'd you fall?

Badly.

No, how does one fall off a fucking stepladder? I'm trying to visualize it. I'm trying to erase another visual in my mind.

Sorry. Your asshole time is up. Now I'm going out to the field to do some stretching.

As I jog out of the clubhouse, I hear him yelling.

Who's an asshole? Who's an asshole! HEY! YOU CALLING ME AN ASSHOLE!

In the playoffs we're eliminated in the first round. During the off season, the team trades Scottie and his inflated salary to the Pittsburgh Pirates for two minor league prospects. Caprice and Scottie stay together for another year before she files for divorce. I don't hear from Caprice again except for a letter I receive during the winter postmarked from Pittsburgh. The entirety of the note reads as follows:

MISS YOU. NO REGRETS. I NEVER TOLD HIM. LOVE, CAPRICE.

When I now think of Scottie's question, I ask myself, who is the asshole? The answer is clearly me. I betrayed a teammate, someone who did me no harm. Because of my betrayal we were quickly eliminated in the playoffs breause our ace couldn't pitch. Because of my betrayal his marriage to Caprice fell apart. Maybe their marriage was already broken. Maybe not. Caprice didn't love me. She was bored, and I was a new sex toy she could play with. What's my excuse? I was young? Yeah, I was young, but my parents raised me to know the difference between right and wrong. I knew what I was doing was wrong. Very wrong. But I did it anyway. Why? I imagine the questions a psychiatrist would ask.

Sounds like a pattern, says the shrink.

A pattern?

I lie on a sofa. The shrink sits behind me.

Yes.

I don't understand.

You have an affair with Caprice, the wife of a teammate. Despite the risks and shaky morality of this action, you find it exciting. Then you have an affair with Sherry, the lover of a powerful man that can and will do you harm. This excites you like no other relationship. Now you are having an affair with Heidi, the wife of a neighbor and friend who is also a prominent officer of the law. Now do you see a pattern?

Could it just be coincidence?

Psychiatrists don't believe there is coincidence in human behavior.

Laurel and Hardy have arrived. That's who the two cops who've shown up at the hotel pool patio remind me of. The older cop is thin and balding in baggy slacks and a mismatched shabby sports jacket that hangs on him like a scarecrow's coat. The younger dick is stout, pink, and wears a well-cut suit that looks a half-size tight. Laurel and Hardy introduce themselves as Detective Stamp (Laurel) and Detective Muggins (Hardy). I'm in the pool patio watching Salem do cannonballs off the diving board when they enter.

Mr. Joseph Bye, we have a few questions, says Det. Stamp.

I'll try my best to answer them, I say, forcing a friendly smile.

May we sit down? asks Det. Muggins.

They pull up chairs and sit a few feet from my wheelchair.

This won't take long. Sorry to bother you, Mr. Bye, says Stamp.

So far they are polite, even deferential. It's to put me at ease. I'm not at ease. There are other people in the pool or relaxing around the patio area. Yet, the cops made a beeline to me. If I'm not a suspect, I'm under suspicion. The other guests look over at us, intrigued by the entrance of these suited men.

We're investigating a death, states Det. Muggins.

A death? Here at the hotel? I ask, looking alarmed.

No, no. But close by. Five nights ago, a man fell onto the freeway. His body was hit by several vehicles before the traffic stopped, says Stamp.

My God! The poor man! Will he recover? I widen my eyes for effect.

Doubtful. The man is quite dead, deadpans Muggins.

Dead? That's awful! How tragic! The detectives are silent and glance at each other. Am I laying it on too thick?

Was the poor man inebriated? You don't think it was a suicide, do you? I ask. Hoping they do.

We believe it's a homicide, answers Stamp.

Murder?

That's what homicide means, sir, Muggins evenly replies.

How do you know?

According to the coroner's report, the victim's neck was broken. Our theory is that the murderer broke his neck then threw him down into the freeway to make it look like an accident.

My gosh! If your grisly theory is correct, this killer must possess super-human strength. He must be a giant, a monster! I say with a slight tremble in my voice. I wonder if Sherry would approve of my performance.

Well... mumbles Stamp, we don't know—

Do you think he's staying in this hotel? Oh, Jesus! I have a daughter!

Nothing to be alarmed, sir, assures Muggins. We have an officer stationed nearby.

That's a relief. Is there anything else I can help you with, detectives? I don't want to keep you as there must be others you'll want to interview.

They don't leave. Instead, they pull their chairs closer to me and lean forward. Interview ends. Interrogation begins. Muggins takes out a surprisingly small notebook and a stubby pencil to take notes. I want to loan him one of my Faber-Castell sketching pencils.

We have some photos we'd like to show you, says Stamp.

Photos?

Of the victim, sir.

You mean *after* his death? Oh, please, I couldn't bear—

The victim's face is surprisingly intact, Muggins helpfully interjects.

From a leather pouch, Stamp takes out some 8 x 10 photos and hands them to me. The images are in grisly color and sharply detailed. The forensic photographer did a good job. The head is rather mashed up, but the face is discernible. I quickly glance through them.

Please, take your time, Stamp says almost angrily.

Sorry, I don't recognize him, poor soul.

I hand the photos back to Stamp, who snatches them out of my hand and shoves them in the pouch. He looks at Muggins.

Where were you five nights ago – that would be Tuesday, sir – between the hours of 7:00 and 9:00 PM? asks Muggins as gently as asking what I had for dinner.

I don't understand, I say, looking confused.

We just want to eliminate all parties.

Does that mean I'm a suspect?

The detectives chuckle, shake their heads, as if the very idea is preposterous.

Oh, no, Mr. Bye. You're not a suspect, says Muggins.

But I'm under suspicion.

Not exactly.

Because Laurel and Hardy aren't smart enough to play it real smart, they're playing it dumb. Hoping I'll slip up. So, I'm playing dumber, which hopefully is smarter.

Now I'm really confused, I sigh.

We have a witness, says Stamp in a flat tone.

A witness?

A driver, he adds.

A driver in a vehicle who was driving?

One of the drivers who stopped just short of the body. She says she saw someone in a wheelchair on the sidewalk across from the freeway, expounds Mullins.

What did this witness actually witness?

We just told you! snaps Stamp.

We believe that there could be a connection, Mullins gently clarifies.

Damn straight! adds Stamp.

Boy, if seeing someone in a wheelchair on a sidewalk can raise nefarious questions, then my life would surely be nothing but big trouble, I say almost with a chuckle.

Laurel and Hardy are silent. Mullins has stopped taking notes.

Surely, I'm not the only wheelchair-bound person in the area or even in the hotel.

There is one other wheelchair-bound individual staying in the hotel, says Mullins. She's seventy-nine years old.

Have you questioned her? The detectives look stonily at me, wondering if I'm joking or being stupid. I'm betting on the latter.

Not yet, Mr. Bye, but she's on our list, lies Muggins.

Can you tell us where you were Tuesday night between 7:00 and 9:00 PM? asks Stamp.

I was here.

You mean the hotel? Muggins suggests.

Yes.

Where in the hotel? Stamp presses.

My room.

Can anyone verify that? Stamp presses harder.

Verify? I ask, staying dumb.

Muggins intercedes again. Can anyone vouch for that?

I can.

We all turn to the verifier. It's my daughter, drying herself with a towel, looking like a walking mermaid. The cops gaze on this stunning teenager with the legs and shoulders of a *Sports Illustrated* swimsuit model.

And who are you? asks Stamp.

I'm his daughter.

The detectives look at each other. Muggins stands up to offer his chair. Salem ignores him and walks over to stand beside me.

Please state your full name and tell us when you were with your father that night, says Stamp. Muggins prepares to take more notes.

Salem Heather Bye. I was in his room at around... 7:15 PM. Then we went down to the hotel's restaurant bar at around 8:30 PM. I went back to my room at around 9:00 PM. Anything else?

What were you doing in your father's room for over an hour?

We were having a personal daughter-father conversation, which is none of your business.

We could make it our business, Stamp bluffs.

Daddy, do I really have to talk about missing my period with the police?

You're right, young lady, Muggins quickly intercedes. A personal conversation with your father is none of our business. We'll be moving on.

Pete, I have a few more questions, grouses Stamp. But Muggins shakes his head.

Thank you for your time, Mr. Bye, says Muggins then heads for the exit.

Stay in the area for the next seventy-two hours, are Stamp's parting words before following his partner.

I look at Salem, who meets my gaze.

Are you going to lecture me on telling falsehoods to the fuzz?

Fuzz? Has she been reading my Raymond Chandler books?

No, I say.

Good, she says.

Then Salem promptly climbs up the high springboard and

does a back dive with one revolution. Nice takeoff and flight but her entry in the water has too much splash.

SATCHEL IS one of our most popular paintings, says Taylor.

The next day, Salem and I are inside the Museum of Contemporary Art (MOCA) in downtown Los Angeles. I had not planned to come here, bringing my daughter. Call it an impulse. We're being guided by Taylor, a lively young female curator with an elegant gold nose ring.

The *Satchel* postcards literally fly off the rack in our museum shop, Taylor continues. I must admit that it's a favorite of mine. And I'm not saying that because I'm speaking directly to the artist. I love the way you used browns, blacks, and reds to roughen and intensify the fierce joy in the subject's face. And your handling of text in the painting is masterful. I think it's fantastic.

Thank you, Taylor.

I'll leave you and Salem here to view the other galleries. Let me know if there's anything else I can do. It's such an honor to have you visit MOCA.

The honor is all mine, I say. Taylor takes a quick glance around.

I feel silly asking, Mr. Bye, but can I get a selfie with you?

My daughter will be happy to take our photo.

That would be super.

Taylor hands Salem her cell phone. Salem takes our photo. Then Taylor waves and is gone.

I painted *Satchel* ten years ago. Talk about competitive fire and love of the game. During his prime through the 1930s and 1940s, Satchel Paige was one of the greatest pitchers of all time. Joe DiMaggio said Paige was the greatest pitcher he ever faced. Satchel had a wicked fastball, pinpoint control, a variety of windups, and he was a natural showman. It is reported that he would sometimes bring his outfielders in to sit behind the pitching mound then proceed to strike out the side. His prime years were spent pitching in the Negro leagues. In 1948, at the age of forty-two, the Cleveland Indians signed him to a contract. He not only helped break the racial barriers in Major League Baseball, but helped lead the Indians to a World Series championship.

I remember you working on this one, says Salem.

You do?

Yes.

You couldn't have been more than four or five years old.

I still remember it. Maybe it's the name. Satchel. It was different from your other paintings.

I didn't think you paid much attention to my work.

I did.

I never knew that.

Now you do, Salem says, not unkindly.

Besides the name, how else was it different?

You took a long time with it.

Did I?

Yeah, you did.

I guess so.

Longer than the others.

Hmm... That's probably true.

It was on your easel like forever.

A couple of years.

Seems longer.

Maybe it was.

Why'd it take so long? she asks.

I don't know. Trying to get it right. Make it work. Some pieces take longer. It's hard to explain.

I don't tell her that I almost gave up on *Satchel*. I was ready to paint over it or just toss the canvas in the trash. After a few months leaning against the wall, I put it back on the easel.

Seeing it in the barn with your other paintings, it stood out for me, says Salem. But seeing it here... It looks even better.

Same painting. Same paint on the same canvas. Just different context.

We gaze at it for a few minutes in silence. People come, look at it, then move on. A few of the older men linger. Salem turns to me with her serious look.

I don't know how you work. How you do this?

You mean my process?

Process... Yeah.

It's not very interesting. Putting paint to canvas.

Tell me something that's interesting, she says, almost as a challenge.

I think a moment. There is something. But should I tell her?

Sometimes... my paintings talk to me, I say. She looks at me to see if I'm joking. She turns her gaze back at the painting.

Did Satchel talk to you?

He wouldn't shut up.

What'd he talk about?

Everything.

Like what?

His life growing up in Jim Crow Mobile, Alabama. Pitching in the Negro League. Playing with and against some of the league's biggest star players: Josh Gibson, Cool Papa Bell, Buck Leonard, Smokey Joe Williams. He talked about the women he loved while on the road. He talked fondly of Bill Veeck, who signed him to play for the Cleveland Indians when he was past his prime, but still great.

Did that make him angry? To have it take that long?

The thing is, he wasn't bitter. Not a bit. He said God gave him the ability to pitch better than anyone else on Earth. Every day that he can go to the mound and pitch, he's grateful.

That's so inspiring! I need to read about him.

He also talked about Babe Ruth.

Wow. He pitched against Babe Ruth?

That was the problem. He never did. They came close a couple of times. Never happened. Both formed all-Star teams and barnstormed around the country. Babe's team played against Negro League players. Satchel's team played against white Major League players. But their teams never played against each other. I believe that was one of Satchel's biggest regrets. Satch kept telling me how he would have pitched to the Babe.

Can I tell you something? Salem asks.

Sure.

Don't be embarrassed.

Okay.

I'm proud of you.

Why?

Seeing your painting here. Watching people stop to look at it. It's the coolest thing.

Thanks. Now go walk around the other galleries and look at more paintings. I'm going to hang out here a bit longer.

Salem kisses me on the cheek and goes off. I try to remember the last time she kissed me on the cheek. I can't.

I didn't tell Salem that Satchel told me how to paint him. Too long and weird a story.

You making me old, man! Don't you make me old! Satchel bitches as I work on his face.

I'm painting you in your rookie year. Cleveland Indians, 1948. You went 6-1.

I don't give a fuck about that. Paint Satchel young and pretty.

When was that?

Jesus, do I gotta paint Satchel myself?

What team, what year?

Lemme think... Second year with the Pittsburgh Crawfords... 1933.

Why then?

I won 31 games, including 21 straight and 62 scoreless innings. You ever pitch a year like that?

No.

Damn straight. I'm a 27-year-old, 6-foot-3, 180-pound Black man.

Best looking, best lover, and best pitcher on the best baseball team in the whole fucking world.

I changed the painting. After some research I found an image of him in his Crawfords uniform. I made him younger, leaner. He had big, soulful brown eyes. Satchel still complained that I didn't make him pretty enough. Didn't like the color of the uniform. Wanted me to paint him in his windup, stuff like that. He didn't like the text I added, even though the quote is attributed to him. At the very top I painted in white over dark background: DON'T LOOK BACK. SOMETHING MIGHT BE GAINING ON YOU.

Satchel the man and *Satchel* the painting both mean a lot to me. One of the things that connects us is the brevity of our Major League careers. His was cut short by beginning at the age of forty-two due to a racist policy. Mine was cut short at the age of twenty-eight due to the jealous rage of a powerful man.

An attractive Black couple in their thirties enters the gallery with their son who may be about ten. They stop in front of *Satchel*. I hear the father explain who Satchel Paige was to his son. The boy nods. The mother stares intently at the painting. She doesn't care who Satchel was. She's studying *Satchel* as a painting. I appreciate that. Then she talks to her son about the composition of the shapes and handling of colors. I'm thinking she took some art classes in college. I'm thinking that being in this quiet space, watching visitors enjoy my painting, may be as close as I can get to pitching in a World Series game with 50,000 cheering fans.

After breakfast the next morning, I head for the pool as usual. As usual it's crowded. And, as usual, that will change as soon as the swimmers see Paraplegic Man. By the time I'm at the water's edge, crawling the last two feet, the pool is empty. I swim my twenty laps, get back in my chair, and wheel under a shady umbrella table. To my right I see a thin, dark-haired young man in baggy swim trunks. He's lying in a lounge chair intently typing on a laptop balanced on his thighs. Screenwriter? I get out my pad and begin to sketch him until I get sleepy. I rest my head back and close my eyes.

How long are you gonna sit around on your ass by the pool? rumbles a voice from above.

Those endearing words can be from no other than Floyd Klebecky, who awakens me out of my light slumber. I slip my sunglasses down my nose and look up. He stands like a giant sequoia, feet apart, brawny arms folded. Undermining this towering image is his attire: yellow Hawaiian shirt with toothy blue sharks swimming around. I try not to laugh.

I don't know, Kleb. I'm getting to like L.A.

Bullshit.

Sitting on our ass is what paraplegics do.

You know what I mean.

I will sit on my ass until I see Lake.

You don't need to see him. You possess the recorded confession of the hired hitman. He names Lake! Hand the recording over to the law. They can charge him with attempted murder. Stop with the O.K. Corral shit. You're not Wyatt Earp.

Maybe not. But you sure ain't Sam Spade, I joke.

Oh, yeah? Kleb snarls, not joking.

Say I turn in the recording. It will still be Lake's word against Slammer's. Who's the Law going to believe? Lake Lemon, the rich and famous sportswriter and celebrity? Or a dying, ex-con who has a grudge against his former employer?

Lake had motives! Jealousy, resentment, hatred, malice a mile long!

He'll call me. I know it.

How do you know, Breeze?

Because I know *him*.

He hasn't called yet.

He'll call.

Set a deadline. Tomorrow! If he doesn't call by tomorrow, we'll go to his house, or you get on a plane back home. Doing nothing is nothing.

Waiting isn't nothing. Waiting is the hardest thing you can do. Waiting can be the most productive thing. Think if Britain and Germany had waited before declaring war in 1914. That may have avoided WWI.

Don't give me any fucking history lessons!

It wasn't a lesson, Kleb! IT WAS A FUCKING ANALOGY!

FUCK YOUR ANALOGY UP YOUR ASS!

The poolside guests stare at us. Mothers with young children direct disgusted frowns in our direction. Kleb meets them with a bestial glare he used when pitching in relief. Everyone immediately looks away. Satisfied, Kleb walks away without looking back. He's pissed at me. Can't blame him. Knowing Kleb, he'll cool down in a few hours. I start sketching a little boy in the wading area, playing with a rubber seahorse. This morning I heard in the news that there's a new wild fire to the east of us, twenty miles away. Firefighters have it thirty percent contained. The sky is a smokey slate gray.

I miss my home. I miss my studio. I despise this hostile world. I fear that I'll never complete my paintings. And Salem will miss the division championship game. But if I don't finish this business now, I'll never finish it. I could wait for Lake to die. No. Then he wins. I won't let him win. We may both lose, but I won't let him win. Sometimes, on rare occasions, your life rises to the importance of playing in Game 7 of the World Series. Yes, I'm using another baseball analogy, but stay with me. The outcome will determine the rest of your life. There's only winning or losing. There are no tie games. There is only glory or disgrace.

If I go home without confronting Lake, I lose and he wins.

If I stay and Lake kills me, I lose and he wins.

If I stay and he confesses... then what? Do I kill him? If I kill him, I lose and Lake wins.

Is there a scenario in which Breeze wins? If there is I don't know it. Therefore, of all the outcomes, the one in which Breeze wins and Lake loses seems the least likely outcome and not to be considered.

I put my pad away and decide to swim another twenty laps. When the guests see dreaded Paraplegic Man approach, the pool empties – except for one swimmer doing laps, switching from breaststroke to backstroke. She's Black, late twenties, ivory-white one-piece suit. Stunning. Then I see Sherry! Spring training. We're standing in my hotel pool, water neck high, our hands running over each of our bodies. She's also wearing a white one-piece bathing suit, and I'm entranced by the stretched ivory-white fabric against her dark skin.

I like you feeling me up in the water, Sherry says.

Think people will mind if we make love in the pool? I ask.

Shall we ask them?

Nah, let's just do it.

You're crazy! she whispers as her hand slides inside my trunks.

I fall face first into the water and begin my laps. White Suit and I swim without signaling to each other. I do my twenty laps, which takes much longer in this larger pool. It's a good workout. My arms ache as I swim to the pool's edge. White Suit is still swimming effortlessly. Breaststroke one lap, backstroke next lap. Impressive form. I reach the pool's steps and prepare to pull myself out.

I can't do the butterfly to save my life, says a warm voice.

A few feet away White Suit, her arms folded over the pool's edge, smiles at me.

I wouldn't do the butterfly to save my life either.

But with your butterfly you could.

It's not that hard.

Can you show me?

Show you what?

Your butterfly.

Gladly. The hands are as important as the arms. You want to push as much water as possible. Some think making big splashes is good form. It's not. Just a lot of noisy, showy foam. Try it.

Okay, she says.

White Suit kicks off the pool wall and tries it. She does it surprisingly well. She's an accomplished swimmer. The guests on the patio watch us. The younger men look resentful that this beauty is paying attention to the middle-aged, disabled man. What a waste! While she does butterfly laps, I pull myself out. I easily get into my wheelchair – no need for a performance – and glide under an umbrella. From there I watch White Suit do a few more laps. I'm impressed by her endurance. Now that Paraplegic Man is out, the guests jump back in the pool, churning the water with jabbering adults and screaming kids. I close my eyes, drowsy from my swim.

Thanks!

I open my eyes and look to my left. White Suit plops herself in the lounge chair next me, happily toweling herself, humming a funky tune.

For what? I ask.

Showing me the butterfly.

You're a natural.

I'm also grateful that you got rid of the other people during my swim.

My pleasure.

I know you didn't do it for me, but it was such a delight to have almost the whole pool to myself. I really needed to unwind.

She rests her head back and slips on a flattering pair of white-framed, cat-eye shades. Very cool. I think this gesture signals the end of our conversation.

It was nice swimming with you, I say, and prepare to leave.

Full disclosure. I know who you are.

Yes?

Joseph Bye, aka The Big Breeze. Am I right?

Hundred percent. But just call me Joe.

I'm Kat-with-a-K Walker.

Hello Kat with a K, I reply, thinking this sounds intriguing.

My father batted against you.

Okay, this sounds more intriguing. A beautiful Black mermaid in a sexy white bathing suit is the daughter of a player I pitched against. How do I deserve this gift?

Who is your father? I ask.

Was. He passed a year ago.

I'm sorry.

He was a beautiful man and an amazing father. I was lucky... very lucky.

She turns her head away, looking what? Sad? Wistful? I gaze at her graceful profile, wishing I had pencil and paper in my hand.

You remember a Rainey Walker? she asks.

Rainey... Rainey Walker... What team?

Pittsburgh Pirates, mostly. He also played for a few other teams.

What position?

Outfield. He could also play catcher and first base in a pinch. Guess you'd call him a utility player. But the outfield is where he shined like a newly minted silver dollar. He ran like a deer and had an arm like a howitzer. He loved throwing runners out tagging up at third base or trying to stretch a double into a triple. His one regret is that he never got to play in a World Series. He passed on his speed to me. I still hold the Pennsylvania high school record for the girls 200-yard dash. Am I talking too much?

You're not and I'm interested.

Dad spoke about you.

Me?

He said when you were on, which was most of the time, you were unhittable. Do you remember him at all?

Vaguely... Rainey Walker... it will come to me.

He did brag about once hitting a bases-loaded triple against you to win the game. He was so proud of that. You'd think he'd won the World Series.

I don't respond because I'm thinking of Rainey's triple and

looking at Kat. For a microsecond her confident manner seems to flag. Then she palms her cheek almost comically.

God, I can't believe I'm talking to Breezy Bye!

I can't believe you recognized me. I'm at least twenty-five years older than my last baseball card.

Well, the wheelchair helps. But you haven't changed that much. Older, yeah. Grayer, sure. But a nice head of hair. And still a good-looking man, if you don't mind me saying.

I don't know whether to thank you or take your temperature. You may be running a fever.

You can thank me.

Thank you.

What brings you to Santa Monica?

Business. Not interesting enough to talk about. What about you?

Pilot season in Hollywood. Yeah, I'm an actor. My agent told me to get my ass to L.A. She got me a nice room here. Good chance they'll pick up the pilot, which would be AMAZING.

Good luck with that.

Thanks.

On impulse I ask, Want to meet for a swim tomorrow?

Damn. I'm checking out tomorrow morning.

Too bad. Guess I'll have to scare off the guests and swim alone.

Tonight I'm going for a swim in the ocean. Come join me.

I'd love to, but I'm strictly a pool guy.

Oh, come on. Please! Our last chance to swim together.

It's tempting, but I don't think so.

You're not afraid, are you?

Afraid? I ask, now watching her carefully.

Sorry, that was rude of me.

When?

Sunset. The sky is glorious. And the beach will be nearly empty.

Okay.

Really? You'll come? she asks, her eyes wide with excitement.

Where shall we meet? The lobby?

The boardwalk, next to the porpoise sculpture.

I'll be there.

Thank you, Breeze – I mean Joe. See you tonight!

With that she gets up, gives me a little wave, and walks off. She has quite a walk, too. Her hips and ass roll with each step. I keep my eyes on her the whole time, as do the other men around the pool, young and old. This feels like a dream. But if it's not a dream, then what is it? I want to stay in the dream. But the dream has already dissipated, and some hard waking questions arise.

Best-case scenario: Kat is a sweet young woman who is delighted to hang out with an older, once famous ballplayer, now nobody painter. Worst-case scenario: She is a hired killer out to lure said nobody painter to his death. She doesn't want to meet in the hotel lobby. Why? Because she doesn't want any witnesses? If worst-case scenario is true, how will she do it? Knife him? Drown him? I say she chooses drowning. They swim out a good distance. She pushes him underwater. He struggles. She's stronger than she looks. Just in case she throws a plastic bag over his head. Glub... glub... glub. How fitting or fateful. A Sherry look-alike mermaid drowns The Big Breeze. Have I been waiting for this moment all along?

I remember Rainey Walker. Like Kat said, he was fast. Had speed to burn. And I remember his triple. I remember all the triples because they didn't happen that often. Triples I could accept. Home runs I hated. They're awful. The batter swings, gets all of it, confirmed by the sweet CRACK! of bat solidly meeting ball. The batter takes a moment to admire the ball's flight, trots around the bases, grinning like a jackass. When the batter reaches the dugout, he's greeted by his fist-pumping team-mates. Meanwhile, the pitcher stands dumbly like a post, trying to remain expressionless. A triple is a different story. The batter must hit the ball hard, sending it over an outfielder's head or in the gap, then run as fast as he can. If the ball caroms crazily off the wall, that gives the batter a few more seconds. It's often a close play at third base, and a good slide can make the difference. Like I said, I don't mind triples. They're hard-earned, and I tip my cap to the batter. Plus, if the bases are empty it's not a run. I still have a chance to get cleanly out of the inning.

Back to Rainey's triple. I threw a horrible pitch. A breaking ball that, instead of breaking outside *off* the plate, broke outer-middle *over* the plate. Rainey went the other way. A right-handed batter, he hit it into the right-field corner where it took a funny bounce. Our right fielder had a great arm and threw a bullet to the third basemen. Rainey slid head first, his hand touching the bag just under the tag. Unlike Kat's version of her dad's triple, it didn't win the game. It tied the game. We scored the winning run in the bottom of the eleventh inning. They took me out in the ninth for a pinch hitter. It's a small error. I figure her father tweaked his story to make him more heroic. Or... he never told her the story. Or... her father wasn't Rainey Walker.

Other than that tiny glitch, I didn't see or hear her reveal the slightest *tell*. Her every word, gesture, and expression sounded and looked sincere and believable. Her performance was flawless. Not once did she pause too long mid-sentence. Never a stumble to find the right words, which came effortlessly. She smiled brightly or wanly in all the right places. Choked up endearingly when speaking of her late father. Wait! Is that it? Is *that* her tell? That she *shows* no tell? Is she that good? Nobody is that good. Even the greatest pitchers had a tell if you studied them long and hard enough. Sandy Koufax had huge hands. When he was going to throw one of his gorgeous, orbiting, unhittable curveballs, I'm told, opposing players could see the impression his hand made in his glove. Didn't matter. The pitch was still unhittable. What if Kat is who she says she is? That would vastly change my world view. Am I prepared for that? Is Fate giving me a second chance. Another swing at Sherry? Even if this woman is a second-rate Sherry.

I try calling Kleb to check up on this Kat Walker with a K. But a woman tells me he's out on a case. Can you leave a message? she asks. I tell her I'll call back.

My thoughts turn to the black ribbon in my double portrait. It's starting to haunt me. Should I have looked to see if a black ribbon hung over Kat? Perhaps the ribbon hangs over me. If it does, would that be a good or a bad sign? Tonight, I may find out.

SIXTEEN

Seventh inning, one out, and nineteen strikeouts! Nineteen batters. Nineteen strikeouts. Still perfect. Hey, Tiny, here's a question as I get into my crouch: If one of the Marvel Comics superheroes you read as a kid was on the mound – like Thor, Iron Man, or Captain America – could any of them pitch better than Breeze is pitching tonight? Better? No way they could pitch as good!

Here comes batter number 20. Center fielder Rocky Kepner. Three years ago, Rocky was MVP. Led the league in homers and RBIs. Everybody drooling over this young white player. Saying he's the next Mickey Mantle. Yeah, maybe Micky Rooney 'cause it didn't happen. This year Rocky's batting .220 with ten lousy homers. Half the time he strikes out. What happened? Nobody knows. One of those baseball mysteries, you know? Like a flash of lightening. It's blinding, but it don't last long. Coming to bat the dude looks lost.

Breeze won't waste time with him. Starts off with a low fastball that kisses the outside corner. Could go either way, but the ump's not siding with a .220 hitter. Strike one. I call for more heat. Inside. Rocky swings wildly, yet somehow makes contact, driving the ball down on his back ankle. He drops like a shot deer, rolling and writhing on the ground. The trainer and manager trot out. Trainer tends to Rocky's ankle. Manager stares down, spitting tobacco juice, some dribbling down his chin. I stand up and walk away, knowing it will take a few minutes before Rocky gets to his feet or hobbles into the clubhouse. I curse the delay and hope it doesn't fuck with Breeze's rhythm. I look at Breeze, who stares at the ball in his glove, locked in his zone. Fucking Breeze.

I gaze into the stands and think of Gamal. All day I try not to think about him. Gamal. Goddamn Gamal. This morning a mutual friend calls me to say that he died of AIDS two days ago. My first lover. Egyptian. Businessman. Educated and cultured. What people call polished. I met him in my rookie year at a gay bar in New York City's West Village. I'm scared shitless yet excited to finally enter a place with men like me. We're in town playing the Mets. It's after a day game. We win 5-3. I hit a double and drive in two runs. Maybe I feel a little cocky... until I walk in. The lighting is dim and the room is long and narrow. The men are a mix of young and middle-aged. Later, I learn that in the back, behind a curtain, there's a well-known cruising room.

I'm not in the bar five minutes when Gamal stands at my side. Wearing a tailored suit, he's a trim man with a trim mustache. Early fifties. Not a bit of gray in his dark curly hair. Later he tells me he dyes it.

My name is Gamal, he says. I'll take care of you.

Thanks, I say. It's all I can think of.

He takes me to a table in the corner, orders a bottle of red wine, and starts talking about himself. Like we've known each other for years. I almost start to cry. It's like I'm home for the first time. I feel safe among all these guys. Sure, some prance around like peacocks in their outrageous outfits. Some look dangerous in their black leather jockstraps and nipple rings. But basically, we're all ordinary men looking for companionship and wanting to be ourselves.

Gamal asks questions about me. He wants to know everything about me. He laughs easily. It's a beautiful laugh that sounds like music to my ears. After we finish the bottle, we go back to his place. Central Park West. Twenty-first floor. Three bedrooms. Furnished like one of those spreads in a glossy style magazine. Floor to ceiling bookcases filled with books in English, French, and Arabic. Where there aren't bookcases there's artwork. He shows me a small Picasso drawing of a nude boy he says is his favorite. After sex he reads poetry to me.

I'm in love. The relationship lasts fourteen months and two weeks. Then I end it… six years ago. I was a coward. He was the first man who cared about me that I loved. He wanted me to live with him during the off season. Gamal talked about taking me to Egypt and France. We would be a couple. I couldn't handle the risk. I saw it happen in the minor leagues. A teammate was seen leaving a gay bar with another man. Next day no one on the team spoke to him. Filthy graffiti was scrawled over his locker. After a week he quit and went back home. Gamal… Gamal. My first love. Forgive me.

After limping around for a minute, Rocky returns to the plate. I get in my crouch. Breeze puts him out of his misery with another heater, chest high and inside. Rocky doesn't move. Strike three. And strikeout number twenty.

Number 21 coming to bat is Butch Gratzinger, third base-men, a redneck sonofabitch from Texas. Built short and wide, he has sure soft hands at the hot corner. You can pretty much count on Butch to hit .290, 30 homers, and 90 ribbies. Probably the most disliked player in the league. He calls all opposing pitchers and catchers *bitches* or *faggots*. He considers pitchers his enemy along with the catchers who enable them. He could tell you he hates queers. I could tell him there's at least a dozen queers playing in the Majors, including one on his team. I could also tell him that maybe he's afraid he's queer, too.

When getting into his batting stance, Butch likes to dig in like a bull pawing the dirt before charging. This gives us time for a little chitchat.

Having fun, Tiny? He calls me by my nickname because I'm a lot bigger.

Doesn't get any better, Butch.

I'm breaking this faggot's fucked-up game.

Don't think so.

Fifty bucks says I do.

A hundred says you don't touch cowhide.

You saying I don't touch cowhide off this faggot?

That's right.

Two hundred says I do.

You're on.

Cut the fucking chatter, girls, and play ball! barks ump McQuaid.

The fool took the bait. He's sure to take three aggressive swings. Breeze starts him with a big, sweeping curve at his eyes that drops to his ankles. He swings his club like a caveman and misses by half a foot.

Hey, Butch? Wanna withdraw the bet?

Three hundred!

Five hundred?

Five hundred and that faggot Breeze is fucked!

For the next two pitches, Breeze goes fast then slow. A 99-mph 4-seamer at his knees. Then an 80-mph change-up. On strike two Butch even chokes up on the bat – something I'd never seen him do. Three swings and three swishes. Butch walks away without looking at me. When he gets to the dugout, I see him break the bat over his knee then slam the broken halves on the ground.

Meanwhile, the crowd is going crazy, chanting BREEZY! BREEZY! BREEZY! Breeze quickly walks off the mound, no expression, not even a glance at the hysteria in the stands. I linger for a moment behind the plate and trace with my ungloved hand the letters G-A-M-A-L.

That one's for you, I whisper.

SEVENTEEN

That night I wear my swimming trunks under my shorts. I tuck a towel into one of the side pockets of my chair. After Salem and I have dinner together at the hotel restaurant, she tells me she's going for a swim in the pool. She asks if I want to join her. I tell her I'm feeling tired. Another lie to my daughter. But she can't come with me tonight.

Kat waits for me at the designated spot. She wears a white sheer sleeveless shirt that hangs open over her bikini. The bikini is black. Black on black. I'm thinking, harder to I.D. at night. The bikini cuts high on her ass. The top barely covers her firm breasts. I may follow the song of this siren to the ends of the earth or to my doom, whichever comes first.

We head down the boardwalk to the beach. Kat walks beside me. Over her shoulder is a black nylon bag, which I suppose holds her towel and other assorted small items. The beach has mostly emptied. There are a handful of surfers far out in the water. The blue surf rolls and crests in white-tipped waves, some fifteen feet high. Most of the surfers wear black wetsuits that make them look like modern dancers in costume.

May I push you? Kat asks.

No thanks. I prefer to motor by my own power.

Can I push you for just a little distance? This will sound stupid, but it would be an honor. Something for me to remember.

Sure, I say, go ahead.

Great!

I brake as Kat moves behind me. I watch a surfer lose his balance and tumble head first into the surf.

What do I do? asks Kat. Sorry, but I've never pushed anyone in a wheelchair before. She doesn't sound panicky or wimpy; rather, she's laughing at herself. If she wanted to sound endearing, she succeeded.

It's simple enough. Grab hold of those rubber handles. They're called push handles.

Push handles grabbed, she confirms.

Place your arms close to your body. Bend your elbows. Keep your back straight. And push with your whole body and leg muscles.

Got it!

Kat starts pushing me, more slowly than if I was wheeling myself, but that's okay.

How am I doing, Joe?

Just fine, Kat.

Neither of us speaks for a couple of minutes. It's a long boardwalk to the water. I don't try to guess what she's thinking. Plus, I can't see her face. Then again, she can't see mine.

This is wonderful! Kat sings out.

I don't respond. I'm too busy wondering if these are my final moments. So far all of this could be perfectly simple and entirely innocent. I would like that. I imagine myself going on a swim with this charming young lady in a black bikini. Kat. She'll push my wheelchair to the very edge of the surf. I will roll my body into the water until I'm afloat. Then we will swim like porpoises.

I haven't swum in the Pacific Ocean since my last series

against the Dodgers. I pitched a good game: 5 hits, 10 strikeouts, 1 walk. The score was 6-1. Early the next morning, I go off by myself to Venice Beach. I remember feeling happy and lucky to be young and a Major League baseball player on a contending team. I must have generated this feel-good vibe because young bikini-clad women walking by my blanket greet me with overtly sexual come-ons. I ignore them. I am in love with the only woman I will ever want to love.

Should I push you onto the sand? Kat asks.

I see that we've reached the end of the wooden boardwalk. There is about ten feet of dry sand before turning wet.

No. It's easier if I do it. But I'd first like to get my shorts off. Can you help me?

Of course.

She comes around, bends down, deftly unzips my shorts. While I lift my butt up, she grabs the bottom of my shorts and pulls. They easily slip off.

Tada! she cheers and holds them up like a flag.

This makes me laugh. I like this kid. I really do.

Walk with me? I ask.

Gladly.

Kat slips off the shirt and stuffs it in her bag. I look at her face. Her smile is partly open. I see a sliver of bright white teeth. The white sliver reminds me of the black ribbon of paint. Above Kat is a ribbon of darkening sky.

I'm on the sand. Pushing through it is more difficult than I thought. My wheels sink, holding me back, almost as a warning. But I push on until I get to wet sand, which makes for easier traction. Kat runs ahead of me, getting her knees and thighs wet. She twirls around like a child, gesturing me to join her.

Joe! The water feels fantastic! Join me!

I put the brakes on Wheels then fall forward on my knees. With my hands grabbing into the wet dark sand, I pull myself forward. Waves rush around me. The salty water feels cool but not cold. Just a few more feet and the water will be over my head. Kat reaches out her hand.

Take my hand! I'll pull you in! Here! Grab hold!

I look up at her. She laughs giddily. Why? Because she's happy? Or because she's trying to hide something? Such as fear.

Don't be afraid! Joe, take my hand! The water's wonderful!

I motion with my index finger for her to come closer. Kat gives me a questioning look. Yet, she squats down in front of me. Our heads are a foot apart. I take her all in. Gorgeous. She smiles. Her tongue darts out to wet her upper lip. She thinks I want to kiss her. I do. Oh, God... I do want to kiss this Sherry-sister on her soft, moist mouth.

Instead, I slap her across the cheek. I slap her with such force she would have gone spinning into the surf – had I not grabbed her hair with my other hand. Before she has time to think, I release her hair and slap her other cheek even harder. Her body does a 180 and flops into the green blackish brine. She rolls away, turns to face me, and screams:

WHAT THE FUCK! ARE YOU FUCKING CRAZY! WHAT'S WRONG! WHAT DID I DO!

She's on her feet now and far enough away that I can't reach her. I am silent but keep my gaze on her face. She's playing outrage, confusion, and humiliation. But so far she hasn't left.

SAY SOMETHING, YOU BASTARD! TALK TO ME! WHY! WHY?

Kat starts crying. The tears are real. Her sobs sound real. Her legs sink to the ground until she falls on her knees. She covers her face with her hands. Her shoulders shake. I wait a few more moments for her to quiet down. I want her to hear me.

Tell Lake that this is strike three.

Lake? she whimpers, raising her head. Blood trickles from her nose.

LAKE LEMON!

I don't know what you're talking about.

You know exactly what I'm talking about, Kat. If that's your real name.

This is bullshit!

I hired a private investigator. He tapped into your cell phone. It's not that difficult these days. I know that Lake Lemon hired you. Were you going to drown me? Make it look like an accident? No witnesses except for some surfers too far away and too occupied to notice. Perfect. Except that my P.I. is somewhere on the boardwalk watching us with a pair of binoculars.

Joe, I would NEVER harm you! I admire you! I like practically fell in love with you!

If you don't want me to press charges for attempted murder, cut the bullshit and tell me the truth.

Okay! OKAY! Lake Lemon did hire me, but I never met him.

How does that work?

It was all through my agent. I needed a job. My agent said there was a rich old dude who wanted me to play a role. Get close to Breezy Bye. But everything else I said was true. And I would never, ever hurt you. Never! Please believe me.

Remember to tell Lake or have your agent tell him: Strike three. Strike three! Got that?

I got it.

Now get the fuck out of my sight. If you haven't checked out of the hotel by tonight, I will press charges.

Kat gives me a pleading look, but I turn my head away. When I know she's gone, I get back in my wheelchair. I never called Kleb's office back. I doubt if Kleb could tap into her phone. But I figured that if I was wrong, Kat would have denied knowing Lake to kingdom come – or furiously stomped off. I took a chance. It paid off. So, why do I feel like shit? I wanted to be wrong. Badly.

I remain in my Wheels on the wet sand watching the waves come in. She was right. The sunset horizons are spectacular – pinks, reds, yellows, and a streak of indigo. In the distance a lone surfer tries to catch one more bomb of a wave before night falls.

But the bomb never arrives. The surfer gives up and slowly paddles his way to shore. I start to head back when I feel a crushing pressure on my neck and shoulders. That goddamn black ribbon pressing down.

When I enter the hotel I go straight to my room. As I pass Salem's room I can hear something on the TV. Feeling hungry, I call room service and order a chicken sandwich. While I wait for my order, I receive a text on my cell phone: *Will call 11:59 PM. Be at pool. Alone. L.*

At 11:50 PM, I wheel down to the pool. There's a sign on the gate that reads POOL OPEN 8:00 AM TO 8:00 PM. I expect the gate to be locked. But it isn't. I glide in. There are no pool lights on. It's dark except for the reflection of the full moon in the water. At exactly 11:59 PM, my cell buzzes.

Lake?

Are you at the pool?

Why all the mystery?

What mystery?

Midnight. At the pool. Be alone.

Precautions.

From what?

Never mind.

Precautions from what?

I have enemies.

I'm silent. Let him lead.

Are you at the pool now? he asks.

You know I'm at the pool, I say.

How would I know that?

Did Kat give you my message?

Kate? Kate who?

KAT. Like the animal but with a K.

I didn't get any message from anyone named Kat.

Interesting coincidence that you want to talk tonight.

Let's cut the bullshit. Did you want to see me?

It's you who wants to see me.

There's a pause after our round of batting practice. I don't expect a straight fastball from Lake. He'll throw something off-speed with a lot of movement, hoping that I'll chase. For a pitcher I was a pretty good batter. I could lay down a bunt when needed or at least make contact to drive a runner in from third base. One year I hit three home runs. For a pitcher, hitting a home run is sweeter than pitching a shutout.

You shouldn't have come to L.A.

I get that message a lot.

I've got nothing to say to you.

It's happening, I thought. I'm going to face the man I've hated for over twenty-five years.

As a pitcher I hated only one player: Red Roettger, third baseman for the Cincinnati Reds. He was a good hitter with pop. Hit two home runs off me. When he hit a home run, he did a little dance with his bat. He'd twirl it like a cheerleader's baton as he trotted to first base, hand it to the first base coach, then continue his jog around the bases. It was a cheap, showy performance, unworthy of the flashiest hot-dog. Every pitcher in the league despised him – including the pitchers on his team. Roettger was a freckled, redheaded, baby-faced lout from Wisconsin. He liked to crowd the plate to intimidate the pitcher. Because he leaned over the dish, he got hit a lot. He seemed to welcome that. Wouldn't even try to get out of the way. I never hit him. Some pitchers did. But I threw him chin music on occasion. Eventually, a 95-mph fastball found its way into his face. It smashed his cheekbone, fracturing it in three places. After that he was never the same.

You can make this all go away, Lake says.

Really?

That's right.

How would I do that?

Pretend it never happened.

Hard to pretend in a wheelchair, Lake. Could you pretend in a wheelchair?

Lake goes mysteriously silent, though I hear him breathing. My eyes dart around the pool area to see if I'm still alone. Hotel windows spill a faint blue-gray light into the pool's water.

Hello? I ask.

Still here.

It's too late to pretend.

You could have stayed in New York. Middelburg? Fucking name for a town. Could have just lived your life. Paint your paintings. Raise your daughter. Watch her grow into a young woman. Go to college. But no. FUCK NO! You had to come HERE!

Silence. Catching his breath? Mopping his brow? Let him finish his aria to the end. I hear him clear his throat.

For what? To do what? To finish what? It's over, Breeze. It's done. Been done for twenty-five years. I regret nothing, I repent nothing, I apologize for nothing. The past is the past. The dead are dead. The living will be dead soon enough. Even the most beautiful flowers shrivel and die.

Pretty words, I say, not hiding my sarcasm.

I've been reading poetry in my old age. Suddenly I'm in love with Walt Whitman, who was also a newspaper man: *Let your soul stand cool and composed before a million universes.*

I'm not leaving until I see you.

Silence.

Lake?

You know where I live?

I know.

Tomorrow at 8:00 PM.

Why at night?

So, we can be alone. I'll make sure my staff and help are gone.

Okay.

You better come alone.

I'll be alone.

I mean it!

See you tomorrow.

I return to my room. Between my dance of death with Kat-with-a-K and my midnight dialogue with the Devil, I feel like I just pitched a 10-inning 1-0 nailbiter. I don't bother changing into PJs. I just sink into the bed, feeling my muscles begin to relax and my mind let go of the crazy events of the day. Outside my window I hear a noise that's weirdly familiar. It's a singular sound I haven't heard in twenty-five years. It is the din of a full baseball stadium cheering a single player, repeating his name over and over, spaced out like ocean waves.

MAT-TEE! MAT-TEE! MAT-TEE! MAT-TEE!

Hello, Breeze, says that mellow, tenor voice.

I don't want to move or even open my eyes. I desperately want to sleep, to fall into the deepest blackness and blankness of slumber. But I push myself up against pillow and headboard.

In the far corner of the room, a figure stands. I switch on the bedside lamp. Christy Mathewson. But he's a Matty I barely recognize. He's older, thicker, grayer. He wears the three-piece suit, 1920s vintage, of a small-town businessman. On his head, absurdly, sits a gray fedora hat. In his right hand he holds a cane. His skin is sallow, and his eyes have no life.

You can't be Matty! I think but dare not say.

It's okay to think that, he answers anyway.

I want to see you in your uniform!

'Fraid my uniform wouldn't fit anymore.

What's wrong!

I died, kid... I died. Happens to all of us.

I know you're dead! 1925. You were only forty-five.

I had a good life. Better than most. When the Good Lord called me, I heeded His call.

Why are you here?

I think you know why.

Matty takes his hat off and sits down on the only comfort-able chair in the room, a slim wingback that half encloses his face. He looks tired and covers his mouth often with a handker-chief to suppress a cough. He died from TB, but it was the mustard gas he accidentally inhaled during a training exercise in Chaumont, France during WWI that killed him. I hate seeing him like this. In my hour of greatest need, this is how he appears? Like a chamber of commerce zombie? Jesus! Why the fuck did he come? Don't act stupid, Breeze. You know why.

What do you plan to do? Matty asks.

What choice do I have?

Choices have consequences. If you choose to not sleep, you will be tired. If you choose to not eat, you will be hungry.

And if I choose to kill... there will be consequences. Right, Matty?

All choices have consequences.

Do I wait around for another hired assassin to finish the job?

I can't advise you to kill.

I'm not asking for advice!

What are you asking?

I don't care if I die. I've lived a life longer than my father's and yours. Plus, death will save me from going to another god-awful art opening.

Matty chuckles at my joke before bursting into a ragged coughing fit. There are bloody splotches on his handkerchief. To see my hero, my champion, as a dying old man of forty-five shatters me. I want to go over and hold him in my arms. If only my legs would let me.

When his coughing subsides, he asks, Then why do you want to live?

To protect Salem. To protect the one I love the most. Wouldn't you do everything you could?

You'll find a way to do the right thing.

How will I know?

If you believe there is only one choice then that leaves you with one choice. If you're open to all possible choices, well...

And if my best choice is to kill Lake? And if my second best choice is to die? Then what?

Matty stands and moves closer to my bed. He starts to put

his hat on, changes his mind. He seems to gather himself up, and for a moment I can see an echo of his old glory. The silly fedora in his hand is a baseball glove. The bloody white handkerchief in his other hand is a scuffed-up baseball. He stares at the batter, deciding whether to throw a fastball or his famous fadeaway. The moment passes when he starts to cough again. After his coughing passes, he gives me a look that I will never forget. It is a face stripped of all emotions, scraped down to the barest bone of existence a being can expose.

Then he says, I never saw any action in France. But I witnessed the result of that horrific war. Tens of millions of civilians killed, including women and children. Millions of soldiers killed, dismembered, maimed, and disfigured. If you're asking me whether it's better to kill or forgive one evil man, the Good Book says to forgive. But if you forgive and the evil man still intends to do you harm, then the choice is clear.

I get out of bed, feel my feet touch the floor. I stand up, walk over to Matty, and hold him in my arms. He feels smaller than I thought, and I can smell the faint acrid odor of decay.

Matty?

Yeah?

What inning am I in?

You're in the ninth.

Are you sure?

Hang in there, kid.

I don't remember letting Matty go or of him leaving. The next thing I know is I'm lying on the floor shielding my eyes from the morning sun. I pull myself up back onto the bed. I phone Kleb's office, and this time I reach him. I tell him about my call with Lake. Kleb says he'll pick me up at 7:30 PM. Then I tell him to check up on a woman named Kat Walker who claims to be the daughter of former Major League player, Rainey Walker.

Rainey Walker, I remember him, says Kleb. Pretty good fastball hitter, but he couldn't touch my sinker.

Let me know what you find.

Will do.

Thanks.

I lay my head back down and fall instantly asleep.

I wake from a deep sleep... and a bad dream. I'm painting –
standing on my feet – dipping a house paint brush into a bucket
of black tar. I slap it on the canvas. Behind me are stacks of
canvases all covered with sticky black tar, nothing else. A nude
model sits on a stool. It's Jackie! And her body looks surprisingly
young. But all I paint are canvases covered in black tar. Jackie
gets up to look at the painting. But when she gets closer, I see
the face of Sherry! I try to stop her from looking. She easily
pushes me aside. Then my phone rings. I'm half asleep and not
in a good mood.

Hello? I say, but it comes out a garbled hell... ahh.

Good afternoon, Mr. Bye. This is Tommy Shannon.

What time is it?

Twelve-thirty P.M.

Well, it's nine-thirty A.M. in L.A.

L.A.? Is that where you are?

Tommy... Wait! You're the journalist.

Yes, sir. Tommy Shannon. We spoke–

You don't fucking give up.

This is not about an interview.

Then what? What!

I just learned some news I wanted to share.

Can this sharing wait?

No, sir, I don't believe it can. And you should hear it.

Then make it short.

The Hall of Fame–

No! Not the Hall of Fame! We're done!

Can you just listen a minute? he asks.

One minute, I say, ready to hang up.

The Hall is considering making you an exception of the 10-
year eligibility rule.

What?

If their Board of Directors decides to make you eligible, sportswriters will be permitted to finally vote for you. The Board's decision could come down any time.

I say nothing as I try to process this information.

What's your reaction, Mr. Bye? How do you feel?

I'm sitting up in bed. I want to pee, but that would take me five minutes of maneuvering. I always stick a bed pan under the bed, just in case, but that will also take five minutes of maneuvering. Peeing can wait.

It doesn't make sense, I say. Why make me an exception?

They got pressure.

Pressure from where?

The highest authority.

God? I ask.

Close. The President, Tommy answers.

President of what?

President of the United States, sir. Turns out he's a huge fan of yours. Apparently, you were his favorite player. He grew up in Iowa listening to the Chicago Cubs on the radio. He also went to Harvard Law School with the Hall of Fame's president. According to my sources the President has been communicating with the Hall on your behalf, reminding them that their educational programs receive some federal funding.

I'm silent as I try to process this bizarre news, but my brain keeps getting stuck on *President of the United States*.

Mr. Bye? Tommy softly asks.

Why are you telling me this?

I don't know... Guess I wanted to be the first to tell you. The Big Breeze belongs in the Hall. The injustice has gone on too long. Eventually, they would have come to their senses, but when? After you're long dead like some of—

Tommy! You're sure about this?

A hundred percent.

Thanks. I owe you.

Nah.

If... when I get back to New York, and you're still interested, I'll consent to an interview.

Still interested? Hell, yes! Give me a date and I'll be there!

I was pretty shitty to you.

No harm. I figured you're shitty to everyone.

You figured correctly. You can come up to my house. I'll show you around my studio.

May I bring a photographer?

Sure.

Mr. Bye, may I ask you a journalistic question?

Okay. And call me Joe.

Why are you in L.A.? I've heard that you're such a recluse. It strikes me as highly unusual for you to travel so far.

I came to visit some old friends before they die, I reply. Not a complete lie.

That's it?

Yep.

I think there's more. I smell a story and my nose never lies.

Hope to see you in New York.

Hope?

Goodbye, Tommy, I say, and hang up.

What just happened? I ask myself. And how should I feel about it? I don't know.

Cut the bullshit, Breeze. How do you feel?

Sick. Sad. Angry.

Why would they consider you an exception?

I know! It's like the Vatican considering the canonization of a Jew to sainthood. Yeah, right. And never mind that the Jew is also gay and an atheist.

Ha-ha! But he did live a devout life helping the poor and needy.

And went to kindergarten with the Pope.

I try to go back to sleep for maybe another hour. But I can't. Instead, I think of Ron Necciai. I should have told Tommy about Ron Necciai. Who is Ron Necciai? In 1952, he pitched for the Bristol Twins, a low-level minor league team affiliated with the Pittsburgh Pirates in Virginia. In May of that year, Ron Necciai struck out 27 batters in a 9-inning, no-hit game. It wasn't a perfect game, but he was the first player to strike out twenty-seven batters in professional baseball. To me, it makes my so-called Immaculate Game rather less miraculous.

At the time, Ron was a 19-year-old, hulking 6-foot-5 pitcher from PA with a blazing fastball. His nickname was Rocket Ron. The front office was excited by his talent and potential. Branch Rickey, the Pirates general manager, called him the next Dizzy Dean. But in 1953, he was drafted into the Korean War. Later, the Army released him on a medical discharge for chronic bleeding ulcers. Then he suffered a torn rotator cuff preparing for the season. When he asked the doctor his chances of getting back on the mound, the doc told Ron that he better buy a gas station. At the age of twenty-two, his baseball career was over. He didn't buy a gas station. Instead, he spent his life selling sporting goods equipment.

Did Ron Necciai have a full life? Did he have a good life? I read that he had a long marriage, a family, a home, a steady profession. And his 27-strikeout game is in the record books. Who's to say Ron Necciai didn't have a good life?

My Immaculate Game was no miracle. It has happened before. It will happen again. Maybe next year or in fifty years. That's baseball.

This morning I can't find Salem anywhere. Not in her room, not in the restaurant, not at the pool. On a hunch, I wheel myself to the beach and roll down the boardwalk to the water. It's a gray, foggy morning. The air smells fresh, tangy, and clear of smoke from the wild fires. Perhaps the winds have shifted.

Wearing a gray hoodie and her black denim shorts, she sits on the sand near the surf, chin resting on upraised knees, arms wrapped around her legs. I can't see her face yet, but her balled up body signals how forlorn she feels. I can guess why. I stay parked at the end of the boardwalk and wait. After a while she turns her head toward me. I raise my hand to her. She does the same. I smile and wait. She stands up, brushes the sand off her shorts, and comes over.

Oriole is gone, she says.

I figured.

I asked at the front desk. She and her mother checked out early this morning. She didn't leave a message for me.

Oriole didn't tell you she was going?

Yeah, but she made it sound like it wasn't for another week. I feel like such a loser.

Why?

Because I don't think Oriole really cared about me. She just used me. And I let her! I LET HER!

Can I ask you–

I HATE HER!

Can I ask–

I FUCKING HATE THAT BITCH!!

Salem turns away and breaks down into tears. The only other time I've seen her cry, not counting babyhood, was when Sherry died. That was more like weeping. This is full out wailing. She tries to stop but can't. She's been keeping it in all morning. And now that her sorrow has overwhelmed her, she can no longer hold it back. I know how bad it feels when your heart weighs like a frozen stone.

I wait until her crying subsides. I wait until she wipes her face with the bottom of her hoodie. I wait until she looks at me.

Why didn't you warn me? You're the adult! You could have said something. WHY DIDN'T YOU SAY SOMETHING!

Salem... can I ask you a question?

Okay, she says with a deep sigh.

If today wasn't today yet... If today was still yesterday, would you say you had fun with Oriole? Would you say you felt happy being with her and that perhaps she understood you in a way no one has in a long time?

She pauses to consider my question and to wipe her nose on the hoodie sleeve.

Maybe... I guess, she says with a minimal French shrug.

Don't let a sad ending of a relationship spoil the previous 95 percent that was joyful.

I hear you, Breeze. But I still feel like shit.

Understood.

We did things to each other..., she says, and I prepare myself as she continues.

... stuff I'd never done before. We kissed and touched each other. Not just on the lips... but other places. It felt like... I mean I'd touched myself before, but not with another... There's a long word for it.

Oral sex?

That's not the word.

Means the same thing.

Does that make me a lesbian?

Would it bother you if it did?

No... Would it bother you?

No. But maybe it's too early to give yourself a label.

Salem nods then turns to look at the ocean. The surfers are back. So far, the ocean is not cooperating, offering only middling waves.

I watched you and Oriole. From my viewpoint she was enjoying being with you as much as you were with her. You know it is possible that her watchful, protective mother forbade Oriole from contacting you.

Oh... Hadn't thought of that.

May I use an analogy?

Okay.

I'm pitching a game against the Colorado Rockies in Denver. They don't call Coors Stadium a hitter's park for nothing. Balls bang out of that mile-high ballpark like launched rockets. I hated pitching there. But on this day my stuff is filthy. I'm pitching a perfect game for seven innings. Ten strikeouts. Only two balls hit out of the infield. Eighth inning, score is 1-0. In the eighth inning with two outs, the batter strikes out on a slider but the ball bounces in the dirt and skips away from the catcher. Batter runs to first and beats out the throw from the catcher. There goes the perfect game. Okay, still got a no-hitter. I get two quick strikes on the next batter, Marsh Davis. Bats on the left side and a dead pull hitter. I throw him a four-seamer on the outside corner. What's he do? Goes the other way! Looks like a lazy fly ball. In most ball parks a can of corn near the warning track. Not in Coors. In the thin air the ball keeps going and lands just out of reach of our leaping left fielder's outstretched glove against the wall. No-hitter gone. Shut out gone. My win gone. Except for one pitch, I threw a gem of a game. But all people will remember is that I lost. Is that fair? No. But it's base-ball. It can be a cruel and humbling game.

Are you saying life is like baseball?

It's just an analogy.

There you go again!

What?

Talking baseball! Having long meetings with old baseball players; seeing a woman you knew when you played baseball; flying clear across the country because of what happened to you when you were a baseball player. Ever since we got here it's been nothing BUT baseball!

Yeah, so?

You always, *always* say that you hate baseball. Now do you see the contradiction?

Hungry? I ask.

I expect a shrug, but instead she nods.

Let's go back to the hotel and have breakfast.

She gets behind my wheelchair, grabs the handles, and pushes me.

Of course, I see a contradiction. Does it concern me? No. As Emerson once wrote: *A foolish consistency is the hobgoblin of little minds*. I've always liked that quote. But I don't say this to Salem because it's beside the point. What is the point? I ask myself. Maybe there *is* no contradiction. Maybe I don't really hate baseball? Maybe all these years I just liked saying it. Is it possible that I'm still in love with the game that betrayed me? Much like a jilted lover who is furious, heartbroken, and grieving from the rejection. Yet deep down he remains in love with his betrayer.

I won't tell Salem this either. Better, I think, that she believes I contradict myself.

EIGHTEEN

We're eating breakfast in the hotel restaurant. I order a cheese omelet, bacon, and home fries. It's the breakfast I always ordered on the road the day I was scheduled to pitch. I wolf down the food, preparing myself for battle. While I won't be pitching, I will face an adversary. As arranged, Kleb will pick me up at 7:30 PM. I haven't yet told Salem of my plans. I don't expect the conversation to go well.

I'm going to be gone for a couple of hours tonight.

Salem gives me a queer look I recognize as a red flag.

Where are you going?

Just for a drive with Kleb.

Your Sherlock Holmes dude.

He's a private investigator.

You're just driving around?

That's right.

Sounds kinda weird.

He's going to give me an update on his investigation.

Cool. Can I come with you?

It will be dry, boring stuff.

I don't mind.

I'll be back in two hours.

Two hours seems like a long time for an update.

Probably less than two hours.

I want to come with you, she says more insistently.

Then I make a tactical mistake.

It's safer if you stay here.

Safer?

Shit, I almost blurt aloud.

How is it safer if you're just going for a drive?

It just is... as a precaution, I reply.

Salem's nostrils flare just like Sherry's whenever she caught me in a lie.

You're going to see Lake Lemon. And don't tell me again you're just going for a drive.

All right. I have a meeting with Lake. We'll talk for thirty or forty minutes. That's it.

Then I should absolutely go with you.

Absolutely not. I'll be fine. Kleb will be with me. I want you here.

Breeze—

Don't argue.

But—

No.

She just looks at me, as if we're having a staring contest.

Promise me that you'll stay in the hotel.

Salem continues staring. I stare back. We *are* having a staring contest. If she thinks this tactic will help her, she's wrong. Meanwhile, my eggs are now cold.

It's 7:50 PM when I gaze at Lake's gated beachside villa: tiled roof, stucco walls, impressive arches. A 4-foot stone wall with another three feet of wrought iron surrounds the property. Tall palm trees, Italian cypresses, and a lawn obscenely green during a record drought. We sit in Kleb's parked van a block away. Kleb turns to look at me then at Salem, who sits in the back. He's not happy with Salem's presence. I made her promise to talk as little as possible.

The mansion was built by a big-time silent screen star, says Kleb in a low voice, though there's no one in sight.

Constance... something, he continues. She was famous for throwing extravagant parties. A lot of booze, sex, and drugs. After one party a body was found floating in the pool. The studio hushed it up. This was the '20s. When talkies arrived, turns out Constance had a voice squeakier than Minnie Mouse. End of her career. She soon sells the place. It goes through several owners until the villa sinks into disrepair. Lake buys it dirt cheap and has the whole thing restored.

Not to my taste, I remark.

Mine neither. But what do I know about villas? I was a middle reliever.

I think it's gorgeous! pipes Salem.

Shhh! warns Kleb.

Did you check up on Kat Walker's story? I ask.

Oh, yeah. Her name is Katrina Walker, unemployed actor. She does go by Kat professionally. Everything she said about Rainy is true, except that he was her uncle, not her father. He batted a buck-65 off you with no homers and one triple. And she doesn't hold the PA high school record for the girls 200-yard dash. She came in third in the state finals.

Thanks, Kleb, I say, now feeling guilty about being so rough on her.

At 7:55, Salem and Kleb help me out of the van. I unfold my Wheels and get in. Kleb attaches a wire beneath the seat. He's coolly efficient. Then he climbs inside the back of the van, puts on a headset, ready to check that it records.

You're all set, Kleb says.

Roger that, I respond.

Kleb doesn't smile. He's all business now.

Say something smart, he tells me.

Hitting against Klebecky was like taking batting practice.

I said smart, not smartass.

He jumps down from the van with a grin. The bastard is

enjoying this. Why not? As a reliever he loved being the stud that saved the starting pitcher's ass. Now he gets to be the stud that saves a client's ass, such as mine.

As long as you can hear me, Kleb.

Get Lake to confess that he hired the driver that ran you down. Then get the hell out. Fast. I hear any sign of trouble, I'm coming in. Understand?

Understood.

Let me go with you, says Salem.

No fucking way, Kleb quickly interjects.

Who asked you, Sherlock?

Lake said alone, I tell her. I promised I'd be alone. I can't break a promise, can I?

I could hide inside. No one will see me.

Surveillance cameras on the fence, says Kleb.

Time for me to get going.

Wait. Take this, he says. Kleb holds a sleek, black, biggish handgun.

What is it? I ask.

What's it look like?

What kind?

Beretta 92FS. LAPD has been using it since 1988. Some cops don't care for the bulky grip. But with my big hands, it's a perfect fit.

Is it loaded?

Fifteen rounds.

I don't want a gun.

Take it, damn it, growls Kleb. He holds it by the barrel, offering its big, sexy grip.

I won't need it.

Just in case. A little insurance.

We're talking. We're not dueling.

Do you know how to use it?

My father had a lot of guns on the farm. He raised me on guns. But I haven't held a firearm in thirty-five years.

It's like sex and bicycles. You don't forget. Aim, hold breath, squeeze.

He slips the Beretta into my side pouch. I'm about to give it back to him, but something stops me. Like a force holding me back.

I'll be in the van, says Kleb. Call or text me for any reason. If you don't come out in an hour, I'm coming in.

Still my reliever.

You rarely needed one. Such a fucking showoff.

Be careful, Dad, says Salem. She puts her arms around me. I almost make a wry comment on her *Dad* but I don't. That same force stops me. She thinks this might be the last time she'll see me. Sweet girl. She's right to think that.

Don't worry, is all I say to reassure her.

I wheel myself across the street and up to the gate. I hear a soft clank. The gate magically opens like something out of a fairy tale. As Kleb had instructed, I slap a 6 x 6-inch square of sticky sided 1-inch cardboard over the lock plate, preventing the gate to lock. I roll up the long driveway until I get to the front of the house. Unexpectedly, in addition to the stone steps, there's a wooden ramp to the front door. The wood looks like pressure-treated lumber, the best wood for outdoor ramps. I know my ramps well. Did Lake have this built just for me? Unlikely. Does he live with, or is visited by, a person with a disability? Next, the front door, a hugely built entryway made of carved oak. As I reach for the doorbell, the door swings open all by itself. Hmm. If this really is a fairy tale then it's one from Brothers Grimm. I slap another square of cardboard over the door strike plate. As the door closes behind me, I hear no click of the dead bolt locking in. So far, so good.

I enter a wide hallway and wheel forward. The hall leads to a large, lavishly furnished living room. To the right is an elegant staircase with an elaborate iron-wrought banister. A crystal chandelier floats above the staircase. On the walls hang pricey artwork from the '60s, '70s, and '80s – clearly the selections of an art consultant. I recognize prints by Andy Warhol, paintings by Jasper Johns, Jean-Michel Basquiat, Eric Fischl, Julian Schnabel, and a small, framed photograph by Cindy Sherman. The Sherman photograph is an early self-portrait and the only piece that interests me. I lock the brakes.

What the hell. Lake knows I've arrived. Five minutes pass. Ten minutes. Patience. He'll come when he's ready. He's Mr. Lake Lemon, and Lake must make an entrance. I hear the hum of an elevator. I wheel to my left, reset the brakes. Partly hidden behind the stairway are the doors of an elevator. The doors open. Inside, in a power wheelchair, sits a bald, bearded, obese, elderly man. He wears a burgundy cashmere bathrobe over green silk pajamas. The deep folds of the robe almost bury him. His gray beard is unkempt. The power wheelchair moves out of the elevator and into the living room. I never liked the sound they make. Like hateful bees in a hive. I notice only one foot on the footrest, tucked in a fine leather slipper. From the impression made inside the bathrobe, it looks like the other leg ends midthigh. Could this one-legged, wheelchair-bound, fat, old man be Lake Lemmon? He turns his wheelchair to face me. And I smell the pungent odor of an unwashed body. A cold smile draws a deep crease across his Jell-O-like cheeks.

Are you savoring the irony? he asks. The voice, though cracked, is unmistakably Lake's.

Irony?

Oh, come on!

Because you lost a leg?

There you go! But I didn't LOSE IT! They fucking cut it off. Like you'd cut away the fat on a tender sirloin steak.

Diabetes?

Very good, Breeze, very good.

You had harmful habits, Lake.

That's what the doctors and specialists said. Quit smoking cigars, quit drinking expensive liquor, stop eating rich foods. I told them they could go fuck themselves. They said if I didn't change my ways, I risked losing a leg. Change my ways? Too late for that. In addition to diabetes, I have a bad heart, high blood pressure, a prostate the size of an Idaho potato, and I haven't had an erection in three years. And they expect me to worry about a leg.

You have a prosthesis?

Dumped in a closet somewhere in the house. I tried it. Went to physical therapy. Once. Hurt like bloody hell. Told me it could take a year to get used to. Thanks, but no thanks. I'll take the wheelchair.

I'm sorry.

Sorry that I didn't lose both legs? Well, I'm working on it. Still smoking, drinking, and eating real food. Speaking of which, can I offer you a drink?

No thanks.

Lake's wheelchair moves to a bar cart I hadn't noticed. He pours himself a generous glass of bourbon. I notice that his hands tremble as he pours. He takes a long swig, spilling a few drops on his bathrobe.

You used to favor single-malt whiskey, he says.

I don't drink anymore.

Good. For. You. But really, Breeze, what's the point? You can't walk.

True, but I still have both my legs.

They wanted to cut them both off, didn't they?

How the fuck does he know that? I ask myself. Myself answers: Because he's Lake Lemon. He must have kept tabs on me during my recovery.

You would have liked that. The surgeons could have sent you one of my legs to hang on your wall as a trophy.

HA-HA! You're a sick man, Breezy. But funny.

Why'd you do it?

Do what?

It's just you and me here. How did my pitching hurt you? I was winning games for your city's ball-club. Since you took me out of baseball, the Cubs haven't won a pennant. So, how did my pitching hurt you? By destroying me, you destroyed a great team.

One player doesn't make a champion team.

Tell that to the Boston Red Sox. Two years after winning the 1918 World Series, beating the Chicago Cubs by the way, they sold Babe Ruth to the New York Yankees. We know how that turned out.

You have the balls to compare yourself to Babe Ruth! When we first met, you were just a conceited punk. After a few good seasons, you thought you were the next Christy Mathewson and Bob Gibson rolled into one.

His reference to Matty makes me smile.

What are you grinning about?

I don't answer, which makes him angrier. He touches a button on the electronic controller, grabs the joy stick, pulls it forward, and moves closer. We're ten feet apart. Two crippled men in wheelchairs. One old, the other older. He points his index finger at me.

Whoever drove that car did baseball a big favor, a huge favor for the team, the league, the fans—

What car is that? I ask, but Lake has begun a rant and isn't slowing down.

Thought you were too good for the Chicago sportswriters. You treated them like they were scum. They *made* you into a star. Every time you won a game, they wrote it up like you did it all. You were lucky to play on power-packed teams. Any pitcher with decent talent could have done the same. You thought you were on a highway straight to the Hall of Fame, didn't you? You got close. Once. Guess who stopped that nonsense? Make you an EXCEPTION? To even consider... NO! Unacceptable! There are a thousand players who had a few great years then fizzled or got hurt. Herb Score. You know about Herb Score?

Yeah.

Tell me about him, he says.

This storytelling time? I quip, wanting to steer him to a confession.

Herb Score. What do you know?

Ace pitcher for the Cleveland Indians in the 1950s. A line drive struck him in the face.

And?

It pretty much finished him.

That it? That all you got?

Isn't that enough?

FUCK NO! Lake yells, his one foot stomps on the footrest. He takes a sloppy swig of his drink before beginning his aria.

It's 1955. The Cleveland Indians call up from the minors a 21-year-old kid named Herb Score. He is nothing less than a sensation. Strikes out 245 batters, a rookie record that stands for thirty years. He's the first starting pitcher in Major League history to average over one strikeout per inning. Sophomore year he's even better. Wins twenty games and strikes out 263 batters. People are calling him the left-handed Bob Feller. All this by the time he's twenty-two years old. He's on his way to being one of the league's most dominant power pitchers for the next ten years. Then bad luck strikes as it usually does to those most blessed with brilliance and great talent. It's 1957, his third year. Yankee shortstop Gil McDougald hits a line drive that shatters Score's facial bones and injures his eye. He plays five more years before retiring. He wins a total of fifty-five games. Should Herb Score be inducted into the Hall of Fame because of what he *might* have accomplished?

I'm silent.

I asked a question!

Sounded rhetorical.

It's a fucking question.

The answer, of course, is no. He shouldn't be in the Hall of Fame.

And neither should you. Flash in the pans. Careers cut short. It's a cruel fact of any sport, but none as cruel as baseball.

You're right about everything – except for one thing.

What's that?

I *am* going into the Hall of Fame.

Dream on, he says, laughing at the ludicrous idea.

Not a dream, Lake.

The laughter dies in his throat. I wait for a response, but there's none.

The Hall of Fame has decided to reconsider my eligibility.

Bullshit! The Hall has never reconsidered any player's eligibility. Period. Full stop.

Except for this one time.

Joke's over, Breeze.

Pressure from very high authority came down hard on the Hall. That authority said that Breeze deserves to be considered, seriously considered. Clearly, the Hall buckled to that pressure. Kinda cool, Lake, ain't it?

I haven't heard anything about this.

It hasn't been made public yet.

You know this for a fact? he asks, biting down bitterly into each word.

Got an inside source, I answer. Lake is quiet. I continue.

The news will be made public in a day or two. My source says that when the baseball writers vote it will go overwhelmingly in my favor. What's truly ironic is that I never wanted it. I see the Hall of Fame as a public relations gimmick to bring tourism to Cooperstown. It's all a hundred percent PR bullshit.

Lake stares at me for several moments then breaks into a hideous grin.

Hah! Had me there for a minute, Breeze! But you gotta do better than that.

I don't need to convince you. Read it on the Hall of Fame's website. They must have posted it by now.

Lake's grin withers into a scowl.

Keep pissing on yourself, Breeze.

Check it out. On your cell, Lake. Go ahead!

He takes out his cell phone but just stares at it. Just as I thought. He doesn't know *how* to search on it! He's even more tech-dumb than me.

No problem, I tell him. I'll find it. I take out my cell, quickly find the Hall's website, pray that an announcement IS posted, and go to Future Eligibles.

I'm in their website, Lake. I'm clicking on Future Eligibles. Got it! I'll read it out, I say, which I do, loud and clear:

After weeks of discussion, our Board of Directors has decided that the National Baseball Hall of Fame should make Joseph Bye, known as The Big Breeze, an exception to the 10-year rule for eligibility. In our unprecedented decision, we considered two factors that outweighed the rule. First, his unique, record-setting career is almost without parallel in Major League Baseball history. Second, the tragic circumstances that abruptly ended his brilliant career left him only one year short of eligibility. Considering the unique contributions he made to Major League Baseball, his name will be added to this year's list of candidates immediately.

I stop reading. In truth, I stop *not* reading. There is no post about my eligibility or any mention of my name. I made the shit up, phrasing it as a Hall of Fame executive flunky might phrase it. I quickly put away my cell. There is a long silence until Lake breaks.

NOOO!! It's not possible! They can't do this! They FUCKING CAN'T!

Glad I'm the first to tell you. What's also ironic is that you thought running me down would be the end of Breezy Bye. Just the opposite. I learned a new vocation that brings me as much joy as pitching a baseball. I married the woman of my dreams. And I have a daughter that I love as much as I loved Sherry. That's my life. It's a full life. A life I'm happy I lived. How's your life, Lake? From where I sit, it doesn't look too good.

IT'S NOT FAIR! IT'S NOT FUCKING FAIR!

Lake throws his glass of bourbon across the room. It shatters against the wall.

I'll stop it! I CAN STOP IT! I still know people at the Hall!

Too late. Their board of directors already voted. It's a done deal.

THEY CAN'T DO THIS TO ME! THEY CAN'T! THEY CAN'T! Lake howls.

He pounds his fists on the chair's arms repeatedly, his flabby face twists into a baby's bawl, turning a color that almost matches his burgundy bathrobe. He looks like an overstuffed toddler stuck in a stroller having a tantrum. It's a surreal and sad sight. Is this why I flew 3,000 miles to this god-awful place? To witness the pathetic meltdown of a man I detested and feared for twenty-five years?

I wish Slammer had killed you! But he always fucked things up!

I can't believe you actually paid Slammer to kill me.

Waste of money.

For a lousy five grand.

He's a fucking liar! I paid him ten grand!

He said it! A confession! Thank you, Lake. You swung right over my curve ball. That's what you wanted to hear, isn't it? I ask myself. Before I can answer, I see the black ribbony line floating a few inches above Lake's head. How can he not notice? But he doesn't. What is the meaning of this sign? Is it a warning? An affirmation? Both?

Isn't this enough? Black Line asks.

Is what enough? I ask back.

Witnessing how your deception crushed Lake, Black Line answers.

I am silent.

What more damage can you inflict on this rotting, one-legged old man? asks Black Line.

I could kill him, I answer, and I feel my fingers itch to hold the Beretta.

Better to let him wallow in his pain... to his dying breath... to his dying breath... to his dying breath... Black Line whispers until it disappears.

It was Lake's life-long dream to be admitted into the Hall's wing of legendary sportswriters. At the height of his power and popularity, he had a legitimate shot. Then the scandals killed that dream. I put myself in Lake's shoes – or rather, shoe – and feel his annihilating pain. If he still has a soul, it is ground to dust. He's a dead man not walking but crawling. I almost want to take out the Beretta and shoot him in the head as a mercy kill.

You won't get away with this... You won't get away... Lake mutters between sobs.

Did I really mean it when I told him I had lived a full life? Or was it just to goad him? No. I *did* meant it. Even if it is the first time I ever said it, let alone thought it.

See ya, Lake, I say as I release my brakes.

Think you're leaving, Breeze?

We're done.

Like hell! Lake holds a small revolver in his pudgy hand, pointed at me. I'm guessing a .22. Small gun, small bullets, still lethal.

Pointing a gun at me won't change anything, I say, trying to sound reasonable.

Unless I pull the trigger.

Lake looks nervous and sweaty. The odor is now a rancid stench. How do I get out of this? How do I stop him from winning? Haven't I already won? Getting into the Hall of Fame is what *he* badly wanted. And now he lost. He knows he lost. Ergo, he has nothing to lose. And where the fuck is Kleb?

Lake, I know you don't want to kill me.

You should have let me write your biography. All you had to do was say yes... YES! And how different your life would have been. But no, you couldn't do that.

Wait! You didn't have Quincy run me down because of Sherry?

Sherry? Kill you because of a woman? Over a piece of ass?

Sherry was a great piece of ass, but do you take me for a sentimental fool?

I stare at him, hating him even more and thinking that I must be the sentimental fool.

Any last words, Breeze?

What do you gain by killing me? My violent death doubly ensures I'll get into the Hall. Think of all those pity votes. Plus, you'll go to prison for life.

What I gain is depriving you the experience of Cooperstown. The ceremony, the pomp, the crowds, the speeches will still go on. But you'll be six feet under. Go to prison? For life? Ha-ha! I'm going to die soon. I might even be dead before they send me there.

Here are my last words, Lake, before I go: I pity you... and I forgive you.

Forgive me? How dare you forgive me! HOW DARE YOU!

I spin a 180 and push my Wheels forward. Will he shoot me in the back? I'm betting he hasn't the balls. Even if he shoots, I'm betting his shaky hands will miss their mark.

I hear the almost cartoonish POP of a .22. He missed! Then I feel a hot searing sensation across the top of my right shoulder, as if sliced by a red-hot machete. Shit, I can't move my right arm! I can't move my wheelchair! Another POP. This time a real miss that shatters glass somewhere.

DADDY!

Salem stands at the living room's entrance. She stares at me then looks past me at Lake.

GET DOWN! I shout. But she doesn't move, paralyzed with shock and fear.

My mind stunned, my body takes over. I lock the brakes, put one foot on the floor then the other foot, stand upright, and run to Salem. With my good left arm, I grab her around the waist and pull her down beneath me.

A moment passes. A third POP rings through the room.

Then silence. I listen for the beehive sound of his wheelchair. Silence. Where the fuck IS Kleb!

Don't be scared, I whisper to Salem.

You're bleeding! she whispers back. I see a pool of blood on the floor and blood on Salem.

It's... nothing, I say, the pain of my wound making it hard to speak.

Don't die, Daddy... Please don't die.

I... won't...

Better not.

I love... you... Salem, I manage to say, in case I pass out.

I love you too, Daddy!

Kleb runs in, gun drawn. He stares in the direction of Lake then slides his gun in a shoulder holster I hadn't noticed before.

Everyone okay?

I still have Salem wrapped in my arm. I roll away to allow her to move.

Where... were you? I manage to ask.

Delayed because your daughter ran ahead of me and let the gate and the door lock behind her. I had to climb over the fence and pick the front door lock to get in. Anyway, doesn't matter anymore.

Lake...

You'll never have to worry about Lake Lemon again.

I hear the loud siren of a police car outside. So soon?

Kleb... How... Cops...

I still have friends at my old station. Before we left, I asked them to post a car a few blocks away. I knew you would screw it up and get shot.

Fuck... you.

You're welcome!

Daddy, you ran to me! You RAN to me! exclaims Salem. Then she starts crying.

I... ran?

Kleb looks at my wheelchair twenty feet away.

Either that or you flew.

Shiiit, I sigh.

Then I pass out.

Three days have passed since my fateful meeting with Lake. My right shoulder and chest are heavily bandaged. Luckily the bullet went clean through. No bones or critical arteries are damaged. Salem misses the regional championship game because she stays with me in the L.A. hospital while I recuperate. She only goes back to the hotel to shower and change clothes. I tell her to fly back to New York in time to pitch the game. She refuses. I beg her. She refuses.

During her visits we share our most vivid memories of Sherry. For Salem, small quiet moments stand out: Sherry's stories of growing up Black, female, and poor in Chicago's Southside; her advice in dealing with white people, the law, and men. I tell Salem of the times Sherry kept me from quitting on myself: I'm not giving up on you, she would say, so you damn better not give up on yourself. Basically, she kept me alive.

Today, at the end of one of our conversations, I ask Salem a question. The question that's been rising like a breaching whale ever since we arrived in L.A.

What is my biggest failure as a father?

You never made me laugh, she answers without hesitation.

That's my *biggest* failure? I ask.

As I think of my pyramid of failures as a dad, I would not have put that one at the top or even near the middle.

Yes, she replies.

Never?

Did you ever try?

I'm silent for a long moment, trying to think of a time I tried. I can't.

Of my many failures, why is that one the biggest?

Because it would have been the easiest failure to fix. Because you *are* funny and witty, when you want to be. I've heard you. But you never bothered.

After a moment she adds, Kids tell me I'm gloomy.

You're not gloomy.

I think I am. When I'm hanging out with some girls and someone tells a funny story and everyone laughs, I don't. When a teacher makes a joke and all the students laugh, I don't. I never do!

I'm sorry, Salem.

It's not your fault. Maybe I'm naturally gloomy.

Should I try to be funny with you?

God, no! That would be too embarrassing. Just be you.

A nurse walks in to take my temperature. Salem browses through the *Seventeen* magazine she brought. By the time the nurse leaves, Salem has fallen asleep.

Later that same day, after sending Salem back to the hotel to get some rest, I'm sitting up in bed, jabbing my fork at the unappetizing lunch tray – chicken-something, I believe – when two familiar suited men pay me a visit. It's the Laurel and Hardy duo, Detectives Stamp and Muggins. Each carries a large Styrofoam cup of coffee from the hospital cafeteria. I had already given a statement to a different pair of detectives who visited me. I didn't tell them about Lake's taped confession of hiring someone to kill me. Kleb told me that turning in the recording would just open a can of worms that could keep me in L.A. for weeks.

My advice is to let it go, Kleb says. Lake is dead. He confessed to you. It's what you wanted, right? I follow Kleb's advice.

Mr. Bye, we meet again, darkly greets the sardonic Stamp.

What a pleasure, I say, trying to look pleased.

And once again you're linked to a mysterious death, adds Stamp.

There was never evidence I was linked to the first death, I'm quick to correct.

A fair statement, says the more reasonable Muggins.

But you're damn well tied to *this* death! Stamp trumps with a satisfied smile.

I'm still shaken by that awful experience, I say. For effect I shudder and push away my lunch tray.

The detectives look at each other then sit in the only two chairs for visitors.

What was your connection to Lake Lemon? Stamp asks.

I've already answered those questions from your colleagues.

We may have a few new questions to ask, reassures Muggins, already writing in his little notebook. Stamp slurps his coffee. It feels like the three of us meet regularly to have chitchats about recent homicides.

Lake and I met twenty-five years ago. He was a sportswriter in Chicago when I played for the Cubs.

Why did Lemon shoot you and then himself? asks Muggins.

You'd have to ask him.

That a joke? Stamp barks.

I am silent.

Because it ain't funny. A man is dead! You think that's fucking funny?

Easy, Bill, easy, cautions Muggins.

Why do cops continue to play the good cop/bad cop routine? It's old, stale, and a cliché. Why not vary it, such as bad cop/bad cop, good cop/good cop, or funny cop/dreary cop, happy cop/sad cop?

Why were you in Mr. Lemon's home on the night of his death? Mullins asks.

I had called him to say I was in town. He invited me to his house.

How did Mr. Lemon seem when he saw you? presses Stamp.

Nervous... no, maybe upset is a better word.

Stamp's body leans toward me, as if he's about to leap onto my bed.

Ballistics determined that he took two shots at you before putting the third bullet in his head. Seems he was *very* upset.

We argued.

About what? Muggins asks.

My late wife was formerly his girlfriend. She left him for me. I guess he never got over it.

You *guess*? Muggins asks drily, no longer the good cop.

Yes.

Okay, let's cut the bullshit! shouts Stamp. Was Lake blackmailing you?

No.

Were you blackmailing him? Muggins asks.

No.

Did you threaten him? Stamp asks.

No.

Did Lake threaten you? Muggins asks.

No.

Did you and Lake ram wheelchairs into each other?

No.

Did you taunt him with graphic details of fucking his former lover? Stamp asks, trying to taunt me.

Get the hell out of my room, I reply softly.

C'MON, BYE! What the fuck are you hiding! Spittle flies out of Stamp's curled lips.

A nurse enters and orders them to leave. On their way out, Stamp warns, Don't leave town for the next seventy-two hours, Bye. We'll be coming back.

Kleb tells me the cops are bluffing and I can go home. He gets me in touch with an L.A. lawyer in case the cops play hardball. A week later Kleb calls to say the LAPD ruled Lemon's death a suicide. Case closed.

NINETEEN

Here we go, Tiny! You ready, man? I ask myself as I stand in the on-deck circle. Ready as I'm ever gonna be. Take in the moment, I tell myself, won't never be another like it.

It's the bottom of the eighth inning. The score is still 0-0. Felix is pitching a helluva game. He's a Dominican brother. Cool guy. We once had a couple of beers together. Too bad he's pitching against Breeze tonight. Thing is, he hasn't pitched a complete game this season. He's already thrown over a hundred pitches. Grimes, our shortstop, just grounded out. Two outs. My turn. I slowly walk to the batter's box as I collect my thoughts. Felix has gotta be tired. It's always the legs first. When the legs get a little wobbly, so do the pitches. I dig in, take a couple of practice swings, thinking, he's gonna try to crowd me with the slider. But it won't have the same bite it did in the third inning when he struck me out. Felix shakes off the catcher's sign. He shakes off the next one. Catcher wants a fastball. But I'm betting Felix wants to throw a slider 'cause he got me to swing at two in the dirt. I'm ready for the slider. Keep your hands in. Wait. Quick hands. Wait. Hands in. Wait. Quick hands. Wait... wait... SWING! Oh, baby, the beautiful sounding CRACK! of getting it all. I watch the ball's flight for only a moment, drop my bat, take my trot. The crowd is on their feet cheering. There is no better feeling on Earth. I glance at Felix who stares with dead eyes at the ground in front of him. I see my teammates ready to pound my back and helmet when I enter the dugout. Still got one more inning to play.

Top of the ninth inning. The twenty-seventh batter comes to the plate after twenty-six straight outs – all Ks! If this is a dream I never want to wake up. If this is real then it's the greatest day of my life.

Santo Santiago digs in at the plate, pinch hitting for the pitcher. Santo is a speedy Panamanian. In his prime he was the best shortstop in the league. Now he's thirty-seven years old, and this season he's a part-time player. He'll never complain, but I know it stabs his pride like a dagger. One day that will happen to me. In two or three years they'll bring up a hot-hitting, young catcher, and I'll be the backup. How will I handle that? I hope with class. Santo digs in some more. He was always a tough out, still is. Rarely strikes out. Chokes up on a big bat. Short, compact swing. Gets a ton of infield hits. Can he lay down a perfect bunt? In his fucking sleep. He never chases, walks a lot, and can steal a base. He glances down at me with a wolfish grin and says, *Él no me está golpeando. De ninguna manera*. In English: He ain't fucking striking me out. No fucking way. They ain't empty words. Four years ago, Breeze was pitching a no hitter into the sixth inning. Santo came up. With two strikes he slapped a fastball at his shoelaces up the middle. It was the only hit in the game. Breeze showed no reaction. But I know it bothered him because he struck out the next five batters.

Just before Santo gets into his stance, he makes the sign of the cross. No surprise. He does that at every at bat. Then I do something in a baseball game I've never done before. I pray. I pray to Jesus. Not to God, not to Mary, though I love Mary. They couldn't care less about a baseball game. But Jesus? He just might. Because if Jesus was once a real man, then he was once a real boy. And every boy loves baseball. So, I pray to Jesus. Like I said, I've never prayed in a game. I'm a good Catholic boy. Go to church every Sunday morning, even on the road. But I get disgusted at seeing all my Latino brothers doing the sign of the cross before they bat, after they get a hit, after they score a run. Looking up to God, all that holy shit. I'm thinking, you gonna waste all that prayer power on baseball? C'mon, man, God has no time for games! But maybe Jesus does.

Jesus, I'm not asking you to help Breeze strike out Santo. Breeze don't need it. But if Santo prayed to you, please ignore it. You got way more important stuff to do. Thank you, Jesus!

Sure enough, Santo fouls off three wicked fastballs and two devastating curveballs, just getting a piece of it. Like I said, a tough out. I know he's thinking, Be the twenty-seventh strike-out? Fuck no! Be the fool who completes the most amazing game in history? Hell no! If I know Santo, he'd rather eat his own shit than be in the record books for what he *failed* to do.

Breeze throws a slider that just misses the outside corner. Santo somehow lays off. Breeze throws a curve that's an inch too high. Santo lays off again! The counts 2-2. Breeze throws another curve. It's a beauty on the outside corner. Santo lays off. The ump hesitates and calls it a ball. I curse under my breath. It's the first close call that goes against Breeze. The counts 3-2. One more called ball and this miracle is over. Santo steps out of the batting box to adjust his gloves.

What's he gonna throw next, Tiny? Santo asks with a cocky smile.

Fastball right down Broadway. You ready, Santo?

Ha-ha! Funny man.

Ain't no joke. Waist high, okay? Want it little lower?

Shut the fuck up! Then he curses me in Spanish and gets back in his stance.

Maybe I got him thinking fastball, waist high. Or maybe I got him thinking breaking ball. What I hope is that I messed up his thinking. Fucked up his concentration just a hair. I call for a sinker. Breeze stares at my sign but doesn't move. I call it again. Breeze has a good sinker, but rarely throws it because he doesn't have to. A sinker looks like a fastball until it gets to the plate. Then it drops into the dirt. It's a risky pitch. If Santo doesn't swing, it's a ball. Breeze doesn't shake me off but goes into his windup. The pitch travels over 98 mph right down Broadway just like I told Santo. He swings and MISSES as the ball drops to the dirt!

STEEE-RIIIKE! McQuaid shouts, pumping both fists up for emphasis.

MIERDA! Santo wails and drops to his knees.

The crowd goes berserk. I throw my mask aside and run to Breeze. We hug each other tightly before we're buried by team-mates. Then they lift Breeze up and carry him aloft as fans shout, scream, laugh, cry. And I'm crying, crying with happiness.

Through my tears of joy, I think, I'll tell Breeze tonight. I'll finally tell him.

TWENTY

'm in Syracuse, attending my first live baseball game since the last time I pitched on the mound. Despite Salem being stuck in L.A., her team still won the conference championship game without their ace pitcher. It was a stirring come-from-behind victory, scoring 3 runs in the ninth inning. Her team is now playing in the New York State Tournament to determine the state high school baseball championship. The winner of this game will move on to the finals. We're in the fifth inning. On the mound, Salem Heather Bye is pitching a gem. Her team, the Hawks, and a team from Buffalo, the River Rats, are locked in a 1-1 tie. I'm sitting in the bleachers, fourth row. That's right, *fourth* row. No wheelchair. I'm using a walker.

Yesterday, I saw Dr. Rishi Gupta, my orthopedic surgeon.

Congratulations, Mr. Bye! Well done... well done!

He's as excited as I am. He tells me if I diligently continue with the physical therapy, I can start using a cane in a month. After I answer a few of his questions about how I feel, I ask him a question that has been on my mind since I left L.A.

Dr. Gupta, is this a miracle?

Is this a miracle? he repeats thoughtfully. Dr. Gupta is a

ruminative man, so every statement he makes sounds prudently thoughtful.

Is it? I ask again.

Rishi leans back behind his cluttered desk, lacing his fingers together.

Yes... and no, he answers after a pause.

What do you mean, Doctor?

Rishi picks up a lovely glass paperweight on his desk. The object is in the shape of a resting tiger. It looks handblown and vintage. He sets the tiger down and looks at me.

Sometimes atrophied muscles and nerves grow back over a long period of time. Even over many years. It helps if the patient exercises regularly. Your daily swimming regime is no doubt a factor. However, when motor nerves are severely damaged, as yours were, a significant recovery is extremely rare. You are a rare case, Mr. Bye.

Why couldn't I walk sooner? I ask him.

You probably could.

What? I don't understand.

I could use fancy neurological terms to explain, such as efferent neurons and neurotransmitters. But let me speak in plain, simple English. Your body knew you could walk. But your brain did not know. Or did not know yet.

You mean if I had listened to my body instead of my brain, I could have been walking a year ago, or three years ago, or five years ago?

That I cannot say with any certainty.

When I asked you if this was a miracle, you said yes and no. What is the yes part?

Ah, that is an excellent question, Rishi gleefully replies. The yes part is extremely interesting, he adds, nodding his head with delight. Then he goes silent, adding nothing more.

Dr. Gupta, please go on, I urge.

What happened to you is also a miracle. The miracle is what the human body can do. We doctors and scientists believe we know the body's limitations, then it keeps surprising us. Mr. Bye, you are no long a paraplegic. I do not want to ever see you again in a wheelchair. Is that clear?

Yes, Doctor. Thank you.

We're in the seventh inning. Salem has pitched a fabulous game: 4 hits, 10 strikeouts. She has also singled, doubled, and driven in a run. I've already made a dozen quick charcoal sketches of her in my drawing pad. The bad news is that she's losing 3-2 due to one bad pitch.

In the sixth inning, the River Rats' number 3 hitter is at bat with a runner on first. He's a big bruiser of a kid. After throwing him nothing but fastballs, with the count 2-2, Salem throws a curveball. A good curveball is deceptive and has bite. Slower than a fastball, it dips down just as it gets to the plate. A bad curveball has no bite. It hangs over the plate like a pair of wet underwear hanging on the line. This was a bad curveball. The batter crushed it. What I'll remember most about that moment is Salem's response. She turns to see if the ball goes out. When it does, she bends down, picks up the rosin bag with her pitching hand, gives it a squeeze, tosses it down, and asks the ump for a fresh ball. First pitch she throws is a strike on the inside corner. She shook off her mistake and got quickly back in the game.

Salem's team loses 3-2. It's a tough loss. Some of her teammates are in tears. Not Salem. After the final out, she walks over to the opposing team, in mid-celebration, and shakes hands with the winning pitcher. I could not be prouder of her if she had won.

Soon after returning from Syracuse, I walk down the driveway one overcast morning to pick up my *New York Times*. It takes me longer with the walker than when I scooted my Wheels down in seconds, but I don't mind. I pick up my *Times* and glance at the gloomy headlines. Down the block I see Warren Stillwater slowly heading my way. I haven't seen him since getting back from L.A. I notice that he's using a cane and has only one dog with him. I'm sure Warren has not spotted me yet, which makes for an easy getaway to avoid the annoying old man. But I don't head back to the house. I remain where I am and wait. Below the fold of the *Times*, I look to see if the news is any brighter. It is not.

Hey, Joey! Joey! Warren calls out. You waited for me!

Morning, Warren.

What happened?

Happened?

I mean, how come you didn't skedaddle?

Why would I do that?

Because I'm a sour, bitter old man?

Not at all. How are you?

Not so great... not so great. I fell on my face two days – no, three days ago. Walking the dog. I lost my balance, BLAM! I'm eating asphalt. But I got up all by myself.

That sounds nasty. You alright?

Didn't break any bones, thank God. But, boy oh boy, is my body sore. The doctor told me to use a cane for a few days.

I know about falling. Glad your bones held up, I say.

Warren stares at me for several moments, looking puzzled.

Hey... You look different.

I do?

Yeah. Something changed.

Not changed. Missing.

Missing?

What is it you don't see?

Warren stares more intensely at me.

Should I give–

No clues! Give me a damn minute. Missing... missing... something missing...

Warren leans on his cane. It's now a game that he wants to win. I recall how he liked playing games with me when I was little, in which he *always* won. He was not a gracious winner either. I can still hear his mocking laughter as I stormed off.

Your wheelchair! he shouts triumphantly. Where's your wheelchair?

In my studio.

What's it doing there, Joey?

Don't need it. I can walk now... or getting there.

Since when?

A few weeks.

He scratches his head, fingers raking through the sparse white hairs. His eyes look red and watery. His old dog, which I think is Peanut, lies on the ground.

Where's Vinny?

Vinny? He don't take walks no more.

Is he okay?

Yeah. I let him out in the backyard. He can climb up the stairs to my bed. But I gotta carry him downstairs.

Sorry to hear.

Vinny's just old... like me. He's had a good enough life. My wife doted on him something awful. Like you'd dote on a favorite grandchild. I don't dote. But I took care of him.

Warren smiles. His enormous false teeth cover almost half his face. But his eyes look sad. He might deny it, but walking both dogs brought him some joy. I realize that in a year or two, Warren may not be walking by the house anymore.

I won't keep you, Joey. You got paintings to paint. Baseball pitchers, right?

I nod.

Peanut, time to go! Warren tugs on the leash until the dog gets to his feet.

Hey, Warren, come by sometime and pay a visit. We'll have coffee and there's always some cake or cookies around. Just knock on the door. I'm always around, either in the house or the studio.

Can I bring Peanut?

Of course.

Thanks, Joey. It's been a long time since I've been in your house. Guess last time was when Sherry was alive.

You take it easy, Warren.

I watch him walk down the street, Peanut following behind.

Back in my studio, I stare at my second double portrait. I finished the first double portrait, which I retitled *Pitcher in Mourning I*. In the new painting, titled *Pitcher in Mourning II*, there is no figure of a catcher. This is about the pitcher and the thing that haunts him. A woman that is gone, yet not gone. A memory shattered into fragments. In the background I added white jagged rain drops against the gray somber tones of the background. Above the pitcher and the other figure, I painted across the canvas the words I'LL NEVER LEAVE YOU. Words Sherry often told me shortly after we wed when I thought I would never walk again. Unlike in the first double portrait, I paint the pitcher in full figure.

You've never done that before, says Salem.

She stares at *Pitcher in Mourning II*. She's now allowed to enter my studio any time.

What?

Painted in the legs.

True.

I like it.

Good.

Why is that? she asks, still staring at the painting.

What?

Why'd you paint in the legs.

I wanted to paint a full-figure portrait.

Yeah... But why didn't you do that before? Why did you wait so long to paint in the legs and feet?

I guess I always wanted to model them after the Renaissance portraits I loved.

Salem is silent for several moments. Her eyes still on the portrait, she backs up, takes a moment, gets closer, takes a moment, then looks at me.

I think there's another reason.

Another reason?

Maybe you didn't want to be reminded.

Reminded of what?

You know, she says.

I shake my head and say, That had nothing to do with it.

Right, she says then walks out.

I sit down in the paint-splattered chair, look at the painting, put my hands on my thighs, and squeeze them as hard as I can.

In *Pitcher in Mourning II*, the second figure evolved from the black line I painted above the pitcher. The form still hovers above the pitcher, but it is no longer a line or a ribbon. It is a fully-formed figure. Adding more black paint and more of Sherry's ashes, the shape thickens and expands. I push and rub the paint with my palate knife, my fingers, the palms of my hands until the ribbon forms into a female figure with womanly legs, hips, breasts, and long flowing hair. I lean on my walker and stare at the canvas. The figure is unmistakably Sherry.

You're back, I say.

I never left, says the figure.

Does that mean you'll stay?

I'll never leave you.

A cot is set up in the studio so I can work longer with shorter breaks. I spend two days nonstop on the hovering figure. The paint and ashes become hotter and hotter like ashes from a live volcano. They burn my fingers as I push the thick, black material around. Salem brings me my meals. I feel weak and sick and fear the painting will kill me. When the portrait is done, I sleep like the dead for sixteen straight hours.

I left several messages on Heidi's phone when I returned home. I have not yet received a response. Going to her house is out of the question. I hope that she's safe. Tonight, I start working on my last painting for the show. It's late, past 11:00 PM, when I hear a familiar pounding on the studio door. I grab my walker and head to the door. When I open the door, as I feared, stands Larry on the other side. He's dressed in street clothes, not his uniform. But the bigger change from his last visit is in his demeanor. I sense a seething animosity, which doesn't surprise me. I've been expecting and dreading this visit since my return.

You can walk?

Yes.

No point getting into the degree of my progress, short of real walking. Larry looks disappointed by my answer. He doesn't speak for a long moment but just stares at my upright legs as if they have turned into gold. He shakes his head.

How... When did...

While I was in L.A.

You just started walking one day?

Not exactly. It's hard to explain.

Try me.

I started listening to my body instead of my brain.

Larry nods, but I know he has no idea what I mean. Doesn't matter. The subject of his visit is not about the condition of my legs.

I'd invite you in, but I'm in the middle of—

Outside is fine, he snaps.

I push my walker out the door so that both of us can better face each other. Whatever it is he wants to say or do, I want to get it over with. I want to get back to my painting. Right now that's all I care about.

Heidi and I are back together, Larry announces with unhidden smugness.

I'm glad, I reply. What more can I say? I see he's not happy with my answer. Perhaps he expected his news would deliver a shattering blow upon his rival.

Glad? Really?

Yes. I hope it works out. I sincerely do.

Right.

I mean it.

I don't want you to contact Heidi ever again.

I won't.

I'm fucking serious.

Got it.

Because if you ever—

Got it!

You know what really kills me, Joe?

I'm silent.

What kills me is that I trusted you. I trust very few people. Very few. Comes from being raised by criminally deceitful parents. So, I guess you'd say it's ironic that the two people I trusted the most in the world are you and Heidi. You know how that makes me feel?

I don't answer, wondering why I get myself in ironic situations.

It makes me feel like the dumbest sonofabitch in the world. Then I think Joe must also think I'm the dumbest sonofabitch in the world.

I never thought that, I quickly retort, but Larry is no longer listening.

One of my strengths as a cop, something I have prided myself in, is my ability to judge people. It has saved my life more than once. Tell me, Joe, how the holy fuck did I get you so wrong?

I don't answer.

Because of your disability? Because you were wheelchair bound? Because your wife, who I adored, is dead? Thus, making you a wheelchair-bound widower raising a daughter all by yourself? God, you must really despise me.

Larry, I never meant to—

I TRUSTED you because you were always kind to me.

I don't think I was especially kind—

You WERE! You were kind. And in turn I trusted you.

Larry looks up at the sky. It is a clear night, full of stars and a thumbnail of a moon. I feel for this man. I want to hug him, but

I know that would be wrong and misunderstood. Larry starts to say something. I hear a deep sound, but I can't distinguish words. The next moment I'm lying face down on the ground. The entire side of my head aches. Then I hear Larry's words.

I would never hit a paraplegic. But since you can now walk, I can punch out your face.

He kicks me in the ribs for good measure.

I'm glad you can walk, he says then adds, But I liked you better as a cripple. Then he leaves.

I lie on the ground for a few more minutes. The ground feels safe, even comforting. When I get up, I will go back inside my studio and continue working. I am thinking that I'm not glad Heidi and Larry are back together. And I don't regret my time with her. I believe being with Heidi and making love with her got me listening to my body again and not my brain. In exchange for that gift, a fist in the face and a kick in the ribs is a small price to pay.

Today I resume work on my newest painting. It will be different from all my previous baseball pitcher portraits. I am painting a portrait of Salem, based on the sketches I made of her during the game in Syracuse. It will be my last finished painting before my opening in one week. If I like it I'll include it in the show. I have never painted so quickly. Does standing upright free up more movement in my painting hand? Or, like a surfer catching a big wave, I'm riding a bomb of inspiration? No matter. I'm content that the work goes well.

I haven't yet told Salem that I'm using her as a subject. I'll wait until it's finish before showing it to her. I want to capture her fearless confidence pitching the biggest game in her young life. This girl is all business on the mound, poker faced from beginning to end. No fidgeting or walking around the mound. I can't recall seeing Salem wipe her face once during the game. You can't teach self-control like that. Unlike me, she has very little leg kick and minimum windup. It's all about her hips and legs. She stands upright, straight as an iron rod. No bending down at the knees or waist to read the catcher's signs, like some pitchers do. If they bend down, then they must straighten back up; that makes two extra movements.

Watching her pitch during the game, I observe the remarkable power she generates from her slim frame. The source comes from her legs and hips, the way she uses them. The sequence of forward movement is as follows: first the legs, then the hips, and then her pitching arm. I liken it to a sling shot. Pull back the stone as far as you can before letting go. I am also reminded of Billie Holiday performing a song. She is always just behind the beat. That delay helps give the lyrics such compelling expression. One more observation: Just before Salem goes into her windup, there's the briefest moment of stillness, like a bird about to take flight, then a quick intake of breath, then the pitch.

What are her pitches? Good curveball. Sneaky fastball. Changeup is a work in progress. The changeup is the most difficult pitch to master. The arm slot and arm speed must be consistent to fool the batter into thinking the slower pitch is a fastball. Her release point is the same for all the pitches. Makes it difficult for batters to guess which pitch is coming until it's too late. She works quickly like her old man. I don't know why, but the fact that she's a lefty makes me want to weep with joy. I think of all the great lefties who have pitched before me and lefties I pitched against: Lefty Grove, Whitey Ford, Sandy Koufax, Steve Carlton, Randy Johnson, Tom Glavine. I'm glad I was a righty, but lefties are their own special breed.

Looking for the catcher's sign, she covers half her face with the glove while gripping the ball inside the glove's pocket. The glove veils the lower half of her face. The bill of her cap sits low, just above her eyes. This is the pose I'm painting: in profile, braided ponytail pushed through her cap, hanging down her back.

For the background I brush bruising black, purple, and violet colors. I lighten the tone only around the figure's face.

The title is *Girl on the Mound*.

WITH TREPIDATION I enter the packed Tommy Tom Gallery on opening night of my show. Fashionably dressed people, holding plastic wine glasses, talk loudly in twos and threes. Some even glance at the paintings. Jackie looks wildly exuberant. She's gesticulating, touching arms, and hugging and kissing practically anyone who enters the gallery. Dressed in a deep-blue sequined dress, spike heels, strings of pearls, Jackie has transformed herself into an alluring woman twenty years younger. I've never seen her like this in all the years and gallery openings I've known her. When she sees me enter the room with the walker, she runs over and gives me a ferocious hug that almost knocks me to the floor.

Look at you! I know you told me, but I've never seen you upright before.

It's my new, crazy look. You like?

I LOVE! But do my eyes deceive me? Wearing a tie! Catch me, I'm going to faint.

If you faint I can't catch you.

Joseph! You have made me very happy. Thank you for coming! Isn't it a gorgeous show? The new paintings – especially the double portraits – are BRILLIANT! People can't stop talking about them. We're going to sell a lot of paintings. Are you happy? Tell me you're happy.

I just smile and leave the H-word alone.

Jackie laughs.

Oh, Christ, just tell me how you feel.

I feel... glad you're happy, Jackie.

Are you, Joseph?

Yes.

She gives me a big, wet kiss on the lips. I pull away before she can slip in her tongue. Then she darts off to greet a bearded, dark-suited man, who may be a major collector. I head to a corner and sit in the only chair in the room. It has a sign that reads RESERVED FOR THE ARTIST. A considerate touch by Jackie. People come up to me to rave about the work before they even look at it. I promised Jackie that I would stay for one hour. I stay ninety minutes to see how long I can endure it. It may have been on minute eighty-nine when a young, blond, artsy looking guy in a manbun approaches me.

Congratulations, he says.

Thank you.

Quite a breakthrough. Painting TWO figures on one canvas.

Seeing where this may go, I say nothing.

I mean like WOW. I cannot wait to see if you expand to three figures on a canvas. That artistic leap will surely blow everyone away.

Are you so stupid to think the number of figures is what counts? says a female voice.

Manbun and I turn our attention to the source of this cutting comment. The speaker is an attractive woman of about forty in a red blazer and black leather pants. Her over-sized, pink-framed glasses go well on her oval face and short, pink-dyed hair.

Hey... Who asked you to... to butt in? sputters manbun.

Nobody. You must be ignorant or blind or both not to see the psychology, drama, tension, and humanity impacted in the double portraits. Go look again without trying to count past one. Or just go away and bother someone else with your idiotic opinions.

Manbun starts to say something, thinks better of it, and leaves.

Thanks for the rescue, I say.

That moron? Child's play. Excuse me, she says and leaves.

That was strange, I think. A moment later, she returns with a folding chair from God knows where, unfolds it, and sits next to me. Then she hands me a glass of seltzer. Does she know that I don't drink alcohol?

I've been dying to talk to you since you arrived. My name is

Hannah Landsberger, and I adore your new work. I think it's daring, intimate, and profound. Congratulations!

Hannah has a faint German accent.

Thank you. You know my work?

A huge fan. I write about art for a small art journal you probably never heard of.

Try me.

Art Today and Tomorrow.

I know it.

You do? Amazing! What do you think of it?

It wants to be the hippest kid on the block. That's not a criticism. I like that they try to showcase unknown and underrated artists in America, Asia, and Europe.

I have been to other openings of yours. This is the first time I have seen you.

A long time ago, I made it a point not to attend openings.

Then this is indeed a rare privilege. I know this is not the time, but I'd love to interview you for my magazine. I would treat you to lunch or dinner.

Nice of you to offer, but I rarely come to the city. I live upstate.

Sometimes I drive upstate to go to art shows. May I visit you when I'm in your area?

She gives me her card. I give her my contact info. We chat for a few more minutes before she goes to talk to some people she knows. I look at her card and think that I'll leave now while I'm ahead.

TWENTY-ONE

A year has passed. I'll catch you up. Today is a sunny, late July morning in upstate New York. Salem and I ride in the back of Tommy Shannon's rented silver BMW SUV. Tommy is driving us to Cooperstown for the induction ceremonies. In January, the baseball writers elected me into the Hall of Fame. It's Tommy who calls and first tells me the news.

You're in! You're FUCKNG IN! he shouts over the phone.

I'm in what?

Joe, you are now a Hall of Famer.

You're sure?

No, I'm making it up.

Damn.

Congratulations!

Can't believe I'd get the votes on my first ballot.

Not even close – 92.5 percent of the votes! Should have been a hundred.

Thanks, Tommy.

I'm looking forward to seeing you get inducted.

Yeah... well, I'm not sure I can–

Yes, you can! Because I'm driving you myself to Cooperstown. So, no excuses.

Despite Tommy's well-meaning exuberance, I'm conflicted. After all my years of trashing the Hall of Fame, now what? Do I refuse to be inducted on principle? Do I accept the honor but skip the ceremonies as a compromise? Or do I forego principle and eat my words? It is Salem who makes my decision for me.

OH, MY GOD! OH, MY GOD! Salem squeals like a 10-year-old when I tell her the news. Then she jumps into my arms – fortunately I'm sitting – and starts crying.

Daddy! I'm so happy! I wish Mom was still with us. She'd be so proud. Will you take me with you? Please! Daddy? Are you crying?

Of course, I'll take you with me. Wouldn't go without you, I say. And yes, I'm crying.

That is how I made my decision. Disappoint my precious girl? No way. I'm still uncomfortable about being made an *exception*. But I'm glad to hear that the Hall of Fame is reconsidering the 10-year minimum rule for eligibility.

For the occasion I wear a charcoal suit (my only suit). The last time I wore this suit was at Sherry's memorial. Salem wears a new dress she bought for the occasion, sleeveless and black that reaches just above her knees. She also pinned her hair up to better showcase her mother's gold, dangly earrings. She asks me what I think. I say she looks fetching. When she wrinkles her nose, I tell her that she'll be the most beautiful young woman there. She smiles. Jackie, Kleb, and a few of my old teammates will be attending the ceremonies. Two other former Major Leaguers will also be inducted. They played after me, and both are deserving.

I walk with the aid of a cane now. A woodworking neighbor carved the cane from the wood of a felled maple tree on his property. Near the handle he chiseled the Chicago Cubs logo and *The Big Breeze*. It's a handsome cane, but my goal is to walk without it in three months. Anticipating that day feels akin to the anticipation of pitching opening day of a new season.

Larry and Heidi are gone. Sold their house. Moved away a few months ago. Whether to another town or out of state, I don't know. I saw Heidi only once since Larry's last visit. It may have been just before they moved. On a Tuesday morning, I walk down the driveway with my cane to fetch my *Times*. As I pick it up, I notice Heidi's white Volvo parked across the street. Heidi sits in the driver's seat, wearing sunglasses, her blue nurse's uniform, gazing at me through the open driver's window. She gives me a little wave. I manage to nod, fearing my head will fall off from the effort. We don't move for perhaps a minute, though it seems like an eternity. I walk toward her car slowly at first then as quickly as I'm able with the cane. When I get to the street, she floors the pedal, tires SCREECHING, and drives away. I stupidly try to run after her and fall from my effort, the cane flying from my hand. I lift my head in time to see the Volvo shrink to a white speck. I know that I will never see her again. I had believed I was over her – until that moment. Then all my emotions for Heidi poured out like blood gushing from a knife stab in the neck. The rest of the day I wonder what I could have done to bring us back together. I conclude that there was nothing... nothing I could have done.

Warren has passed. He did come by the house once a week for coffee and cake. We – or rather *he* – talked about the old days when my parents were alive. He told stories I've heard a hundred times. He also told stories I never heard before. Then I didn't see him for a few weeks. On the third week his daughter, Libby, came to the house. She told me that Warren had died of a stroke.

They put him on a respirator, she says. Pop hung on for ten days... until I told the doctors to let him go. It's time, I said. Pop knows it, too. But he always did like leaving a party last.

I'm sorry. I enjoyed his visits.

So did Pop.

Libby, would you like to come in? There's fresh coffee made.

She shakes her head.

No thanks, I got a few more visits to make. The funeral's on Saturday morning at St. Mary's Church. Will you come and say a few words?

I'll be there.

At the funeral I tell a funny story about Warren and my father trying to help me fly my kite when I'm about seven. The kite never gets off the ground. But we all had a great time trying. The male mourners laugh and the female mourners nod their heads. I leave out the part of Warren and my father being drunk as skunks and that it's ten o'clock at night. They smashed my kite, and I ran home in tears. Some things are better left unsaid.

I finally got around to dealing with Sherry's ashes – what ashes are left after my *Pitcher in Mourning* paintings. At my show, the description in the blurb listed the materials only as *oils and ashes*. I never told anyone the source of the ashes, not even Salem. While I suspect she knew, she never asked. It was on Sherry's birthday in May that Salem and I spread her ashes in the garden. I let Salem pick out the spot. She led me to a large Japanese maple on a high rise in the garden. It has a nice view and receives half sun with dappled shade from surrounding trees. As we spread the ashes, Salem sang Sherry's favorite songs. We hugged and cried.

I visit my parents' graves. The first time since I buried my father thirty-five years ago. Their graves lie side by side, just the same as their bodies laid in their bed: Dad on the left side, Mom on the right. From the garden I bring a bouquet of my mother's favorite flowers: tulips, daffodils, hyacinths, violas. I lay the bouquet against her headstone. For my father I bring my first World Series ring. I never wore any of my three World Series rings. Too gaudy for my taste. With a small garden trowel, I dig a narrow hole in the middle of his grave, right above the spot where I think his hands are folded over each other. I dig six inches deep, drop the ring in, cover it, then pat the dirt down with the trowel. I don't pray or sink to my knees. I stand before the graves and say a few words to each of my parents, which are too private to share.

After we returned from L.A., I inspect my studio with fresh eyes. I must admit the place is a filthy mess. On the floor are empty paint cans, used oil paint tubes, debris of tossed canvases I destroyed (usually with rage), old brushes crudded with dried paint, scattered paint-stained rags, piles of artbooks, art journals, stacks of old issues of *The New York Times* I'd saved for later reading that were never read. There's even a mound of dried-up leaves. Why dried leaves? I once had the idea of adding leaves to the painted canvas. Don't ask me why. My Wheels, faithful steed, is parked in the corner. I couldn't fold it up and discard it in the attic. Wheels is a daily reminder of my former life. Despite promising Dr. Gupta to never again use a wheelchair, I sometimes like to settle back in Wheels to think or to gaze at a canvas. It calms me. Half my life was spent in that chair. It is part of me and always will be.

I thought Jasmine would fall over when I asked her to clean the studio. Entering it for the first time, she lets out a shriek – I think with as much delight as horror – by the degree of grunginess and disorder. With furrowed brow she surveys the landscape like a general preparing for battle. Then she turns to me with an expression I can only describe as radiant.

Tank you, tank you, Mr. Bye! Now you go away. I tink this job will take Jasmine all day.

She now cleans and organizes my studio once a month. And I gave her a hefty raise.

During the spring, Tommy drives up from New York City twice to interview me for *Rolling Stone Magazine*. Tommy looks like his father. He's what you'd call Black Irish with a thick mane of coal-black hair, ruddy complexion, and craggy features. Not handsome by any means, but I can see some women falling at his feet. Accompanying him is a photographer named Madison, who I later learn is his girlfriend. Madison is a willowy, pale-skinned, blonde beauty, who wears black-framed glasses, black jeans, and a tan safari vest with lots of pockets and zippers for lenses and related-photo accessories. She's a serious working photographer, who brings three cameras and a trunk full of lighting equipment. It looks like they're making a movie. She doesn't speak much, but Tommy talks enough for the two of them. Madison takes hundreds of photos of me, the house and studio, and my paintings. The article features a full-page photo of me next to my latest portrait of Christy Mathewson. Tommy wants to write an authorized biography of me. To my surprise I agree. Salem enthusiastically approves. He says one publisher is already interested. Another surprise for me is that Tommy and I become friends. His effusive personality has a way of drawing me out. I haven't made a new male friend in thirty years, which tells you what a disagreeable ass I've been and what a sorry state I've lived.

Hannah Landsberger does pay me a visit. I show her my studio. She studies each canvas and makes notes. Hannah tells me she's writing a piece in German about my new work for an Austrian art magazine.

The Austrians are always trying to catch up with the Germans, she says. They've been lagging since the breakup of the Austro-Hungarian Empire. It's sad. But what I like about the Austrians is that they pay better than the Germans.

Hannah stays the weekend. She drives us to a 3-star French restaurant, thirty miles away, that I've never heard of. Hannah speaks fluent French to our waiter and orders for both of us. The food is sublime. She promises to come again when she returns from a trip to Berlin, Paris, and London. I'm not yet sure what I make of Hannah, but I like her sharp, cynical wit and the sex is good. That's all I need right now.

You are now caught up.

Daddy, are you famous? Salem asks after a lengthy silence during our drive to Cooperstown. We both have been gazing out the window admiring the green rolling hills and rich farmlands.

I don't know. Am I?

I think you are.

Famous for what?

You're pulling my chain, she says, a new favorite expression.

Because I'm going to be in the Hall of Fame?

Of course! And because you were one of the greatest pitchers ever.

I'd rather be one of the greatest painters ever, I say half-seriously.

I think you are.

I let that pass, not sure if she's half serious. Madison is also along, sitting in the front passenger seat. She's going to take photos when I make my speech. Her head rests on Tommy's shoulder. It's a good three-hour drive and we're only halfway there.

Still want to pitch in the Major Leagues? I ask Salem.

Of course! she answers. *Of course* is another recent favorite expression.

You need another pitch.

I've got three.

I know.

Fastball, curve, changeup.

Changeup needs work.

No, it doesn't.

Yes, it does. Sometimes it hangs over the middle of the plate. Very hittable. You got away with a few poor changeups.

Why do I need another? Salem asks with a sigh, but spares me the eye roll.

Let me see your hand.

Why?

Show me your hand.

She does. I hold her hand against mine, pressing my fingers against her fingers. Just what I thought. But I wanted her to see it too. Like me, she has unusually long fingers. For a pitcher that's a blessing. Her fingers feel warm, and I don't want to take my hand away. But I do.

What? Salem asks impatiently.

You could throw a split-finger fastball.

What does that do?

Split-finger is an off-speed pitch. It looks like a fastball until it suddenly drops, causing the batter to swing over it. Be a good addition to your arsenal.

How do you throw it?

You spread your index finger and middle finger wide to cradle the ball.

Will you show me?

Yes.

Cool! Did you throw it?

I didn't have to. My other stuff was enough. But I was working on it to save for later. You know, for when I got older and needed new tricks. Looking ahead. I wanted to pitch effectively into my forties like Nolan Ryan and Warren Spahn.

We're both silent for a few minutes. Up ahead I can see the Catskill Mountains. Cooperstown lies at their foothills.

Did you practice your speech? Salem asks.

Some, I say.

Are you nervous?

Not a bit, I lie.

You want to practice it?

Now?

Of course!

No.

It's good to practice.

I'm practiced enough. Besides, I want you to hear my speech for the first time when I give it.

I don't mind hearing it again! Tommy chimes in.

Mind your own business, driver! I yell, which makes Tommy and Madison laugh, which makes Salem laugh.

Madison turns around and snaps photos of us.

Say nothing, Madison says.

NOTHING! Salem and I shout, which makes us all laugh.

Madison takes more photos until I wave my hands in front of my face.

What are you going to say? Salem asks.

It's a short speech. I'll avoid the usual boilerplate about being honored to be inducted and that baseball is still America's greatest team sport.

Well, I think baseball IS the greatest team sport, argues Salem.

Even if it is, though most would disagree, that's still a sentimental cliché.

When it comes to baseball, I *love* sentimental clichés! shouts Tommy.

I'll also keep the thank-yous to a minimum, I continue. No thanking God, Jesus, my parents, my Little League coach.

Did Mom make the cut?

She did.

Yay!

So did you.

Me?

Uh-huh.

What about me? asks Tommy.

Sorry.

Damn!

After we check into the hotel, I'll take you to the Hall of Fame Museum, I tell Salem.

Will your plaque be there?

Your father will be holding the plaque during the ceremony tomorrow, says Tommy.

What will your plaque say? asks Salem.

I'll find out tomorrow.

You don't know?

A committee writes it. It's a long process, Tommy explains.

Why is that? Madison asks.

There's only room for about 90 words. Imagine deciding

what to write when summarizing a player's entire career. Again, in only 90 words.

What do you think the committee will put in? Salem asks.

I'm silent the whole time. I don't want to think about what my plaque will or won't say about me. I don't want to ruin a memory, now forty years ago, of reading the plaques of my heroes. I don't want to smear a clumsy brushstroke of gray paint over that vivid image.

Mostly records, stats, awards and, sometimes, what the player contributed to the betterment of baseball, Tommy replies.

What do you think they'll say about my dad? Salem presses.

Well... If I was on the committee, says Tommy, putting on a campy, profound tone, I'd include the following facts: Transformed the forever losing Cubs into three-time World Series champions, won four Cy Young Awards, led league in ERA six times, led league in wins six times, led league in strikeouts eight times, only pitcher to win two MVP awards, only pitcher to throw an Immaculate 27-strikeout perfect game. As the only pitcher during his career to pitch every four days, he proved to be the equal of the greatest pitchers of the 20th century. I could go on, but as I said, 90 words.

We now enter the quaint village of Cooperstown. Down Main Street we pass many baseball shops and baseball-themed restaurants and bars. As I dwell upon my speech, I consider what the committee *won't* include in my plaque. And it would run more than 90 words. If I should include that missing text in my speech it might sound like this:

Breeze's career was cut short by his wife's murderous, former lover. Afterwards he wasted two years of his life in bitterness, self-pity, and addiction. He tried to kill himself and failed. He tried to become an artist with only modest success. For fourteen years he was an absent father to his daughter. He caused the death of two men. He committed adultery twice. He cheated on his wife once. Were we to consider him on character, decency, and deeds, he would not qualify. However, we will make an exception with Joseph Breezy Bye. At the age of 54, he is sincerely attempting to make a comeback as a loving father and caring human being.

When I do give my speech, I say none of that. I keep it brief and gracious. In closing I add the following line: *Baseball is still America's greatest team sport*. Not because I mean it, but to see Salem burst into laughter.

ACKNOWLEDGMENTS

I must start with my partner and wife, Holly, who never tired of reading yet another draft. A million thanks for always giving me the hard truth of what didn't work and gently pushing me to make it work. A special thanks to my superb editor, Lisa McCoy, whose insightful advice, rigorous editing, and unwavering belief in my novel were invaluable and a gift. Thanks to my brothers and early readers, Randy and Tracy. Tracy, who bleeds Dodger blue, read a rough chunk and provided the regular-guy baseball feedback I needed. Randy, a smart funny writer himself, dove deep in the first complete draft and helped me on the literary front. Thanks to my great friend, Rob Ingraham, who has given me steadfast support through many of my writing efforts, including this novel. His generous and constant encouragement is something I can never repay. I am deeply grateful to the team at Encyclopocalypse Publications. My foremost gratitude goes to President and Founder, Mark Alan Miller. From the beginning, his passion for my novel has been priceless. Mark, a publisher who genuinely likes writers, invited this writer's ideas for the cover – and actually used them. Finally, thanks to the fabulous cover artist, Fabiano Neves, who did a knockout job designing the cover.

ABOUT THE AUTHOR

Steven Fechter is a novelist, playwright, and screenwriter. He co-wrote the screenplay for the award-winning film *The Woodsman* (based on his play) starring Kevin Bacon. For that film he was a Humanitas Prize finalist in screenwriting. *The Woodsman* and his other plays have been staged throughout North America and Europe. In 2022 his play, *The Memory Exam,* premiered at 59E59 Theatres in New York where it had a sold-out run. *The New York Times* called it a "dystopian thriller." His short film, *Miracle Baby,* which he wrote and co-produced, has been an official selection in over 30 film festivals, winning awards for screenwriting, directing, and acting. He lives in the Hudson Valley in Upstate New York with his wife.